About the

Melanie Hughes was brought up in Harrow and trained at the Central School of Speech and Drama. She went on to act in theatre, television and films. She began writing for Ken Russell in the television series "Lady Chatterley" and then worked on further projects for him, the BBC, London Films, and Union Pictures. Melanie loves art, theatre, films, reading and the sea. Her first published book was *Mrs Fisher's Tulip*.

Midnight Legacy is the sequel to *War Changes Everything*, also published by Patrician Press.

"From an impoverished childhood in London to the opulence of Lahore and Delhi at the height of the Raj, journey with Nita through a world at war, political unrest and her life, loves and losses."*War Changes Everything* is a captivating coming-of-age story, which together with the second novel, *Midnight Legacy*, draws you into Nita's fascinating world, which spans two continents, until you feel she has become a lifelong friend."

Penny Culliford, author

Midnight Legacy

Midnight Legacy

Melanie Hughes

Patrician Press
Manningtree

First published as a paperback edition by Patrician Press 2017

E-book edition published by Patrician Press 2017

Copyright © Melanie Hughes 2017

The right of Melanie Hughes to be identified as the author of this work has been asserted in accordance with the Copyright, Designs and Patents Act of 1988.

British Library Cataloguing in Publication Data. A catalogue record for this book is available from the British Library.

ISBN paperback edition 978-0-9955386-7-2

ISBN e-book edition 978-0-9955386-6-5

www.patricianpress.com

Published by Patrician Press 2017

For more information: www.patricianpress.com

For Mike and Ilona with love

In Memoriam
Juanita Serracante Bruce 1916-2005
Kanwar Lal Amol Singh 1920-1982

MIDNIGHT LEGACY

"At the stroke of the midnight hour, when the world sleeps, India will awake to life and freedom."

Jawaharlal Nehru, 15th August 1947

Chapter One

Rikh and I didn't last long in India. Ironic, wasn't it? We, who had fallen in love during a one-sided debate on Indian Independence and fought so hard to bring it about, fell apart when faced with the real thing.

We had struggled to prove our cause, spending long hours in the India League offices in the Strand, writing pamphlets, raising funds, attending meetings of what was, after all, a subversive organisation; being followed around London on dark, rainy nights by the gentlemen of the Metropolitan police, as Krishna Menon called them, only to be pulled relentlessly apart by the onslaught that is India.

I now suspect that is a fairly common experience, but at the time it was a bitter and painful irony and one that was not lost on either of us.

We arrived in Madras in May, after five months at sea, to be assailed by a wall of heat so fierce it felt like a blow.

We were in the middle of what I would later call "the great stoke-up." It was like being inside an oven.

Nothing prepares one for India. All expectations pale, blinded by the light and scale of everything. The sun is too hot, the colours too vivid, the people too many and various. The sights and smells—the spices, the flowers and the open sewers; the pitiful slums, the homeless living and dying and being born in the gutter, the maimed and the lame, and then the throat catching beauty of temples and tombs, the relentless heat of the day and the cool, starlit nights. It was not as I had imagined. Not at all. It was so much more.

It was unexpectedly loud and chaotic—the streets were full of people yelling, car horns blaring, animals bellowing. The people were not silent and aloof, full of mystery—they smiled and laughed a lot, and talked the whole time. An endless flow of chatter that nothing seemed to stem. Despite the most appalling misfortunes, they had an intrinsic good humour that was endearing and exasperating all at once.

Nothing had prepared me for this. My schoolgirl's view of India—all far pavilions and the scent of jasmine in the air—was there all right, but it was elbowed into a corner by everything else. It was only one colour in the spectrum. As the temperature rose, my spirits rose with it. I felt purged of my previous identity, the shroud of disapproval that had smothered me since birth; here I felt younger, lighter, free to be what I wanted to be, not strait-jacketed by convention. Despite its abject poverty and hidebound wretchedness, I loved it. I loved it because it set me free.

When we disembarked from the 'Duchess of Richmond', the converted liner that had brought us safely across the U-boat infested waters of the Atlantic, from Liverpool to Madras, we were met by a harassed looking Staff Officer in shorts who bustled us into a huge shed where we were 'processed'.

"More like cargo than people," Rikh commented. But he was smiling. He was home now and, although it was far from perfect, he was at last where he had always wanted to be.

We were ushered into a long, low building which housed a makeshift Mess, where a lunch of warm beer and ham sandwiches was served. The sandwiches were already dry, the corners curling up in a way that looked oddly oriental, but the whole thing was served on silver trays by a number of Indian bearers in spotless white uniforms, with all the ceremony of tea at the Ritz.

It was a bit of a shock after the years of "make do and muck in" at home.

"Is it always like this?" I whispered to Rikh. Of course, I had seen guests waited on hand and foot at the Waldorf, but I had only ever been staff, and a fairly junior member of staff at that. I was not used to being waited on. So I felt a bit daunted, as a tall, stern looking bearer poured me a glass of foaming beer from a cut glass jug.

Rikh looked at me in surprise. "Like what?"

"Wall to wall servants."

He grinned at me. "Dear child, this is barely the beginning." I said no more and ate my sandwich. It was very good, despite the dry edges. Packed with tinned ham and spread with butter, we'd had nothing like this in England for years.

After the meal, we were given tickets for our respective destinations, and I noted, to my relief, that none of the awful Officers' wives who had been on the ship were headed our way. Our Staff Officer, who announced he would be travelling to Ambala with us, shepherded us onto a bus and we were driven to the station. Luggage, other than one overnight bag each, was to be taken separately in the freight car.

The station was extraordinary. I had never seen so many people in one place in my life. It made the platform in Euston seem deserted. Soldiers with kitbags, pushing and shoving, Memsahibs with noisy children attended by silent ayahs, travellers with bedrolls on their heads, carrying birdcages with live chickens in them, hawkers selling everything under the sun, newspapers, tea in strange metal cups (why would anyone want a hot drink in that climate?), food—brightly coloured and smelling pungently of spices—beggars thrusting their rattling bowls in our faces. My eyes could not take it all in, let alone make sense of it.

Our Staff Officer, whose name was Logan, was sweating profusely. The damp patches on his khaki shirt spread and then joined up, as he struggled to create order out of chaos. Despite his rather brusque manner, he turned out to be rather a dear. Patient but firm, he marched up and down the platform, steering us through the crowds, like a well-trained collie with a group of particularly dim sheep.

What did shock me was the segregation—our waiting room had been clearly marked 'Europeans Only'. As were the train compartments. Rikh told me not to worry, as a serving officer, he was apparently an 'honorary European'. For the time being. Frankly, it disgusted me. He took it in his stride, just dismissed it as part of the hatefulness of the Raj, but his acceptance of such blatant prejudice upset me. It also brought home to me that, despite his RAF rank and service record, he was still a second-class citizen in his own home. He was only an ECO (Emergency Commissioned Officer) like other Indian Officers at the time, so although they bore the same responsibilities and ran the same risks as their British counterparts, they were never accorded the same status or the same pay. They could die for Empire, and they did, in large numbers, but they would never enjoy the recognition their service ought to have entitled them to.

The train was actually very comfortable, if a bit old-fashioned. We were herded into the first-class carriages. The Staff Officer got in with us, which didn't please Rikh but was fine by me, because I knew he would make sure everything went smoothly.

The journey took four days. Four long, hot days. The

nights were best. No black out here. The air streamed in through the open windows—cool at last, as the paddy fields and lush vegetation of the south gave way to the dark immensity of the plain, stretching out endlessly before us, and above it all, the stars clear and bright in an unclouded sky. While Rikh slept, I sat and watched as India unfolded before me.

In the day, the train chugged on, past mile upon mile of half-glimpsed fields, laced with broad rivers and far flung villages, hazy in the afternoon heat.

The hours wore on and we became sleepy with inertia. We stopped at various stations along the way for meals. We poured off the train, melting with heat, our clothes now wet rags clinging to our skin, dazed and dazzled by the light. We were then ushered into specially converted waiting rooms where service canteens had been set up. I was struck by the oddness of eating English school dinners on the baking plains of India. We ate off thick white china, seated at wooden trestle tables and benches and I watched with amused horror, as a huge grey mound of cottage pie with watery, diced carrot was slopped onto my plate. It was just like being back at school. There was even some sort of steaming milk pudding as well, tapioca, I think, for those who could face it. I couldn't. It looked awful to me.

I laughed at poor old Rikh as he forked in the dried up mince, unrelieved by any of his beloved green chillies. He grimaced when he swallowed, like a child taking medicine.

"Is it horrid?"

"Dreadful." For once we were in complete accord.

"Now you know what we had to suffer at school."

"Ours wasn't so very different." He chewed mournfully. "It was run on English lines."

Outside the hawkers touted their wares and the tantalising smell of their fresh spicy snacks drifted in through the open door and was wafted around by the sluggish fans.

"Couldn't we have some of that?" I asked.

"No fear," replied Logan as he shovelled in a spoonful of hot, slimy pudding, crowned with a smear of bright red jam. "Not unless you want a good old dose of Delhi Belly."

I was tempted to risk it. Rikh shook his head, so I didn't persist. I fell silent then. The meal had reminded me of my school days and most, of all, of Yolanda. My dearest friend whose life had ended so prematurely, one of the many killed in the air raids in London. I remembered her bright, sharp gaze. Her sudden shouts of laughter. She would have hated the food too.

The breakfasts were better. Eggs every which way, tinned bacon and, for some reason, Bath buns with butter that melted immediately into the bread. They didn't look very appetising, but tasted very good. I think, after years of margarine, it was just the thrill of real butter.

So we feasted on breakfasts and gave the rest a wide berth. And there was always tea. You didn't have to wait for a meal stop for that. The *cha wallah* would come down the train several times during the day and we drank gallons of his strong, sweet milky tea, all boiled up together, just how Rikh liked it. It was surprising how refreshing the hot tea was in all that heat.

Finally, in the late afternoon of the fourth day, the train puffed into Ambala Cantonment station, hissing and groaning. During the last few hours of the journey Rikh had noticed that the engine had begun to struggle.

"Sounds like it's on its last legs to me." Rikh was, as ever, imperturbable, hidden behind the morning edition of 'The Times of India'.

"Congress is making progress at last," he remarked cheerfully. I didn't enquire. Independence was not a big priority for me at that moment, I was more concerned with survival. The cacophony of squeaks and groans and clanking worried me. It did sound as if the engine could give out at any minute. I sat bolt upright, staring tensely out of the window, willing the train on. I was immensely relieved when, with a final grinding sigh, the train pulled into the station.

We climbed down onto the platform, aching and bent as geriatrics after four long days and nights on the train. Logan jumped down, spry and muscular, barging his way through the crowds of other ranks and attendant hawkers and beggars. We trailed stiffly behind him, "the rag, tag and bobtail" as Rikh called us, the men in sweat-soaked khaki, the women in creased cotton, all of us looking as if we could do with a good wash. We were rather a sorry sight, I felt. And whilst I had no desire whatsoever to be an advertisement for the Raj, for my own sake, I decided to spruce myself up at the first opportunity.

Logan herded us into a jeep, barked an order in Hindustani and we set off at a spanking pace to the base, clutching the numerous small bags, rugs and flasks that Rikh had insisted we bring with us. Rikh sat in front and talked to the driver. In Hindustani. I couldn't understand a word. The Indians at the League at home had always spoken English, even to each other. The driver wore a crisp, clean uniform and sported a starched, white turban with a regimental badge. He was a lot smarter than we were.

Ambala was a huge combined Forces base at that time, a significant part of the build up for the war in the East. It was strategically placed on the Grand Trunk Road, the main highway across the Punjab, close to the railway axis that ran from North to South and West to East.

We were driven through the Cantonment, down long, broad avenues lined with trees and bungalows of varying sizes (allocated according to rank, I imagined). It all looked alarmingly like the Home Counties. They were called 'Fairlawn', and 'Sherwood'. One was even named 'Balmoral'. What struck me though was the deliberate, almost stagey Englishness of it. The gardens especially, with their patch of carefully tended lawn and flower beds full of plants that belonged in a more temperate climate—hollyhocks, lupins and Canterbury bells. Who looked after all this, I wondered? Teams of native servants,

I later found out, who would work around the clock for a hot meal and a derisory wage.

My reverie was brought to an abrupt end when the driver slammed on the brakes with a jerk that nearly sent Rikh through the windscreen and announced triumphantly, "Home, sweet home." I laughed and he grinned back at me. His teeth were superb, gleaming white like Chicklets, and perfectly even. They were so good they looked false. But everything about him was in Technicolour—his dark eyes, his peach coloured skin and the purply pink of his mouth. His appearance was immaculate. He could have been sent by Central Casting.

Rikh scrambled down from the jeep and I followed, with not much more grace I'm afraid. We trundled down the path towards the bungalow that had been allotted to us.

Standing to attention on the veranda were two men and a girl in a clean, but faded sari. The servants. Ours. The driver introduced us and the older man bared his scarlet stained teeth and said, "Welcome home, Memsahib." Golly. Home was never like this. Not mine anyway.

It was a very nice bungalow, in an oddly sprawling format that meant it was open on three sides and only joined to the next bungalow by one wall, so it was a sort of a semi really. But the join was on the side that encompassed the kitchen and the gardens were separated by a tall fence, so we were hardly aware of our neighbours at all.

The rooms were large and shady—two bedrooms, each with their own washrooms, a living room, a small dining room, and a kitchen at the back that I almost never went into. That was the preserve of the servants. Each room had freshly white-washed walls with a few rather grim pictures of the Lake District and standard issue furniture. All necessities were provided, but it was ugly and functional. Everything had been put together with no particular taste so it was very impersonal. Even when I unpacked and put our few knick knacks around, it felt transitory, like a hotel room. In all the time I lived there, it never felt like home.

I felt guilty for not warming to it because compared to our two damp rooms with shared bath and toilet in Marchmont Street, it was downright luxurious. I had bought a few brass ornaments from hawkers at the various stations we had stopped at. Rikh said they were "worthless junk," but I liked them. I bought a Buddha and a curious stunted little man, who I later learned was Shiva, balanced precariously on a brass stand, beating out the rhythm of the world. He was my favourite. I have him still. He and I are the only relics of that time and seeing him on my window ledge now gives me great comfort. He brings the light and colour of India into my chilly little life.

That first evening we bathed and ate a meal, which, although described by Rikh as makeshift, was grander than anything we would ever have had at home. Three courses: mulligatawny soup (I decided that in future we would do without the soup in that climate), an excellent chicken curry and a fluffy rice pilau, followed by ice cream. All served in disapproving silence by Suleiman Khan,

Rikh's batman and bearer, while the cook and general servant, Kutabaksht, peeped round the door and beamed when he saw us eating with gusto.

Over the next few days I tried to get to grips with the servants and their various roles. Frankly, I struggled. It was a very strange division of labour—or so it seemed to me.

At the head of it all and reigning supreme was Suleiman. A tall, slender *Pathan*, with red hair and deep blue eyes. He was a man of very few words and so superior it was impossible for me to engage with him on any level. He was hard-working and trustworthy, Rikh said, and he guarded Rikh more jealously than any lover. None of Rikh's things from his socks to his papers were to be touched by anyone but him. He even did Rikh's laundry for him, spending hours on the back veranda outside the kitchen ironing and starching his shirts and uniform and polishing the brass on his belt to a dazzling shine. He drove Rikh to work in the mornings and then returned to tyrannise the household. Especially me.

He would commandeer Rikh's favourite food and his word was law. I made a tentative request one day for Kutabaksht to make some crumb chops and perhaps a sponge cake? I knew by then that other people on the base ate English food and Kutabaksht was an accomplished cook, but Suleiman silenced me with a glance of withering scorn and just said, "No. Burra Sahib likes spicy food." And that was it.

Kutabaksht was a lot more approachable. By then, in his

seventies, with his betel stained teeth, wrinkly grin and gnarled hands and feet, he was an old man. But he worked from dawn to dusk, lighting the fire in the kitchen range, producing the most delicious meals with the antiquated, labour intensive equipment he was supplied with. I was speechless with admiration for him. He also cleaned and polished. He even shopped for the food we ate—I handed him the money Rikh gave me every morning—they both insisted that was part of his duties and he went off to the market.

Late at night, he would retire to the servants' quarters—a sort of shed at the back of the house with a water tap outside—to smoke his hubble bubble like the caterpillar in 'Alice in Wonderland' and the pungent, old rope smell of hashish would waft gently across the garden and into our room. He was an old rogue, and by the end I was certain he was rooking us on the food money, but I became so fond of him and he did so much for so little, I didn't care. I never told Rikh anyway.

The young girl in the faded sari bothered me the most. She was a *dalit*—an Untouchable—and she was treated like dirt by everyone. I'm ashamed to say I never knew her name. I never heard anyone call her by it. They only called her "girl" – Larkhi. I asked her once in my halting Hindustani, but before the words were properly out of my mouth Suleiman came up and shouted at her and she covered her face with her sari and ran away.

She was given all the tasks no-one else wanted to do.

Every day she washed and swept all the floors, even the garden path which I thought excessive and she scrubbed the bathroom and toilet until it gleamed. She was not allowed in our bedroom, that was Suleiman's domain and I must say he kept it spotless. But right from the first few days, I became aware that nothing could go on in that house without his knowledge, or rather permission. He even slept on the veranda outside our room. After we had gone to bed, he would pick up his bedroll from the back veranda and creep silently to the window outside our room and there he would sleep, his rifle by his side, all night long. It was incredibly inhibiting.

It was a very odd way of life. At least for me. Since childhood I had always pulled my weight with the household chores and then with Rikh, despite my shortcomings as a cook, I had cleaned, washed and ironed and shopped and cooked the meals we ate at home. Suddenly, I had nothing to do. It was a luxury that took me a long time to get used to, not doing things for myself. I could not even go to the kitchen to get a glass of water—Kutabaksht would look concerned at my intrusion and ask me what was wrong and Suleiman would announce he would bring "*pani*" and would serve it to me on a silver tray as if it were a vintage wine. Rikh adapted to it with an ease I found repellent—yelling for an exhausted old man to get him a drink or a snack he could easily have got for himself. He always did in London.

I did ask Rikh how he could square his reverence for

Gandhiji, who was the champion of the Untouchables, with his attitude towards the servants. He sighed as if I were a particularly obtuse child, talking slowly and deliberately in generalities about how Emancipation for "these people" must and would come, but for the moment, to treat the *Larkhi* differently would cause huge offence to Suleiman and Kutabaksht and do her no good at all. In fact, Rikh argued, evoking their resentment without being able to resolve her situation, as he called it, was likely to make her life worse. After which, I shut up. I certainly didn't want to do that.

Chapter Two

First established in 1843, Ambala was one of the oldest and biggest military bases in India. By the time we arrived, it was a hive of activity. The Air Force Base was gearing up for night raids on Burma and this was the reason for the transfer of Rikh's Squadron from the UK to India. In June 1942 the squadrons were re-formed and by the end of the year flying operations on Burma had begun.

After the first few days, settling into my new home and realising that the level of servants was going to mean that I had alarmingly little to do, I began to explore.

Security was tight. Much tighter than in England. Although the Congress Party had in the end backed the war effort, the 'Quit India' campaign had awakened fears of attack on British personal and military property. On entry to or exit from the base, we were checked in and out by the armed sentry in his box, and although for us this was only a formality, it still felt constraining. I was not used to my comings and goings being scrutinised and, frankly, I did not like it. At home the continuous brooding presence of Suleiman made me feel nervous and ill at ease. So I took to taking long walks, at least twice a day, first thing in the morning and late in the afternoon, to get away.

I explored the base first. It held all the usual offices, although on a larger and grander scale than I was used to at home. There was a Naafi, a rather good library with comfortable if worn leather armchairs and yellowing maps of the Punjab and the North West Frontier on the walls, and an Officer's Mess building with games rooms and a bar. Outside was the usual parade ground and cricket pitch and beyond that the Cantonment.

It was an odd place. Nothing was quite what it seemed. The base buildings had none of the shabby homeliness of their counterparts in England. The whitewashed walls were not peeling; everything was bright and well kept. Even the flowers in the neat herbaceous borders with their rows of uniform plants planted in a straight line, seemed to be standing to attention. The lawns were watered and almost manicured, tended to by teams of native gardeners who toiled in the baking sun to keep up the appearance of an English garden. "A corner of a foreign field that is forever Surrey," as Rikh called it. I used to agonise about our relationship on those walks, admiring his cleverness always, but wishing he were not quite so difficult to live with.

I came to see that life on the base and in the cantonment was deeply false. A mummer's show to ward off the dark. A non-stop round of games and parties, dinners and balls, tennis and cricket tournaments. Billiards and bridge, coffee and cake mornings, and whist drives, as they all clung desperately to the Titanic of the Raj. I longed for the end of the war and the independence that must follow. I paced like an anxious prisoner through this facsimile, noting that despite all efforts to maintain the boundaries of home, the scale and grandeur of India could not be kept out—the gardens were too large, the buildings too big, the blue line of the horizon too far away. And I rejoiced in it. Outside the armed camp that was British India was a vast landscape, a place of infinite possibility that would not be denied.

The intensity of the 'Quit India' campaign had shaken British India to the core. It may have been suppressed, but the prisons were overflowing. Nehru had been carted off to jail and nobody, not even his family, was told where he was being held. The crack-down was harsh and unflinching—the police had *lathi* charged groups of women and children who were demonstrating peacefully and the crowds responded by torching public buildings and tearing up railway lines. In Delhi and Bombay the police had opened fire killing strikers and demonstrators. The Raj had prevailed, but it was reeling.

I rejoiced in it, longing for the day when India would be free. I had felt certain that Rikh would feel the same, but since he had arrived in India and taken up his duties on the base, his revolutionary ardour seemed to have evaporated.

He had explained to me on the boat that India would be very different, but I had taken that to mean our way of life, not the principles and beliefs that underpinned it. Perhaps I didn't understand or only heard what I wanted to because he did say that he would have, yet again, to put his pacifism and dreams for Independence in abeyance, or "in hock" I think was the way he put it—until the greater danger, by that he meant a Japanese invasion—had been dealt with. It seemed to me he was trying to square the circle, but I said nothing because I really wouldn't have known what I was talking about and I certainly agreed that this war had to be fought and won.

After we had been in Ambala for about a month we went to a Combined Forces dinner and dance at the Officer's Club. It was the usual type of thing—evening dress for the women, mess dress for the men, decorations worn by those that had them and the whole thing sinking beneath an atmosphere of stilted jollification. Despite the really excellent food and wine, the smartly dressed servants who made sure one wanted for nothing, the regimental silver, crisp white table clothes and Waterford crystal, it was all rather joyless.

It was certainly lavish on a scale we had not enjoyed at home since the war started. Drinks and canapés beforehand, then a meal that seemed to drag on forever as we munched our way through hors d'oeuvres, fish, entrées, savoury and pudding, followed by endless toasts to King and Country, then dancing to a rather dreary band who played selections from 'Rosalie' and 'Evergreen'. It was all very old-fashioned. I began to long for Freddy and the Tango Teas at the Waldorf. I had made up my mind to make a real effort to be pleasant and enjoy myself, but as I was dragged around the dance floor, smiling and laughing merrily as my feet took a terrible bashing from a moustachioed Wing Commander, I was bored witless and wished I had stayed at home with a good book.

However, I told myself to stick it out and by what I hoped was nearly the end of the evening, I hadn't put a foot wrong and was priding myself on my good behaviour. Even Rikh was smiling encouragingly at me. We went into the bar for "one last drink" and a small group of us sat at a table together and practised our small talk. During the course of the evening I had promised to join in with various good works—amongst which were the Knitting for Forces Club (thanks to my mother, I was rather a good knitter at that time) although the thought of all those do-gooding Memsahibs with their endless hanks of khaki wool had rather put me off, but no, I had agreed to join in, and even volunteered to help organise (my background at the Waldorf suddenly an asset) a ladies luncheon in aid of the Red Cross. I had pandered to an entire coven of sour faced old bats and flirted with their boozed up husbands and I felt I had really done my bit. So I allowed myself to relax now as the whole ordeal was clearly winding down. Alas.

I was seated next to Rikh. I suppose there were about five or six of us at the table, and we were talking in general about life, India, hill stations and so on, when one army officer, who was younger and had seemed quite reasonable, took a long drag on his cigarette and remarked,

"I do think Mr Gandhi and his chums might have had the decency to wait until we'd won the war for 'em before they started all this 'do or die, liberty or death' lark."

A colonel's wife, an alarmingly thin lady whose grey silk dress matched her skin and hair, piped up, " I know... absolute stab in the back after all we've done for them."

"What exactly have we done for them?" I asked innocently. Rikh frowned at me in warning. I looked away.

"Everything," she replied lugubriously, "rule of law, justice." I thought there hadn't been much of that lately what with all the imprisonments without charge under the Defence of India Act, then she waved her arm vaguely in the air, "the Grand Trunk Road."

I nearly laughed out loud. They always trotted that out as if it were on a par with the Pyramids or the Acropolis. I looked across at Rikh, wanting him to remember when we first met and a similar, silly argument had been made, longing for him to respond as he had done then, but he was silent and would not catch my eye.

The army chap ground his cigarette viciously into the ashtray, putting it out, nodding his agreement.

"Exactly, and our chaps are dying to keep them safe."
That was too much.

"And two million of them are fighting with us."

They all turned and looked at me. "And presumably also dying? And they volunteered. They didn't have to be conscripted. Is it so very wrong for them to want to be free? After all, isn't that what Mr Churchill says we are fighting for?"

The Grey Wraith gave me a rictus-like smile, "My dear, I don't think you quite grasp the nature of war," she trilled.

That did it. "Oh believe me, I do. I grasped it right enough in London during the Blitz – when we were being bombed night after night, hiding in holes in the ground and only coming out to bury our dead."

I had flayed myself on the raw. I remembered my friend Yolanda's death. Her mother's face flashed before my eyes. Mama Barroni. I saw again her grace, her profound kindness and her towering grief for her dead child. I hated those people in the bar, with their armchair platitudes, safe and smug in their hill stations and cantonments, far from the stink and suffering of war.

We glared at each other—the Grey Wraith and I—with the instinctive, visceral loathing of Cain and Abel. Rikh broke the silence.

"Whisky, Nita." He announced loudly. I couldn't believe my ears. It was an order. I stared at him, dumb-struck.

"Whisky"—this time with the clear enunciation you would use to a dim-witted child.

Now I can see that he was only trying to defuse a pointless confrontation and get me out of the firing line, but then I was aghast. Not only would he not defend me, he was adding insult to injury by treating me like a servant. I had never imagined that this denial of our real selves would be so total. I stood up.

"*Et tu, Brute.*" I must have drunk more than I thought. Blinded by tears of rage or alcohol, I wasn't terribly sure which, and feeling very alone, I made my way to the bar.

My head down, I tried surreptitiously to wipe my eyes, hoping mascara was not making tramlines down my face.

"Whisky, please," I whispered to the bar tender.

"Who's the oaf?" a cheerful voice asked. Oh God, everyone in the bar must have heard Rikh barking out orders at me.

"My husband."

"Ah, sorry."

"At the moment. So am I."

A spotless white handkerchief was passed along the bar. I sniffed and wiped my eyes, leaving black smudges on its gleaming white. I handed it back.

"God, I've ruined it. I'm so sorry."

"I'm not. Gave me an excuse to talk to you. There. Much better now without the panda look." He stuffed the handkerchief back in his pocket. "They're such lovely eyes." I smiled tremulously at him. I felt as if someone had thrown me a lifeline. I grabbed it with both hands.

The bar tender had put five glasses of whisky on a tray. I reached for it, determined not to make anymore of a scene that night.

He took it from me. "No. I'll do that." He nodded at the bar tender "Patiala pegs—two. Don't move." Then he took the tray to Rikh's party. I stayed where I was.

The bar tender filled two tumblers with a huge amount of whisky. The man returned.

"There we are. Patiala pegs. Mud in your eye. Or rather his."

Despite my humiliation, I was still married enough to feel pain at that. I turned to look at the man by my side.

He was small and slight, not much taller than me, with eyes so dark they reflected light like mirrors, a fine-boned, elfin face and a mischievous grin. He reminded me of Puck, my idea of him at any rate, taking a wry amusement at the folly he saw all around him.

"The name's Abdi."

I told him mine.

"What a lovely name. Almost as beautiful as you."

"Come off it."

He laughed.

"I didn't come up the Clyde on a bicycle." Mother's old expression slipped out. God, how I longed for her. Her cool, calm gaze, the soft Scots lilt of her voice, the way I belonged wherever I was with her.

"What a wonderful expression. Say it again." I did. He looked round the room, taking in everyone present.

"God, what a morgue! How did a creature like you fetch up here?"

"I could ask the same of you."

He nodded solemnly, then raised his glass. "War does terrible things to people." I looked across at Rikh and thought how right he was. "Let's hope this one is over before it turns us into the living dead, like that lot."

"I'll drink to that." I stayed talking to him for some time, and when I reluctantly slipped down from the bar stool, saying "back to the morgue," he took my hand to steady me and then kissed it. "You are very naughty," I admonished him.

"I hope so," he replied. I returned to Rikh's table feeling more cheerful than I had felt since we left the Goldmans in New York.

"I see you were having quite the little tête-à-tête over there," sniped the Grey Wraith.

"Abdi's a rogue," announced Bertie Trevelyan, Rikh's new Squadron Leader. I decided I liked Abdi even more.

The evening wound up soon after that, with huge thankfulness on my part and a terrible false conviviality all round, as we lied in our teeth and declared what a wonderful evening it had been. As I was saying good night to the Grey Wraith, she reached for my hand, and held it tight as if I were a four year old and said, "don't worry, dear, you'll soon slot in." I could have kicked her. I didn't want to slot in. Anywhere. Least of all with her.

We drove home in silence. A silence which was maintained as we entered the house. Rikh went into the living room. From his ramrod back and pursed lips, I could see that he was furious. I went straight to bed, arranging the voluminous folds of the mosquito net around me. It was like a pall. Through the gauze, I could see Suleiman taking up his position on the veranda outside.

Rikh came up about an hour later. I pretended to be asleep, but he knew better. He sat down on the chair and began to unlace his shoes.

"You have to make allowances," he began reasonably enough. "All these strikes and riots have terrified them."

I pulled back the net so that he could see that I was listening.

"They're afraid we'll form a fifth column in their midst. Within the Armed Forces—it's their worst nightmare." He bent down to take off his socks.

"They're arresting everybody." I knew that. He stood up to take off his trousers and looked at me sternly.

"They know all about us and the India League, Nita. We'll be on file somewhere. The only thing keeping us out of jail at the moment is my service record. Because of that, and that alone, they'll give us the benefit of the doubt. But only if we pull along and don't rock the boat. Do you understand?"

He folded his trousers neatly and laid them over the

back of the chair. Old habits died hard. I said nothing and that seemed to annoy him.

"They're not playing games, damn it. If they can chuck Nehru in jail, what makes you think they'd spare you?"

He buttoned up his pyjamas. My silence only made him crosser.

"Do you have any idea what an Indian jail is like? Or how hard it would be to get out of it? They'd bury us alive."

He was, as ever, almost certainly right. He went on to assure me that his dreams for a free, independent India were still the same, but we had to change our expectations of how and when it was arrived at.

What he failed to see was that what had stung me most was not the change in his political stance, that was pragmatic good sense, but a hardening of what had already begun in London. His view of me as no longer his equal partner in our struggle for a brave, new world, but rather as an inferior, an irritation, a mote in his eye. That was what hurt me.

I was increasingly lonely after that. The word had gone round that I was "unreliable, a bit of a loose cannon" and despite my volunteering for more or less everything, no-one seemed to want either my help or my company.

After that evening, I was resolutely ignored. I was never invited again to the round of tennis teas, luncheons or charity drives that a new wife on the base is showered with.

I don't suppose I would have enjoyed them much, but

the point was I was not asked. All my attempts to build bridges by chatting at the Naafi or the club were met with polite but cursory replies that lead nowhere.

So I spent most of my days and some evenings alone, taking long walks through the cantonment and spending hours in the library reading the papers from cover to cover to stave off the time when I would have to return to Suleiman's unflinching stare and Rikh's sullen silences.

I liked the evenings when Rikh was flying best. Then I had a solitary dinner, served in state by Suleiman. I had suggested that if I was alone, we could make the whole thing less formal, a sandwich or something on a tray in the living room, but he shuddered with horror at the very thought and continued to serve every dish standing behind my chair in the dining room, refilling my glass and watching me fork in every mouthful. Only after that could I go into the sitting room and read, which I did with great pleasure. I began reading my way through Dickens, relishing every description of my damp and dirty London, delighting in the setting of familiar places and characters known to me since childhood. Pip and Miss Haversham, Bill Sykes and Nancy, Little Dorrit and her appallingly feckless father. Winter twilights on the marshes, the fishing boats setting out to sea in a grey dawn, the river and the lamplight—they all returned and were a huge comfort to me, like the family I had never had.

Some of my most loved books I had won at school for prizes I had long forgotten. For excellence—was written in one frontispiece. It was just as well to be reminded of that because I was getting it all wrong in India. I had arrived at my dream and no-one here seemed to like me at all. Not even my husband. No-one except the imp in the bar seemed to think I was worth the time of day, from the Grey Wraith, who it appeared was the Queen of the Cantonment, to the girl who swept the floor. I couldn't put a foot right. I had hoped that India would bring Rikh and I closer together, that he would be happier, and he was, but not with me. I was beginning to learn that you can't save an ailing marriage with a change of location. Geography alone won't do it.

So I was rather forlorn until a remarkable woman saved me. One morning, a short, dumpy lady, all smiles, with a crumpled cushion of a face, watched me attempt to pay for some goods at the Naafi and came to my rescue. She explained that everything on the base was signed for, not paid. A chit was issued, one signed it and at the end of the month the chits were sent to one's husband for payment. Cash never changed hands, she explained. No filthy lucre, she smiled, only a promise to pay, which is all cash is anyway, she went on airily. I said it seemed very alien to me, that I was used to managing my own money, not having to run to my husband if I wanted to buy a cake of soap. She smoothed my ruffled feathers and invited me into the bar for a drink. I found, despite my ungraciousness, that I could not really refuse and, in any case, she was the only person who had asked for my company since I arrived.

Over a very large gin and tonic (another Patiala peg, I supposed) she introduced herself. She was Mrs Pepe, call me Amelia, she said. Her husband was an injured soldier from the First World War, he walked with a pronounced limp and wore the sort of built up boot we often saw in London during the post war years. Now he ran the Officer's club on the base. I couldn't place her at all. She certainly wasn't English, but she was far too pale to be Indian or even Anglo Indian. She had a background accent, but it was so slight I couldn't identify it. Later I learned that she was from Goa, of Portuguese descent. She wore a worn fox fur in all weathers, its sunken eyes and bared yellow teeth no longer a threat to anyone, and she was the kindest woman I have ever known.

She must have heard of my outburst in the bar, although she never referred to it. Instead, she asked me how I liked India.

I told her I loved what I had seen of India, but I never seemed to be in it, only stuck in a Gilbert and Sullivan travesty of it. She smiled at that and didn't seem to mind my tactlessness, which was big of her.

"I was like you when I first came here. I didn't fit in either," she ventured, putting down her glass. I had a sudden vision of her as a Twenties bride, all short skirts and dangling pearls. She still wore the pearls in fact, although they sometimes got lost in the deep wrinkles around her neck and the fusty haze of the fox fur.

"It took me a long time to get the hang of it." She made it all seem quite natural.

"Were you a flapper?" I asked, remembering Mother and Mrs Lomasney teaching me the Charleston in the kitchen in Peel Street, skirts and long ropes of beads flying.

"I certainly was. No-one could Charleston like me. I was famous for it." I believed her.

"I hate the Memsahibs," I dared tell her, not for a second accusing her of being one. She nodded in what I felt sure was agreement, "but the Indians don't really want to know. They're perfectly polite and everything, but they don't want to be friends." She nodded again. She was a very good listener. "Even the Indian officer's wife who lives next door, runs a mile when I try to talk to her."

"She would."

"Why?"

"Because, usually, Memsahibs look down on them."

"I'm not a Memsahib!"

"I'm afraid you are, my dear, and therein lies your dilemma. The English are dinosaurs to you, and not very lovable ones at that, but the Indians haven't caught up. They will, but not yet." She looked at me seriously, "you are a modern woman in a not quite modern age."

I stared at her in astonishment. "The war will probably fix that. War is a great catalyst for change." I was silent. I thought of the First World War and its catastrophic effect on my mother's life. My absent father and the disgrace of my birth.

"Pariah seems to be my default position." I wasn't going to tell her any more than that. Not yet anyway. I wished Mother were here. But she was many miles away, risking her life in a city full of ruins. A world apart.

Mrs Pepe smiled gently, "Never mind, sweetheart." She raised her glass.

"To a modern gal. Try not to ruffle too many feathers at once, but don't ever stop disconcerting people. It's good for them."

As I came to know her better, I liked her very much indeed. But what I failed to notice at our first meeting was how ill she was. I should have seen it. Her face, beneath the powder was sallow, her ankles were swollen, and her lips had a bluish tinge. Her heart was failing, she told me cheerfully at our second meeting, and there was nothing to be done about it, so she didn't think about it. She just told me she would not be accompanying me on my walks, my route marches, she called them. Then she defused the seriousness of what she had just told me by adding that she had never liked walking very much. Riding in a tonga was more her style. So, together, not every day, because some days I would call for her and she would be too ill to go out, but when she was well, we would go for a ride and talk.

She found resting a great bore, so on those days when a ride by the river was out of the question, she would lie on the fat, chintz covered settee, covered by an embroidered silk shawl, and we would talk there, in her home. The place didn't matter, she said, the talk did. We became great friends.

She lived in a fussy, over-decorated bungalow. A place where every surface was covered with knickknacks, mostly china dogs and horses. Beswick, she said. She collected them and they were valuable. They looked awful to me.

I soon discovered there was very little I could not talk to Mrs Pepe about. She was my first friend in India.

Chapter Three

Late one afternoon, driven out of the bungalow by Suleiman's towering silence (that man could create an atmosphere that was like walking into a brick wall without saying a word), I called on Mrs Pepe, but her bearer told me that she had been very unwell that morning and was asleep now.

So I walked through the cantonment and on into Ambala proper. It was a shock. Until that point the India I had seen was always at one remove. From a train, in a car, safe and sound at all times since I had arrived in the suffocating cocoon of the Raj. Now for the first time, I saw poverty. I walked among it. The people living on these streets had nothing. A few rags and maybe a brass pot. They lived on the street in squalor and disease. I saw people living as I had never seen before. I watched a Muslim lady, completely unashamed, standing at a broken stand-pipe, careful to keep her face veiled while she washed her naked body, I saw sadhus with long ropes of hair, their nakedness only camouflaged with streaks of yellow paint, beggars baying for alms, and thin and faded women, in torn cotton saris cooking meagre meals for their families on open fires, and defecating cheerfully in public.

I saw a child who had been dead for some time, simply lying in the road among the other detritus, the vegetable and human waste, and through it all, the sacred cows wandered, undisturbed, placidly chewing whatever they could forage.

And all this was half a mile from the leafy avenues and manicured lawns of the cantonment where we lived in a state of affluence we could never have enjoyed at home and all of it, the crisp white linen, the spotless houses, the perfectly served meals on silver salvers, was paid for by this vast undertow of misery and filth, while we proudly boasted about the buildings we had built that they were not allowed into. Our civilisation—the obscene advancement of men like the District Commissioner, a decent enough man, but one of very average abilities, had the power of life and death and could incarcerate at will men like Gandhi, Nehru and Krishna Menon. Krishna, who could have wiped the floor with every one of them without breaking a sweat. It made me sick. We had not created poverty in India, but we had done nothing to break its iron grip. I walked on, determined to turn my back on the Raj whenever I could.

Totally preoccupied, I wandered, without direction, like one of the ruminating cows, creatures of insane privilege, far above their natural state, not noticing that the light was changing. Twilight comes quickly in India, the harsh bright glare fades into a soft, golden glow and then, quite suddenly, dusk. A deep forgiving blue descends.

I blundered into the bazaar, drawn perhaps by the light of hundreds of fairy lights strung about to illuminate the stalls. I saw here a girl, who looked no more than fourteen, carrying a sickly baby that was clearly her own, watching as two enormously fat Banias, resplendent in turquoise and orange silk, their pudgy hands bristling with diamond rings, bought sticky sweets that dripped with syrup. I smelled the stink of sewers and spices and the heady scent of dying flowers, while skinny cats and mangy dogs rummaged for food alongside the beggar children, on a mountain of rubbish.

I walked on through an Aladdin's cave of colour and sound, of treasure and junk. It was total chaos. I was instantly surrounded by a group of ragged children, the youngest about six and the oldest no more than twelve, who demanded *pice*, and offered to carry my bag, skipping along, falling over each other, calling, cajoling, pleading.

"My uncle, my uncle... look, here, he will give you the best price."

"I can show you best place for silk, you want scarf, or fruit, anything you want, Memsahib... Lifebuoy soap, you want Colgate with dental cream?"

Always surrounded by voices, shrill or soft, engulfed by waves of a language I could barely understand. At first it frightened me, these insistent children who came too close and clung to me, steering my steps, who would not go away.

I felt as if I must slip, faltering in the heat, the dust, the garish colours and blaring music from a hundred tinny radios all tuned to different channels. I stumbled on with my escort of devouring infants, like a flock of birds pecking at my hands, my bag, my skirt, until I came reeling to rest by a stall, whose owner clad in grubby white pyjamas and a lace skullcap, dazzled me still further by insisting I see his display of silks.

Scarves, saris, salwar kameez, he laid them all out, in silks of every colour and hue, white tunics with silver embroidery, deep crimson, shocking pink, deepest indigo, bright yellow and orange, and a rich jade green.

I was taken by a red silk scarf with a deep border of gold embroidery. It seemed quite beautiful to me. Then he showed me one of a peacock blue with an iridescent sheen and I hovered, undecided, until a voice in my ear announced ironically, "I didn't think I'd find you here." It was the imp, he of the Patiala pegs and the penchant for rescue.

I tried to collect myself. "Why ever not?" He didn't seem convinced. The baying children's voices reached a crescendo.

"They'll pick you clean." Without looking down, he

grabbed a small brown hand that was already working its way stealthily into his pocket. He took out a handful of small change and flung it onto the ground. The children scrabbled for the coins and then ran away.

He grinned at me. "Isn't this a bit... real for you?"

"Not at all." I lied.

We walked together through the bazaar.

Past stands piled high with exotic fruit—plump pink guavas and little green mangoes, hands of bananas, so scarce at home, and black, wrinkled passion fruit. Others selling clothes and fabrics from the finest silks to homespun white cotton, *chappels*, shoes and everywhere the smell of hot fat and spices, of freshly cooked pakoras and samosas mingled with the scent of rose water and sandalwood. Stalls of ground and whole spices in bright pyramids: chilli and turmeric and the heady, sweet undertow of the aromatics, cardamom and cinnamon and cloves. The people were no less various—tall Sikhs in bright turbans, Muslim women veiled and burqa-clad, naked saddhus old as the hills. The crazy wealth and vicious poverty, diamond rings and rags, the top soil of misery atop the strange grandeur of India.

I was silent for most of it, trying to take it all in, desperate to make some kind of sense of it. At one point he said, "Don't."

"Don't what?"

"Try to understand. It's too soon."

He took my arm and I let him. Much later he asked me if

there was anything I wanted. I told him I had seen a scarf, a blue scarf with a sheen like a magpie's wing. He asked me where I had seen it. "Where we met." He took me back. The stall holder insisted on showing me again his entire stock.

"I only want the scarf," I said.

"Really?" Abdi sounded doubtful. "Are you sure?"

"Yes," I said, taking out my purse. "Put that away," he hissed.

The stall holder smiled, inclining his head towards me with a gracious gesture. "For you, Memsahib, only fifteen rupees." I took out my purse.

"Seven." The voice was clear and strong.

"I am taking the food from my children's mouths. I am robbing my grand-mother to give you this," he wailed. Then looking sharply up at Abdi, "ten."

"Eight and not one anna more." The stall holder looked sad. A group of kids obligingly gathered round.

"You are robbing them, Memsahib," he warned, shaking his head. They looked tearful. It worried me. But not Abdi.

"Take no notice. They're probably nothing to do with him. Eight rupees."

The stall holder nodded mournfully. "Premier quality," he intoned as he wrapped the scarf in crumpled and slightly greasy brown paper. Abdi took the money from me and handed it over. The stall holder instantly cheered up.

"Memsahib, when you wear this scarf you will capture

every man's heart and you will remember me." I doubted that. All of it.

"I only sell best quality…" but Abdi was steering me on, far more firmly than my little flock had. The stall holder's voice faded into the background and others, more strident, took over and drowned him out.

I spent a long time with Abdi that evening, walking, talking, sometimes just silently together. He was not an intellectual like Rikh, but he had a bright incisive mind and a sharp eye. He missed very little. He had certainly got the measure of me. He knew I didn't want to go home, so he helped me draw out the long evening, taking me a different way home and showing me the cantonment gardens in the moonlight.

He didn't kiss me that night, but I wanted him to.

One evening, about a week later, I walked down one of the long avenues in the cantonment, past some of the grander bungalows, staring in at the lighted windows, watching the officers and their wives being served drinks or their elaborate dinners, servants in starched white in attendance. Other people's lives, viewed from outside as they listened to the radio or simply sat in companionable silence reading their books, had always fascinated me. The cosy, cheerless minutiae of domestic life—a life shared, but always essentially separate. Watching them made me feel sad and suddenly very alone. I had travelled to the place of my childhood dreams, but I still felt as much of an outsider here as I had in Kensington Gardens. A rootless intruder, yearning to belong.

Whenever I felt lonely I would conjure up my Mother's face, she after all had always been my only home, and now I missed her so much it felt like a physical pain, but she was better off without me. Without me she could move on, no longer be shackled to a painful past, but actually have a future. Perhaps she would find a partner, she was certainly young and attractive enough. A man who would not hurt or disappoint her and they could make a life together. Without me. The thought was unbearable. Even then, so far away, I was not ready to relinquish my place at the centre of her life, which probably meant that somewhere, despite my various attempts to pull away, she was still firmly at the centre of mine. It was a depressing thought for both of us. I trudged on, past the backdrop of other people's lives and wondered how I could have got it so wrong. I wished I could talk to Yolanda.

I walked on past the last bungalow and into the gardens, among the tall trees, wanting to hide in the kindly dark. A figure leapt out at me and clapped his hands over my eyes. I screamed. It was Abdi.

"God, you frightened me."

"Good." Utterly unrepentant, he was still holding me. His arm was now round my waist.

"I was..." He didn't let me go on. He leaned in to me, his eyes alight with what? Desire? Malice? I never knew. Then he kissed me. Hard. I pulled away.

"You've got a nerve."

He kissed me again. A long kiss that lead to a longer embrace and I found that I wanted him too. I was desperate for love – from anywhere and almost anyone, and he was determined to prove his skill, his mastery.

We met often after that, constantly running into each other, not really by chance, in the Naafi, the library, once even as I was leaving Mrs Pepe's. He seemed to know by an uncanny instinct where I would be and when I would be alone. He always seemed to avoid Rikh.

Mostly, we just walked and talked. Inconsequential chatter that staved off loneliness. He was an inveterate gossip, with a nose for scandal and an eye for detail that was unerring. He said he was a mosaic man; he stored up colours until they formed a picture.

On one of these walks, he asked me why I was so oblivious to my surroundings. Stung, I replied I was not. Not at all. We walked on in silence. But then, flinching from such a trenchant and accurate observation, I had to admit to myself that my interior clamour was so great that I was often unaware of what was going on around me. Then he asked if I had ever noticed, for example, that the Grey Wraith's eyes were always sore and swollen. I had not, and even if I had, would not have cared greatly, I announced in a rather lordly fashion.

"Oh Memsahib, how much you miss when you when you have your nose in the air and your head in the clouds." He minced along beside me, doing a rather cruel pastiche of me walking through life, deep in thought and missing it all.

"You are rotten." But I had to laugh because he looked so silly.

"Certainly, but do you know why she's always turning on the waterworks?" He was like a dog with a bone; he wouldn't give it up.

"No. Haven't a clue," I snapped.

"Well," he went on, unstoppable, " her two sons were killed early on in the war – one at Dunkirk and the other at the fall of Singapore – and her only daughter was sent to Canada with the WAAFS and has just announced her intention of staying on after the war. For good. Met a Canadian running around with logs. A lumberjack, I presume. Must be a marvellous change after the giddy excitement of the Mess teas."

"Nothing left for her but to go home and die in Cheltenham," he declared cheerfully.

"What about her husband?"

"The Colonel? Can't stand the sight of her. Haven't you noticed? They barely speak. He never dances with her on a Saturday night or even sits at the same table in the bar." That much was true. Even I had clocked that.

"Separate beds for decades."

That was a thought too far for me. "How do you know?"

"Common knowledge. Everyone knows."

"You are shameless."

He considered or pretended to. "True, but then so are you because you are laughing."

I couldn't argue with that. I was.

Abdi was sometimes away on Ops, but nothing like as often as Rikh because he was not a good pilot. He told me that he had crashed a plane during a training exercise and that they were now loath to let him loose on another. The co-pilot had been badly injured, apparently.

Abdi said he had the luck of the devil and had escaped with only cuts and bruises, but the other chap had serious injuries and was taken to the big military hospital in Poona. He had looked like a penitent child when he said that, his huge dark eyes wide, appalled at his crime. That and his pronounced widow's peak gave him the air of a sorrowful elf. But not for long, because he soon perked up and said that although he was now regarded as "a bit of a Typhoid Mary, only fit for emergency reserves," the silver lining was that he was comparatively idle and had plenty of time for me.

I knew, from my days on the station at Welwyn, how superstitious airmen are and was sure that they would avoid flying with him if they possibly could.

But Rikh was home sometimes. I remember particularly one evening when Suleiman served Kutabaksht's delicious curry with all the trimmings, a special meal to celebrate Rikh's being at home for dinner, but somehow Rikh could not eat and just pushed the food miserably around his plate. I asked him several times if he was feeling ill, because the food was so good I could not imagine any other reason for not eating it, but he shrugged off my concern, saying nothing was wrong.

I didn't believe him for a second. In the end, in an effort to find the reason for this silent misery, I took his hand.

"Rikh, what's up? Why won't you tell me?" I was beginning to get really worried, so my tone was gentle and it worked. He looked away, then swallowed as if it hurt him.

"Bengal." It was almost a whisper.

"What about Bengal?"

"They're starving."

I couldn't believe it. Since we had arrived in India, the profusion and quality of the food had surprised and delighted me.

"How is that possible? Most of the rice comes from..." I dredged up my facts and figures gleaned long ago from the Kensington library.

He turned to face me and although his voice was harsh, his eyes were glittery with tears.

"Exactly. Even with a bad harvest they should have enough. But Churchill has decreed that the entire crop must be diverted to feed the troops."

"But they don't need it."

"Doesn't matter. It's all been taken and the people of Bengal are starving. It's been hushed up, but they say between one and three million."

I couldn't speak, I was so appalled the words stuck in my throat.

"Wavell did try, he appealed to Churchill. But the old bastard won't budge."

"Is there nothing we can do? Surely Congress..."

"Congress is hog-tied—Defence of India Act. Most of them are detained and those that aren't know damn well if they open their mouths they'll go straight to jail. We're bound and gagged, our people starve, we cannot say anything. And I defend these bastards."

I took him in my arms. There was nothing I could say or do. I tried to be kind to Rikh from then on. But the next morning he had taken refuge in a cold, remote silence that nothing could penetrate. When I tried, he snapped at me. Then he went out. That night he did not come home. I didn't know if he was on Ops or just wanted to be alone. I never knew. Perhaps he was just trying to avoid me. Business as usual. Our brief rapprochement was over.

Mrs Pepe was often too ill to see me now. Our drives had ceased and she was often too tired even to receive me in her home. She sent frequent little notes and messages delivered by hand by one of her servants, but they were no substitute for her company. Although I had known her for such a short time, I missed her.

But then there was always Abdi—waiting for me, popping up unexpectedly, always chatty, good company, always wanting to be with me. An increasingly welcome interlude in an otherwise dreary life. I was frankly grateful for the attention. And if all he wanted in return was company and sex, well, why ever not? It was not as if my husband wanted me.

Chapter Four

As summer wore on the heat became unbearable. When you went outside it was like walking into a wall. The air was dry and dusty and the gardens, so verdant and carefully tended, were now parched, the earth yellow and brown. Going out was only really possible very early in the morning, which had never been my style, or late at night.

In the day the sky was cloudy, everything seem to slip and falter in the heat haze. The horizon, formerly a clear blue line, now looked fuzzy, a distant blur. Nothing seemed sure. We kept the fans on all the time in the bungalow and Suleiman arranged for what Kutabaksht assured me was "the old fashioned remedy, tried and true, Memsahib." This proved to be the appearance of the *bheesti*—a native water carrier, bent almost double beneath the weight of a huge goatskin bag full of water, who went around the bungalow, damping down the clouds of dust in the garden and sprinkling the slats of the blinds in a vain attempt to cool the interior down. It didn't seem to me very effective, just an awful lot of labour for a minimal result, but Rikh also set great store by it. I couldn't see it myself. I thought it smacked more of the male hierarchy wanting to feel that they could do something to combat the heat, which by noon felt like a furnace, but this archaic practice was about as effective as throwing tennis balls at a tank. The heat was relentless and inexorable.

In the evening the atmosphere inside the house was still oppressive, as the buildings retained their heat. I marvelled that Rikh could sleep; it was so sticky and uncomfortable. I certainly could never nod off before three in the morning, sometimes even later. But then he was working flat out and I was idle.

In the early hours of the morning, when the whole cantonment seemed asleep, the first hint of relief was the raw, green smell of the parched grass, now cooling, and the call of distant birds. Then I would rise, quickly put on a thin cotton dress, and go outside. It was lovely then. The sky was dark and velvety, and a huge orange moon, hung low in the sky, cast a glimmering, uncertain light. Then I could walk. I only seemed to wake up at night.

Abdi accused me of being "an old vampire, out on the prowl for blood." I wasn't thrilled by that comparison, but he seemed to find it exciting, so I played along.

He was fed up of walking along darkened streets, he said, and suggested we meet in the park. So one night we did. The gardens were cool and deserted. The lights of the airfield runway flickered in the distance.

I looked for him under the trees, but could not find him. Then a ray of light shone across the grass and I saw him, standing in the arched doorway of one of the ruined Moghul tombs the park was dotted with.

"Come in." I walked up the crumbling steps.

"Don't be afraid. No snakes here." He shone the bright torch around the tomb and the lizards darted away into cracks in the walls. Then he put it out and we were in the dark.

I had draped my silk shawl around my shoulders and he took the edges of it and pulled me towards him.

"Going native, Memsahib?"

I could feel him looking at me. Then we kissed and he held me. We were neither of us children, nor inexperienced. We both knew exactly what we wanted. His desire seemed to illuminate him, to bring him to life. He was an attractive man, but when he wanted me I found him irresistible. At that moment everything about him excited me.

He was a skilled lover, his embrace decisive and sure. I felt as if I were falling, but it was not scary, it was a release, a liberation. For those few brief moments everything else ceased to exist. It was not love. There was nothing kind or gentle about Abdi's love-making. It was rough, cathartic, full of passion. It was not like the impersonal love I had had with strangers in London during the bombing. That was a brief coupling, nothing more. This exhausted and drained me, but it also brought me a strange kind of peace.

After the first time, he walked me home. We hardly spoke. A few doors down from the bungalow he stopped and looked at me almost sadly. Then he said,

"Will you be my slave, Memsahib?"

"Yes. But not for long," I replied without thinking. He nodded, as if I had confirmed something he already knew, then he turned and walked away.

After that, we met almost every day. Abdi was fast becoming an addiction.

I needed him to want me; his desire made me real. Without him I felt incorporeal, untethered to anything or anyone in my life. His love-making was raw and urgent. Holding me too tightly, he would bruise my arm, kissing me, he would bite my lip. His taunt "kiss me, you bloody Memsahib," was a joke, but it was barbed, it stung. Yet, at the time, it was the only thing that made me feel alive. Without it I was a rudderless ship, veering round in circles, alienated and unloved.

Being involved with Abdi was an altogether bruising business. Sometimes it felt like combat, as we struggled and strained, almost despite the other, to reach that brief moment of bliss, that fleeting second where nothing else on earth mattered. But it was a collusion, at times not even based on liking.

I had got used to Rikh's love-making—mild and affectionate, eyes closed, face slightly turned away—dare

I say almost paternal? It didn't feel really incestuous, just removed, distant. With Abdi it was the opposite. His eyes were always wide open. He watched my response to every caress. Sometimes I felt I was being monitored, but I didn't really care. I was too absorbed in finding my own delight.

I realised that he liked the idea of fucking a Memsahib, that for him this reversal of roles, a sort of transplanted Figaro, give our union a frisson that others may have lacked. As Memsahibs went, I supposed I was the most palatable—I was young, reasonably good-looking and my sympathies were all with the other side. His side. Although he never mentioned politics to me. Not then, anyway. I was probably just his best bet. At least, that's what I think now.

He told me a little about his family in Lahore. Not much, rarely mentioning names or describing events, just that they were a wealthy Muslim family who owned a bank and that they expected him to marry "appropriately." When I asked him what that meant he scowled and snapped "a cow with money." Then said no more.

He told me more about Lahore than about himself or his friends and family. He insisted that I would love it because it was a proper city, tolerant and cosmopolitan, with restaurants and bars, grand hotels and shops.

"It's full of the kind of people you'd like to know," he stated.

"What kind is that?" I asked.

"Rogues and intellectuals," he replied, "the brainy and

the bounders, princes and paupers, right up your street," he replied then added, "not at all like the chintz morgue," which was what he called the cantonment.

He promised to take me to Lahore one day. He told me its history and what he called its ways and byways. It sounded fascinating, He asked a lot about London. He said he wanted to go there.

I asked him once if he had ever loved anyone. Real love, which was neither lust nor a romanticised ideal. He mentioned a girl, a quite young girl, who he had "loved" and who, in the end, had rejected him. It didn't sound like love to me. It sounded more like a need to possess.

I didn't tell him about Lal. I didn't trust him enough for that. His involvement with me was intense, but he always had a mischievous edge that verged on spite, so I never told him about Lal or Yolanda. I loved them too much to risk their memory in his hands.

In the end, I thought he was unreachable. I didn't feel that he was capable of an altruistic love, an abnegation of self. But I didn't care. He was attractive, funny and he wanted me. For a long time, that was enough.

One night I slipped quietly back into the darkness of the sleeping house, undressing as I always did in the bathroom so as not to wake Rikh. Before sliding into bed I often looked out of our window, wondering if Abdi would pass by on his way back to the base. This time I waited for a few moments, saw no-one, then tired and replete, looked out across the silent garden past the recumbent form of

Suleiman. As usual he was asleep and unmoving outside our bedroom window. Then, as I turned, I looked down and saw, to my horror, that his eyes were wide open.

I felt sick. I wondered how many times he had watched me. I wondered if he had told Rikh.

If he had told him, Rikh said nothing. So I continued to see Abdi. I knew I was being a fool—I was risking everything for very little. I did not love him and he certainly did not love me, but I loved how he made me feel, and because of that, I needed him.

On the rare occasion that Rikh did wake up I told him I couldn't sleep in this heat and he seemed to accept that. At least, he merely grunted what could have been assent and turned over and went back to sleep. I thought it was just the way it had been in England—either he was adept at turning a blind eye or he didn't care, as long as I was discreet. And I thought I was. But I was a fool to believe that I was the only one who could not sleep. And the conventions of the cantonment were far stricter than those in England. On the cantonment the proprieties were religiously adhered to, but Abdi did tell me that life in the hill stations was very different. He told me that in the Charleville Hotel in Mussoori, a charming place which was one of his favourite haunts he said, a 'separation' bell was rung at 4am to warn the adulterous guests to return to their spouses or their rooms in time for early morning tea.

I now wonder how many people were aware of what I was up to. How many fading matrons, tormented by loveless marriages and the menopause, spent their sleepless nights peering through the blinds, watching me? Was I the subject of malicious or even truthful gossip at the countless coffee mornings and whist drives that my earlier outburst had excluded me from? I imagine I was. Where I was a real idiot was not to have expected their titillated malice. The vicarious delight in crucifying others for what you most long for. But no, all of this was lost to me and I sailed on, blind and oblivious, into the next brick wall.

Chapter Five

As I have said, the Memsahibs didn't like me. I thought it was because I was a rebel, albeit a timid one, clinging to the coattails of the Raj. I thought they saw me as a maverick, who wouldn't toe the line, but now I think their dislike was entirely caused by their perception that I was having my cake and eating it. And I'm not sure they were wrong.

Paradoxically, I was always far more aware of racial prejudice in India than I was in England. Not because it was any less there, it was probably more, but there were then so few opportunities for it to be evoked. Rikh in London was a rare bird. There were very few black faces in London at that time and even less in England as a whole. Black men played in bands in clubs in the West End and their music was sublime, but you didn't meet them. Even when present, they were kept at arms' length.

I was an oddball to have Indians as my friends, but then my illegitimacy made me a pariah and my best friend was a Wop. The Freddies and Veronicas of this world (my English co-workers at the Waldorf) would not have been caught dead dining with Rikh. They only tolerated Yolanda because of her economic and social superiority. They would have loathed all foreigners if they had thought about it, but they didn't have to because, even in London, they encountered so few.

In India it was different. Brown faces were all around and by and large, with the exception of a few princes and some of the educated minority, they were treated appallingly, especially when you remembered India was their country. We were the strangers here. Rikh had been right. The Memsahibs were the worst: they saw themselves as the guardians of the flame of Empire and any behaviour that did not rigidly preserve that was a disgrace and a desecration.

The Memsahibs patronised their servants shamefully, even the ayahs who had complete charge of their children, and were genuinely loved as surrogate mothers. The Mems lauded their dog-like devotion and trustworthiness, but were always careful to introduce a negative note as a counterweight. Ayah might be entrusted with their most precious gift, their children, but she would be relentlessly sneered at because she couldn't read or write. They would have been outraged by Kutabaksht's petty pilfering while completely failing to see the immorality of an old man waiting hand and foot for eighteen hours a day on those many years his junior. It staggered me. In his shoes, or rather lack of them, I'd have murdered us all in our beds.

Kutabaksht was capable of such thoughtful kindness. I once received a letter from Mother, a rare event as the wartime post was always uncertain. When he came in to discuss the day's menu, he found me in tears. I told him I missed my mother and he nodded sympathetically, but said nothing. At teatime that day Suleiman had brought my tea as usual, but this time it was accompanied with three tiny, perfect lemon curd tarts. I remembered that I had told him months before that they were my favourite and my mother had always made them for me. His silent comfort moved me, but would have been taken utterly for granted by the Mems, who refusing to grant him equality, were correspondingly blind to his empathy. When I didn't loathe them, I pitied them.

I wondered if the common practice of sending their children away when they were so very young, usually seven or eight, as they always did in the days before the War, not to see their parents for years, made the Memsahibs hard and brittle, husks really, the best part of them torn away.

The heat wore on, wearing me down with it. One baking morning, when we had run out of nearly everything, necessity drove me out of doors. Rikh had complained bitterly over breakfast about the lack of his favourite mouthwash, which had run out weeks ago, and when he asked me sardonically if I could spare the time in my busy schedule to get him some shaving soap and shampoo from the Naafi, I felt I could hardly refuse.

I always tried to avoid the Naafi, dreading the polite cold shouldering that would greet me there, so as I set off towards the base I considered walking on and braving the Bazaar, which would provide me with life and interest, if not the authentic branded products Rikh craved. However, ten minutes of walking in that heat, when even the air I breathed was hot and dusty and made my chest ache, persuaded me that that was folly and I entered the cool of the Naafi with its ceiling fans and cool marble interior with relief.

It was an odd place. It had the elegance of an Edwardian department store, with gilt mirrors and glass fronted cabinets. I almost expected to see hansom cabs waiting at the door. But I got Rikh's provisions, signed the chit and, loath to brave the searing heat of the walk home just yet, strolled into the bar. I was sitting at a table on my own, waiting for a cool beer and plate of freshly made game chips to be brought to me, when the Grey Wraith walked in. She gave me a chilly little wave, her lips puckered into the grimace that was her smile and ordered a gimlet. Then she sat as far away from me as she could. It struck me that maybe the reason the Memsahibs were so awful was that they were rarely sober. As we had kept going in the Blitz on tea and cigarettes, so the Raj kept afloat on a sea of gin. I pondered this as I drank my beer and ate my chips.

I looked out of the window at the dying grass. I was

bored witless. I really did not want to go home, so I went outside and braved the heat for the few minutes it took me to get to Mrs Pepe's.

I found her pale and unwell on her couch, but still smiling and pleased to see me.

"You look blooming," she commented.

"Wilting more like. How do you stand this heat? Do you ever get used to it?" I moaned.

"No, not really, but you do get better at dealing with it." She looked down and pulled up the thin lawn shawl that covered her legs. "Like not walking round in the midday sun, for instance."

We laughed and said together "Mad dogs and Englishmen!"

After a moment, she looked at me searchingly. "How are you, my dear? Really?"

I wondered if she had heard about Abdi.

She looked down and folded her the edge of her shawl into tiny pleats. "Forgive an old woman's bluntness, but I hope you know that nothing on this base can be kept private for long."

"Are people talking?"

"Yes. But that's not my concern. This place is a hornet's nest of gossip and always has been. The scandal of today is the bore of tomorrow." She looked down again.

"You are very lonely, child, aren't you?" she said softly.

"Yes."

"Be careful that your loneliness doesn't lead you into bad company."

"Oh, I don't care about that. The Mems will never approve of me. They think Rikh and I are an abomination."

"Perhaps. But they'll forgive him because of his service record, whereas you..." She didn't have to finish.

I shrugged. "I don't care. Give a dog a bad name... and all that. Rikh could be Jack the Ripper and they'd make excuses for him, and I could be the angel Gabriel and all the Heavenly Host but my name would still be mud."

She smiled. "Perhaps."

Her bearer came in with iced *nimbu pani* (lime squash) in a crystal jug, beaded with moisture, and two tall glasses decorated with slices of lime. We sat in silence as he poured our drinks.

His entrance had broken the thread. After he left, we talked of this and that, the progress of the war, the heat, her longing to go to the hills. She had refused to leave her husband because he needed her support, she said, bewailing the fact that she could be of very little help to him now.

"Then why don't you go? It might do you good."

"He needs me here. Someone he can talk to. His oldest friend who keeps him company when he can't sleep."

"You really love him, don't you?" I found myself envying her.

"Yes, I do. But what is perhaps more important, I like him."

"Is that enough?"

"Yes. In the end, it's the only thing that counts."

And remembering guiltily Rikh and I and the silent, interminable evenings we endured together, each other's company an irritant rather than a comfort, I knew she was right. Rikh and I shared a home, but not a life.

I rose to leave, unhappy and confused. She took my hand when I bent to kiss her withered cheek. She had a wonderful, old fashioned smell of roses and papier poudré.

"Be careful of this man. He is neither kind nor a gentleman."

"I know." I was too ashamed to admit that that was what attracted me.

I walked home, thinking, and as usual, going round in circles. Not really surprised that she knew, knowing that what she said was true and I should act on it – knowing that I would not.

I was deep in thought as I walked up the recently swept path towards the house. Then the front door opened, Suleiman appeared in the doorway and hurled something into the garden.

"*Bicchu*," he cursed. It only just missed me. It was a shoe. One of mine. Then he shut the door. That was too much. I was always afraid of him, especially since I had found him awake. I was terrified that he would follow me and tell

Rikh, but he had nearly hit me with that thing and I was angry.

When Rikh returned that evening, I was ready for battle.

"Your bearer called me a bitch today." Rikh looked at me in astonishment.

"He threw my shoe at me and called me a bitch." He picked up his drink with what looked like relief.

"We really do have to get you some lessons."

"I don't need anyone to teach me not to put up with that."

He smiled wanly. "Did he say *bicchu?*"

"Something like that. He never says the words properly. His English is rubbish."

"Like your Hindustani. *Bicchu* means scorpion. He probably found one in your shoe. The poor blighter was trying to save you."

Rikh sat down and took refuge in his paper, no doubt feeling huge sympathy for his compatriot for having to deal with such a stroppy ignoramus.

Later that evening I came across Suleiman in our bedroom. He was violently shaking Rikh's shoes. He looked up, "*bicchu,*" he said grimly. "Yes. I know," I replied.

Shortly after that Rikh went to Chittagong for specialised flight training. I was now alone and my loneliness became acute.

I loved Mrs Pepe and sought her company whenever I could, but her ill health meant she often could not see me.

As her illness progressed, she also acquired that strange remoteness that only very sick people have. She seemed tired and detached now, as if she inhabited a half-way state—a limbo between life and death. She was a brave woman and she tried very hard to be animated and amusing when we met, but somewhere her heart was not in it anymore, and there was now a terrible waiting, a listless absence where my warm and vibrant companion had once been.

The next brick wall wasn't long in coming. This one was provided by Abdi.

We had both grown tired of a love affair of "shreds and patches" as he called it, always worrying about being seen meant that our snatched moments never reached their natural end, but were always broken off mid-way. It was becoming profoundly unsatisfactory.

One night, as we embraced in the dark shadows of the deserted tomb, he whispered,

"The love that dare not say its name."

I had to laugh. "Don't think that's quite what Oscar had in mind."

He frowned: he was not as cultured as he liked to make out and he hated being laughed at.

"I've found a solution," he announced importantly. I wondered what on earth he would come out with.

"Come away with me. Just for one night."

"You must be mad."

"No. Just one night. Rikh's away on ops. I'll take you to Lahore. You'll love it."

I was sure I would. I had been longing to go there since I was a child. I shook my head.

He kissed me again. "You'll love me too."

"Don't flatter yourself."

He pulled back to look at me in surprise. "Well, that was unexpected."

"Did you expect me to gag with gratitude?"

"Yes. I have been lead to expect it." I gave up. You couldn't trump him. And God only knew, I was dying to go. I wanted to be with him despite his conceit. To have a whole night with him, to lie in his arms and half-waking, half-sleeping, make love as if we had all the time in the world.

"You're army, aren't you?" That broke my reverie all right.

"What?"

"Found out. The Colonel's daughter!"

Now that did make me laugh. "I'm not anyone's daughter."

"Yes. You are."

He trotted out his "proof" triumphantly.

"You speak well. You're obviously very well educated. When you want to you know how to behave and..." with the air of a magician producing a rabbit out of a hat, "you want to risk but not everything."

How could I explain that all of the above were due to the

Godolphin and Latimer School and the Barroni family? Without them I could easily have joined Cornelius, reading "The Daily Sketch" and eating my peas off a knife.

I decided to say nothing. "I thought I had. Marrying Rikh."

"You kicked over the traces all right marrying an Indian. But you picked the only one who is even more of a stuffed shirt than Wavell." He kept kissing me. Then he ran his fingers across my mouth.

"Go on. Risk it. Come with me. I dare you."

How could I resist? I didn't. I took Lal's beautiful chiffon dress out of the trunk, packed an overnight bag and went with Abdi to Lahore.

Chapter Six

Abdi had said that I would love Lahore. He was right. We had boarded the train at the Cantonment station, in a place that was a stuffy replica of the Home Counties, and travelled across the Punjab through the dark velvet night, fitfully dozing and then awakening, we saw very little, but as the train pulled into the station in the clear light of dawn, I saw at last the India I had always dreamed of.

Lahore was not, in those days, the bigoted, decaying backwater it has become. Then it was a bright and bustling city, sophisticated and cosmopolitan. Muslims, Hindus, Sikhs, Parsees, Christians and Jews lived cheek by jowl as they had for centuries. All had their places of worship and ways of life. It also had a lively and rather louche social life, set against a fairy-tale backdrop of mosques and minarets, temples and gardens.

The station reflected this peculiar miscellany of cultures. It was grand and imposing—a red brick Victorian cathedral to engineering, like the great London termini, but it was St Pancras on stilts—bigger, more decorated, a strange hybrid of colonial kitsch and faux Oriental. It was the hub of the Punjab. The smart Europeans and Indian aristocracy who stepped disdainfully down from their first-class carriages (as we did), walked among entire families of coolies, vendors and other human flotsam and jetsam, who lived, washed and cooked their meals within the station walls. I saw my first leper, crouched like a shunned animal in the shadow of the wall, his mutilated face turned away, rattling a tin cup that was tied to the stump of what had once been a hand. He remains in my mind an indelible picture of human suffering; diseased and unwanted, alone in the indifferent crowd.

We took a *tonga* to our hotel. Abdi insisted on it although the Braganza was only just across from the station. He wrinkled his nose and said it would look bad, turning up on foot, carrying one's own box (as he called the tiny overnight case that held little more than a washbag and my chiffon dress.)

We checked into a large and pleasant room, overlooking the garden at the rear of the hotel and then emerged into the bright sunlight to view the city.

First Abdi took me on a *tonga* ride to "see the town." It was a rather grand *tonga*, unlike any in Ambala, with a polished yoke, brass lamps and comfortable leather seats. The driver was smart too, in clean white *salwar*. Lahore was a beautiful city. Graceful and grand, imposing and enticing, combining the power of the Raj and the delicate marble tracery and cusped arches of its Moghul inheritance.

The Mall was then a broad, elegant boulevard that would happily bear comparison to Regent Street or the Champs d'Elysees. It was a joyful paradox. I saw women shrouded from head to toe in black, shapeless forms looking out at the forbidden world through a lattice veil. Clad in their mobile prison, they became an abstract, an absence rather than a presence. Beside them strolled high-heeled, silk-stockinged, Vogue clad ladies, as modish as anything in pre-war Bond Street. Rajas and Ranees, in silks and brocade, plump and be-jewelled, shopped in fancy stores alongside pinched looking Memsahibs, in faded floral grandeur and yellowing lace.

We drove down the Mall, past the temples to Empire and capital—the Reserve Bank of India and the High Court, past the elegant emporia that stocked Swiss watches, HMV records, and grand showrooms displaying the latest models of English and American cars, and cinemas that showed only English and European films.

We had coffee at the Imperial Coffee House and lunch at the Standard Restaurant, whose cubicles had curtains to "ensure their clientele could enjoy an assignation in complete privacy" Abdi told me. He clearly knew it well. By that time the sun was at its height and we were glad of its cool, shady interior. I noted that they also served 'a full tea' and were famous for their sandwiches, scones and cakes. I remembered our honeymoon in Salisbury and thought how Rikh would have hated it. I loved it all so much I could barely eat my lunch. I was too busy watching the people and drinking in the atmosphere. I was as excited as a child on Christmas Eve. I wolfed my food down. A treasure trove was outside and I could not wait to discover it.

Abdi laughed at me, but he enjoyed my enthusiasm for his "home town." We sauntered a little way down the Mall past the Regal Cinema that was showing a Carmen Miranda film. She was very popular in India, he told me. I decided I loved Abdi. He was now not only my lover, but my friend, a soul mate who had seen that I was suffocating in the model village that was the cantonment and had reached in and pulled me out. Enchanted by everything I saw, I felt like a dying man given a second chance at life and loving it with an intensity only the deprived can feel.

Proud and pleased, he stated that Lahore was not just a paradise for sybarites, it was the capital of the Punjab. He reminded me that it had been here, on the banks of the Ravi, that a youthful Nehru had declared that full independence was India's goal. Here too, in 1940, Jinnah had adopted the resolution of an independent Pakistan, a move we both felt was disastrous but unlikely ever to happen. The point was, he declared, this was the place, the buzzing, bustling heart of India, the place where everyone could live together and anything was possible. Alas.

Then he showed me the huge Anarkali bazaar where,

it was said, "anything under the sun" could be bought, but we had no time to linger and browse. I wanted to see everything. He took me to the old city, to the Fort and Badshahi Masjid, and then for a walk in Lawrence Gardens. As we strolled in the shade of the tall, majestic trees, we passed an open-air theatre and in the distance glimpsed the imposing portals of the Gymkhana Club, the haunt of the elite, *burra sahibs* and *rajas* only. Even his family, he said, rich and well connected as they were, were not allowed admittance there. I thought of Lal and wondered if he knew it and where he was now. Abdi showed me, at a distance, the palatial house that was his home, but he did not take me there nor did he suggest that we meet his family. I assumed it was because we had so little time.

By now the heat was intense and the city was becoming deserted as everyone who could took refuge indoors. So the rest of the day was spent hugging the shade and gazing out at the dazzling sunlight. We went back to the hotel and lurked in the shadows, coming out only at night, like owls. A night that was long and cool and filled with stars.

Abdi slept through the afternoon. I was too excited to rest. Too full of the sights and sounds, the wonderful kaleidoscope that was Lahore. I had never seen him asleep before. In repose, he seemed small, almost childlike, his rather delicate features at peace. Awake, he was such a circus of a man—delighting, provoking, exasperating, enchanting, and being involved with such a catalyst one had no choice but to react and never observe. He wanted a response always, he demanded it. If he couldn't arouse one, he would needle and prod until he got one. But asleep, he looked very young and oddly vulnerable. A boy worn out by his pranks. I noticed for the first time he had a rather beautiful mouth. Awake, it was never still for long enough for its shape to become clear.

When he woke, I took a long, cool bath. He shaved at the basin and we were strangely domestic for people who actually knew each other very little, considering our intimacy.

"Dress up. I'm taking you to Faletti's," he said grimacing as he dragged the razor down his cheek.

"Where?" I asked.

"Finest hotel in all the Punjab. Fit for maharajahs and *ranee* sahibs only."

"That's us out," I replied cheerfully, soaping my right foot.

He frowned. An expression whose severity was a bit lost in the Santa Claus beard of shaving foam.

"You'll like the people." He was speaking through one side of his mouth while shaving around it carefully.

"Not if they're all kings and queens I won't." It occurred to me he knew very little of my political affiliations. They hadn't come up much somehow.

"Shut up," he muttered through clenched teeth, "you'll make me nick myself and I am not walking into Faletti's with a bleeding face." He then concentrated on shaving the rest of his face and neck and we spoke no more.

He was already dressed in his mess uniform and waiting for me as I walked out of the little dressing room that led out of the bathroom. For once, I didn't feel too shabby.

"You look... superb." He seemed shocked.

"Where on earth did you get that dress?" It was almost an accusation.

"Bond Street," I answered smugly.

"It's stunning and so are you." I felt a pang of gratitude for Lal, who had bought me this wonderful dress to go to dancing during our brief time together in London. It was so chic it even impressed Abdi, whose main interest in clothes up to now had been to remove them. I went to kiss him, but he pulled back.

"No, no, you can't get crumpled. I want to show you off first."

So off we went. I felt absurdly like Cinderella about to crack the ball.

We dined at Stiffles which would have been wonderful had it not seemed like a brief prologue to the main attraction. Then we went to Faletti's. It was very grand indeed with cool marble interiors that reminded me of the Waldorf. Only this time I was a guest, not staff. I tried to behave with a grace and dignity I did not feel. Actually I was terrified, aware that somewhere this was a test. One if I wanted to keep Abdi, I would have to pass.

I need not have worried. He led me across the foyer to

a group of about eight impossibly elegant people, drinking coffee and whisky. Six men and only two other women. He introduced me and my heart was beating so hard I felt sure they would hear it. A tall, solemn looking man in evening dress gave me his seat. His name was Imran, he said, Imran Siddiqi and he had a voice that was pure Oxbridge. I thanked him and looked around, feeling like a frightened rabbit and then I saw her. Someone I had met before. She was looking at me with a faintly puzzled air as if trying to remember who I was.

Her name was Vicky. She was a vivacious red-head who was the partner of Sir Feroz Khan Noon, a major player in the fight for independence and later to become the seventh Prime Minister of Pakistan. During Rikh's and my time at the India League in London we had met them both briefly. He was then the Indian High Commissioner to London and far above us, but he was a friend of Krishna's. I remembered her clearly because she was so interesting. Of Austrian extraction, she had been raised in London and trained as a concert pianist. We eyed each other awkwardly, I wondering if I should say anything, and she no doubt still wondering who I was. Imran noted our exchanged glances and swiftly moved to introduce us.

"I think I know you," she said tentatively.

"The India League. London." I ventured shyly. Somehow saying the words made me homesick and I longed for the shabby, ramshackle office overlooking the Thames, that smelled of ink and damp and dust. I remembered the hours Rikh and I had spent there, how hard we had worked, debating until the small hours; our fear of the police raids and how jubilant we had felt at each tiny victory snatched from the jaws of Empire. It was another life. A better one. I must have looked sad because she took my hand and said,

"Of course. Krishna's fiefdom. Ah my dear, I remember you well." Her accent was perfect, but her mode of expression and its warmth was all *Mitteleuropa*.

"How are you and how do you find India?"

I was so overawed by her, I could not reply. She was dressed in a jade green silk sari and she looked very beautiful, but she was also extremely intelligent and ferociously articulate. She winked at me and then jumped back into the conversation about Jinnah and the desirability of Partition, a proposition that she and Feroz were reluctantly embracing as the "only viable solution." She was a formidable debater. She and Imran discussed the progress of the war in the East and its likely consequences for India's future. He spoke at length about the INA and Bose. He finished up with,

"It is an interesting notion, but where is our allegiance? With our brothers who fight for the Japanese or our English masters?"

Vicky replied to this contention like a cat pouncing on a particularly witless mouse.

"That's not the burning issue, Imran. Bose has 'folie de grandeur' if he imagines he and his Jap chums can succeed in driving the British out of the sub-continent." In the light of what had happened in Singapore, I wasn't so sure, but I noted with interest that she did not say India, but the "sub-continent" as if the division were already a fait accompli.

I looked at Abdi to see how he would respond, but he said nothing. In fact, he looked as if it was all a bit beyond him. I spoke up. One of us had to.

"It's a bit more than an interesting notion for my husband. He is both a serving officer in the Royal Indian Air Force and a long-time member of the India League. So he could be shot as a traitor by either side. As ever, for many Indians, especially the two million serving in the Armed Forces, it's a situation in which they can only lose. Either way, they remain subject to a foreign master."

Imran turned and grinned at me with delight. Vicky recalled that she had heard that some members of the League had joined the RIAF and were now on active service.

Imran, who was an immensely erudite man of about forty-five, pulled the argument out and talked of the whole effect of "the collision" of East and West as exemplified by the Raj. He pondered the fate of the Anglo Indians, who had been raised in the belief that they were always less than their British masters, but always superior to their Indian brothers, also the vast numbers of native *Jemadars* and *Chokidars*, whose families had served in the British Army for centuries, amounting to a huge population of those utterly dependent on Empire for both identity and livelihood. What would become of them? Even the Princes, he added, had been encouraged to rule absolutely but within the wider framework of British India. Imran was a fascinating man, who wore his encyclopaedic knowledge lightly. Playful and witty, he dominated the debate, combining intellectual rigour with a humanity that was as impressive as it was appealing.

And I was giddy with delight. As the conversation spilled out around me, I felt almost sick with joy. This was the India I had yearned to belong to, the people I longed to call my friends. They discussed the issues of the day and explored the myriad philosophies their intelligence gave them access to. As Yolanda and Rikh and I had in London, they strove to find a path through the tangled nightmare of modern life. Physically inert (I don't think any of them had jobs) they were mentally agile and alert, in a way I had not encountered since I lost Yolanda. She would have loved that evening at Faletti's. Raging against the inequality of Empire, the abuse of power, the vileness of prejudice, she would have been as at home here as I was. I loved these people. I felt more at home here among these strangers than I ever had in the transitory place I lived in.

We talked for hours. Time flew by for me, but I think Abdi became bored. After some time, I mentioned to Vicky that she had once played the piano quite brilliantly – a Beethoven Sonata, I recalled, at the makeshift birthday party of a League member who was a friend of Feroz. I remembered how her skill had far surpassed the out of tune and rather battered piano in the corner of the room and turned a somewhat stilted evening into one of rare delight. She blushed when I said that.

"You remember? How very dear of you." She was really moved, as I was by the sudden memory of a cold, rainy night and the unexpected revelation of her artistry.

She spoke quickly, "you must come to us. Imran will bring you. Feroz will be so pleased to see you again."

I doubted Feroz would even remember who I was, but I thanked her and when she left, much later, gathering up the silken folds of her sari, she made a special point of saying goodbye to me.

"You won't forget, will you? Come to us and I will play for you." She wafted away in a cloud of Arpège, more goddess than woman.

While I had been talking, or rather listening in rapt attention to Imran, who had dominated the discussion with an almost insolent ease, I became aware that the only other woman present was watching me closely. She was tall and blonde with icy blue eyes. Her face was very attractive, but a bit odd. The bottom part of her face didn't match the top. Her jaw was too heavy for the finely chiselled nose and cheekbones. She was very smart in a black crepe evening dress. She looked French to me, or my idea of it, smoking constantly, lighting a new cigarette with the still smouldering butt of the last one.

At one point, she introduced herself to me. Her name

was Eva Maria Roye, she drawled, originally from Belgium. But her voice dispelled the illusion, although pleasingly low and gravelly in tone, it had a ring of false gentility, the over careful articulation my friend Freddy had had at the Waldorf. He came from Ruislip. I smiled thinking her voice was more Lewisham than Liege. She was also older than she wanted people to think. Her skilful make-up and immaculately painted nails made her look younger, but if you looked closely there were lines across her forehead and her mouth had begun to droop. She seemed intriguing, but I didn't really have the chance to talk to her and she herself spoke very little. She was too busy watching.

The evening wound up soon after Vicky's departure. In the *tonga* on the way back to the Braganza, Abdi asked me what I had thought of the evening. I hugged him.

I told him I was in heaven. He scowled and said he thought he was supposed to provide that effect. I laughed and said that I just thought Vicky was wonderful. He didn't comment. So I persisted. I wanted him to share my joy in this magical evening.

"I meant... she is so beautiful. With that glorious red hair and almost triangular, cat-like face, the little pointed chin and rose-bud mouth," I waffled on, ineptly trying to convey the impression she had made on me and I was sure everybody else as well. He didn't reply.

"I can't imagine any man could resist her."

He yawned. "And so few of us will have the opportunity

to try." And that was it. Subject over. Piercing though my euphoria, I wondered if Abdi were jealous. That I had fitted in so well, so much more than he had bargained for. The people there were his acquaintances, but they could never be his friends in the way they could be mine. We shared beliefs and a vernacular that he did not. So was he loath to share the limelight with me or them? This evening he had been out-shone, up-staged by intellects so much more acute than his. Minds that could construct when his could only tear apart. Even I could see he did not like it.

We drove on through the dark, deserted streets. The buildings were shuttered and closed, guarding their secrets until the morning. It was very late—about two or three in the morning. The air was cool and fresh after the stifling heat of the day. The only light came from the moon, a milky orb like a great pearl in the sky. I remember thinking that I wanted to fix it all in my memory—the play of soft light on the white marble of mosque and pavilion, the barely discerned shapes of minaret and dome. It all seemed hardly real, a city of dreams, shimmering in the moonlight as we drove past the delicate tracery of fretted arches and shadowy colonnades. I was drunk, not so much on the whisky I had imbibed, but more with the joy of that beautiful place and the company of like minds.

Abdi pointed out a place he called Hira Mandi—the area where the most beautiful courtesans in India "snared their victims," he said. He emphasized that they were not "just tarts," they were cultured and well read. They sang traditional songs called *ghazals* and danced. Courtesans rather than whores, he said. But he was still very quiet for Abdi, almost withdrawn.

Back in the hotel I tried to reassure him. I asked him if he had felt left out of the discussion and marvelled that he could not see that because he had brought me to this wonderful place, I would only love him more. He almost snorted.

"I don't want your love."

His laugh was bitter. I wondered if he was drunk.

"No, my dear, I am playing for much higher stakes than that."

"Are there any?" I tried to shrug off my growing unease with an attempt at nonchalance.

He looked at me coldly. "God, yes. I don't want your commonplace, schoolgirl dream of moons in June and midnight trysts."

"Then what do you want?"

"Adoration. Worship." I laughed at that, but he took me roughly in his arms and although we made what is called love, it didn't feel like it. It felt more like hate.

It was angry and full of need and although it brought pleasure, it did not bring peace.

That night I slept very little.

The next morning we stumbled onto the early train, both of us massively hung-over, blinking and shrinking from the too bright light.

We had hardly spoken. In the carriage I tried to thank

him, to explain what our brief time in that miraculous place had meant to me. He tried to open his eyes and then shut them firmly. I persisted in my thanks.

"You were right." He half-opened one eye and pulled the blind down all the way.

"I always am." Eyes still shut, he smiled his secret elf smile, knowing exactly how attractive he was, even in his current state. He leaned his head back against the linen covered headrest and assumed an attitude of utter suffering, more saint than sinner, martyred by excess.

"Abdi on the cross."

"I imagine that's blasphemous." At least we were talking.

"Only if you believe in it." He did not reply.

"I love it."

"I take it you don't mean Christianity."

"No. I meant Lahore."

Wincing, he opened a bloodshot eye. "You hardly know it." That was true enough. "You've barely scratched the surface." And with that he retook possession of his home, closed both eyes firmly and said no more.

Back in the bungalow, I sat in the sitting room and stared resentfully at the walls. They seemed to be throbbing in time with my head. Sure that they were actually closing in around me, I bawled for coffee from Kutabaksht, who stared at me in surprise. I had never spoken to him like that before. He probably thought I was showing my true colours. As drunk and discourteous as all the other

Memsahibs. Suleiman just glowered at me, his silence resonant with disapproval.

I went into the bedroom, stumbled onto the bed, fully dressed, shoes still on, and fell into a deep and dreamless sleep. When I woke it was mid-afternoon and the bright sun was glaring in through the window. The pitiless light felt like the anti-aircraft beams that used to pinpoint the German planes while the guns shot them down. My eyes stung and my head rang with pain.

Kutabaksht crept in on tiptoe and took away the untouched coffee. I noticed that he had placed two Abernathy biscuits, my old favourites, on a plate on the tray. Feeling guilty and nauseous, I watched as he left me a foul looking drink. It appeared to be ink with bits of raw egg in it. It smelled strongly of Worcester sauce.

"Hair of the dog, Memsahib," he whispered conspiratorially and then withdrew. I picked up the drink and retched as the pungent aroma hit my nostrils. I thought, "Oh God, I'm turning into my step-father."

I knew I had to pull myself together somehow. Clumsily, and spilling a good deal of it, I poured a glass of water from the carafe on my bedside table and drank. I still felt sick. So I took two aspirins, threw Kutabaksht's vile brew down the toilet and stood under a cold shower for as long as I could stand it.

By the time Rikh came home that evening, I was almost human and ravenously hungry.

That night I tried to talk to Rikh. Knowing somewhere

that this would be my last stab at mending our marriage, a desperate resuscitation of the people we had once been.

I began over dinner.

"I was wondering, Rikh, what you thought of Bose?" It was a clumsy, absurdly formal beginning, more suited to a conversation between people who barely knew each other than a couple who shared principles they still held dear, but my head was aching and the steaming bowl of mulligatawny soup in front of me, in Rikh and Kutabaksht's view the only proper way to start any meal, was making me feel a bit sick.

"Which Bose?" he replied, soup spoon halfway to his mouth. He slurped it appreciatively.

"I didn't know there were two. No, I mean the INA Bose." I was trying to ape Imran. I had over-reached myself.

"Mmm...," Rikh looked grim and drank more soup.

"There is such a clash of loyalties, don't you think?" I went on brightly.

"Not really."

I was getting nowhere. The conversation was guttering, like a candle about to go out.

"Well, they want an independent India and so do we."

He smiled his wintry smile. "Yes, Nita, but they want the Japanese Army to get it for them."

He crumbled the bread on his side plate.

"Bit of a Faustian bargain, wouldn't you say? Swapping

one occupying force for another? Not quite what Gandhi meant by full independence, is it?"

He went on, "And besides, what "freedoms" do you think will be bestowed by the Japanese? They still believe their King is a god."

He drank the rest of his soup, deep in thought. "They are utterly feudal in their outlook. We don't need to import their backwardness. We've got enough of our own."

We both sat in silence as Suleiman cleared the soup course and served our mutton curry. After he had withdrawn, Rikh looked at me and said, "Child, if you had seen what I have in Burma, or had any idea what the Japanese are capable of, you would not even countenance having anything to do with them. They are cruel to a degree you cannot imagine."

Cool, rational, well-reasoned. The hallmark of Rikh. I looked at him almost in wonder. He had, as always, faced an issue and resolved it. At least in his own mind. A mind I could only respect. But also as ever, his argument was a conclusion, never a dialogue. There was nothing more to say. I could play no part in his thinking, even if I wanted to. He had deliberated and reached his conclusions alone, without reference to any other, especially me. I felt like an infant squirming and wriggling in a high chair, spoon-fed, confined.

We ate the rest of our meal without speaking. I—dreading the prospect of another endless evening in the living room, sitting together in silence, he with his newspaper, I with my book, physically close, but emotionally far apart. I wondered how many hours of total tedium I would have to endure before I could make my escape and go for a walk. To see if I could find Abdi.

However before I could go out, Rikh looked at me sternly over the top of his newspaper and said,

"Mess Ball on Saturday. I think we should attend," my face must have fallen because he attempted a brief smile that died before it reached the edges of his mouth.

"Perhaps we can redeem your position here." I didn't hold out much hope of that.

"We should make an effort." It was nice of him to say we; we both knew he meant me.

I looked for Abdi that night in the gardens, but he wasn't there.

When I did catch up with him a few days later he was not helpful.

"I can't think of anything worse," I moaned, "than mincing and capering for the Memsahibs."

"Neither can I. In fact, it's only worth it if you want to save your marriage."

He was curt and impatient. He wanted to get on with the love-making, but I was too pre-occupied with my own problems.

"Bit late for that." I was still revelling in my memories of Lahore, the life and company I had enjoyed there. The bitter contrast between that colour and vitality and the joyless, formulaic life of the base, pandering to a collection of resentful old women, tormented me. I said as much.

"Then don't do it."

"I've got to."

"Why?"

I sighed. "Because I've hurt Rikh enough." I wasn't quite sure where that came from. It had been a very long time since Rikh had displayed any feelings towards me, let alone pain.

"Do you still love him?"

"Of course I love him. Somewhere I always will. But I hate living with him. It's like dying every day."

He looked at me hard. "Then get out. While you're still warm."

He kissed me and then walked away, leaving me alone in the dark.

I don't know how I ever imagined I could get away with it. In a place where an evening walk made me an object of scrutiny, how did I ever think my absence for two whole days would go unremarked? My problem was that although I was aware that my behaviour was the subject of gossip, I was so alienated from the other women on the base, I had ceased to wonder what they might think. Or perhaps the truth is that I didn't think. Full stop; I just grabbed the chance Abdi offered me to get out and leapt blindly into the unknown, without a second's thought of what the consequences might be. It was not out of character, after all.

I was not so oblivious to my surroundings, however, that I failed to notice that the entire base was busy preparing for this ball. Vans arrived at the club, laden with crates of Johnnie Walker Red Label Whisky, Gordon's Gin and Golden Eagle beer, and cartons of Players and Senior Service cigarettes. Memsahibs swarmed about everywhere, taking all the *tongas*, rushing from Bazaar to tailor, lovingly clutching parcels of lace trimming and ribbons. These tailors were called *dherzis*. They were very skilled and would sit sewing on verandas, creating new garments from magazine photographs and refurbishing old. Uniforms were brushed, belts and buckles polished until they shone. The only hairdresser was booked solid and could not fit me in, not even in the afternoon, when the heat turned a hair dryer into an instrument of torture. Everyone was getting ready for the ball.

But not Mrs Pepe. She was not going to be there. I had visited her on my return from Lahore and was shocked by her deterioration. Previously, she had been breathless on exertion, but now breathing at all was an effort for her. She apologised, but she didn't have to explain. She was far too ill to go anywhere. She had never missed a ball or a dance before; in the past, despite her infirmity, she had been well enough to put in a brief appearance after the meal, in her fox fur whatever the weather, and sit appreciatively, watching the dancing.

"I was a good dancer," she had said wistfully. I saw no reason to doubt it. Now the thought of her absence made me feel scared. Without her, I felt alone and exposed, but I knew I would have to go. Rikh had insisted on it. I did not tell her about my trip. I knew she would understand but not approve. I left her resting, a small figure under her paisley lawn cover, already faded, her light nearly gone.

I had refused Rikh's offer of a new dress. I felt too guilty for that, so I unearthed my old black silk, which still had enough of London style about it to pass muster, shook out the creases, endured Suleiman's look of disgust at its crumpled state and accepted his offer to "steam and press" it. He took it away on its hanger, holding it at arms' length as if it were something to be fumigated.

I walked into the Bazaar early one morning and bought a few bits and bobs to jazz it up. A broad black velvet belt which emphasized my waist. It was embroidered with tiny coloured beads in the shapes of flowers, which caught the light. I dug out my old satin sandals, bought a new pair of stockings and a new red lipstick—Fire and Ice it was called—and hey presto, Cinderella was ready for the ball.

I tried my best to look nice. But I drew the line at wearing my chiffon dress. That was too linked in my mind with Abdi and Lal. It also needed cleaning. Its drooping folds had not survived the pavements of Lahore unscathed.

The heat was now intolerable. Even the nights brought no relief. The still air was thick with dust and the low, oppressive sky a dull orange. The ceiling fans turned slowly, churning the stale air. The rooms were stifling, the walls seemed to radiate heat. One morning the distant rumble of thunder woke me, but nothing came of it. The rains were late that year, Kutabaksht said. I hadn't seen Abdi for days.

We arrived late. Dinner was over by the time we got there. I had been ready since seven, sitting in full fig in the living room, waiting for Rikh to return. He came in two hours late, apologising for being held up on the base, then he showered and changed in minutes and off we went to the ball.

It began with the looks. Eyes narrowed, lips pursed, sharp pointed stares. Then the whispering started—words half-heard, sense only guessed at, a hissing monotone that stopped abruptly as I drew near. Everyone turned away. No-one would greet me.

They greeted Rikh with a rich soup of compassion, as thick and meaty as their Brown Windsor soup, then flicked their gaze away to avoid meeting mine.

"Drink, old man?" Rikh's Wing Commander called out too loudly, ushering Rikh over to join him at the bar, a party of two, leaving me alone.

I find it hard now to remember what happened that night with any coherence. What came after blotted it all out, spreading over my life like an ink-stain, dark and angry, obscuring everything. I remember the smell of tobacco and whisky, the sharp tang of male sweat and the dusty scent of Yardley's Lavender.

I saw him seated in an alcove and thought with longing

how beautiful he was. Immaculate in his uniform and clean shaven, his head leaning in to catch the conversation of his companion. I thought I haven't seen him for days. Doesn't he want me anymore? He leaned in to light her cigarette. Her first by the look of it. She inhaled too hard and spluttered and choked. He patted her back and let his hand linger on her bare shoulder. She was a pretty girl, with red gold hair and cornflower eyes. Skin like white velvet. She couldn't have been more than seventeen. A daughter of the regiment with too short legs and tiny feet in silver sandals. She blushed and beamed up at him, batting her beautiful eyes and lapping up his attention, brimming over with excitement. He shifted his chair and turned his back on me. I stood stock still, staring at them, then I walked past them and out onto the veranda. Despite the heat, I felt as if I were full of ice.

After a while, he joined me, but not before he had made me suffer.

"I didn't know you were a sucker for the English rose?" I wanted to be brittle and assured, stiff with sophistication, but my mouth was suddenly dry and my throat hurt.

"Good Lord, are you jealous?"

"I hate you." I meant it. "You are loving every second of this, aren't you?" I wished I could rake my nails across his face. Actually, I don't know why I didn't. Now I wish I had.

He kissed me and then a long embrace that spoke of all we had enjoyed and promised more. As we pulled apart, breathless and shaky with desire, I saw the shocked face of the Grey Wraith over his shoulder. My Nemesis. She screwed up her eyes, drew in a wheezy breath and fled. She had left the dance floor to cool down outside and discovered more heat than was ever inside. She had always hated me. She was no doubt already spreading the glad tidings to all of her acolytes.

I was the Scarlet Woman now all right. I felt lost and alone, a bit sick. I knew I had burnt my bridges; I could smell the smoke.

After that I drank and danced. The wives loathed me, they always had, but their husbands didn't, so I laughed and smiled and one by one they all asked me to dance.

I didn't leave the dance floor, just drank my drink straight down like the good Scots my mother was, and passed from one man's arms to another. I thought. I'll show him. If he thinks I'm going to sit there like an abject little fool, with a tear in my eye, he's damn well mistaken. I drank too much and forgot about Rikh, a blurred figure at the bar, my eyes all the time on Abdi, watching for the effect my conquests had on him. We'd see who was jealous now.

He gave me a run for my money, flirting and dancing as much as I did, but gradually his eyes sought mine more and more and in them I read no more malice and amusement, but rather a weary kind of sadness.

At last, we walked toward each other, sweaty and spent, like two old boxers at the end of a fight, and fell into each others' arms. By this point, I could hardly stand. He was not much better.

"I love you," he said and kissed my ear.

"I love you too."

Denial and subterfuge suddenly seemed absurd, all the lies and secrecy, the creeping about in the dark a silly game neither of us wanted to play anymore. As we dipped and swayed tiredly to the music, we held each other tightly, no longer pretending or hiding, but at last being who we were.

And so we remained on the dance floor, locked in a mobile embrace until the music slowed and the band stopped playing and one by one, the lights above the bar and in the lounge went out. At one point I had been conscious of Rikh, sitting at the bar, glaring at us, but he made no move to break us up and neither did I. I knew what I was doing was wrong and cruel, but we had come too far for pretence now. A line had been crossed and though I knew that it was irrevocable, I was too tired of trying to be someone else and too drunk to really care.

I went home alone. Abdi got me a *tonga*. Never at any stage did he suggest I should go anywhere but home and he did not come with me. The night air sobered me up a little, but not much.

Rikh was waiting for me. In shirtsleeves, his tie undone, his hair askew, he was unrecognisable. He was sitting slumped in an armchair in the living room, an empty whisky glass in his hand, peering into it as if it might provide the answer. Suleiman let me in. He and Rikh exchanged glances.

Rikh then looked at me. I had become used to his looks—of disdain and exasperation, but this was different. This was not dislike, born of a cool distance, this hard unblinking stare looked like hatred.

This was not the Rikh I was used to. He was agitated and angry, a little drunk, his speech usually so studied and precise, was slurred.

"Good of you to come back. Suleiman, get out." He never spoke to Suleiman like that.

He put down the whisky glass and stood up. His hands were shaking.

"I have endured your constant infidelity, your sordid little betrayals, Nita, because you're such a stupid bloody child. But I had hoped to keep all that a private grief. To salvage some shred of what we once had from the foulness of what you have become."

I tried to speak but the words wouldn't come.

"It has been a terrible test of our relationship. God knows, Nita, you've ripped the arse out of it."

Rikh never swore.

"But when you go public. When you turn a private wound into a public exhibition, I will not tolerate it!"

He was jabbing his forefinger in my face.

"I have loved you, though many wondered why. You have hurt and humiliated me. You have punished me for your fathers crimes. Both of them. Your drunken thug of a step-father and the feckless tearaway that sired you. And I have taken it. I have gritted my teeth and tried to remember the abuse you were subject to, but ..."

His voice was shrill and now it cracked. He was in tears.

"Tonight you have made a very public fool of me. One no-one here will forget in a hurry. From the lowliest mechanic to my commanding officer, from the men I work and perhaps will die with, even our own servants, everyone here knew what you were up to. Everyone but me."

He wept. A rusty, choking that sounded as if it hurt him I had never seen him cry before. I moved towards him, but he raised his arm to keep me away, as if fending off a blow.

He left the house that night and when he came back three days later, a woman was with him. An older woman, with iron-grey hair and sensible shoes, wearing a sari.

She looked very stern.

He introduced us. "This is my sister, Lena. She will be running this house from now on."

Suleiman took her case and led her into the spare room. A room that had obviously been prepared for her. Clearly it had all been arranged. But no-one had told me.

Chapter Seven

Lena was not a bad person. In another place, at another time we could easily have become friends. Like her brother she was intelligent and cultured; a considered, thoughtful woman, she clearly felt the awkwardness of her position. But her brother had asked for her help and she would not fail him.

She took over the reins immediately. Kutabaksht now reported to her in the mornings instead of me. She scared him; he crept anxiously about the house, minding his Ps and Qs, casting reproachful glances at me. She also took over the purse strings and I doubt he got away with his little scams now. Even Suleiman took his orders from her and Larkhi just kept her face covered and worked even harder, if that was possible. Lena ran a tight ship and my role became peripheral.

I wondered how much she knew. At first I imagined everything, because the speed with which she had dropped her own life to come to her brother's rescue spoke of necessity rather than planning.

The first morning she and Rikh breakfasted together early before he went to work. I didn't join them. Rikh would barely look at me and Lena and I trod uneasily around each other, wary and hostile, watchful as to the others' next move, like a pair of neighbourhood cats.

When I did not appear, Suleiman brought me my breakfast on a tray. The usual *chota hazri*—bread and butter, fruit and tea. No hard tack and water yet, it seemed.

Later that morning she asked me if I would join her for coffee. And it was that act, inviting me for coffee in the house I had been mistress of that prompted me to ask her straight out why she had abandoned her life to come and live with us. It becoming clear that this was to be a permanent arrangement.

She paused and stirred her coffee. Like Rikh, she took three sugars. Then she sighed and attempted to level with me.

"This was not my idea. I had a nice life."

I realised I knew very little about her. "I don't know... Rikh never speaks about his family."

She sighed again. This was clearly no surprise to her.

"I am a widow. I have four children, now grown up, but living near me. I also have friends. Good friends."

"Then why leave them?"

She looked me straight in the eye. "Because Rikh asked

me. He turned up—out of the blue—in a terrible state, asking for my help because you are too much trouble."

Had he really not told her the details? She went on.

She said she was very concerned at his taking "compassionate leave" at a second's notice. He is a serving officer, she reminded me: he cannot just take off as it suits him. If he were to go AWOL (absent without leave) they could arrest him. There is a war on, she said. He is India League. The jails are full of people like him. Her voice was stern, but her manner was more weary than draconian.

I replied that I knew all this.

"I don't think you realise the state he was in. I have never seen him like that. He was trembling, crying. He asked me to help him."

She looked at me accusingly. "He is my brother. What can I do but help him?"

That was unanswerable. I still wondered what she knew exactly. Although perhaps, seeing his despair, she had not pressed him for chapter and verse. Perhaps she had respected, or even shared his reticence. They were not much of a family for confidences.

After that, the first day passed in sullen silence. Neither of us went out.

That afternoon the monsoon came. My first. The wall of heat outside was trapped by lowering clouds, which spread and blackened. Then a crack of thunder and a streak of lightning that threatened to split the sky. And then the rain, the sweet relief of rain that fell in torrents. I went into the garden and stood outside, completely drenched in a few seconds, underneath that waterfall of rain, cool for the first time in months. Within hours the plants, I had assumed were dead, turned a tentative green and the great dry cracks in the earth became muddy pools. Larkhi's garden path, so diligently swept, was soon a quagmire.

For the first few days, the rain made going outside impossible. Lena and I did not attempt it. In the mornings Rikh charged out of the house to the jeep in his mac and Wellington boots, while Suleiman waited, the engine running. Kutabaksht, held an open umbrella not quite over Rikh, splashing miserably along beside him, the thin cotton of his sodden clothes clinging to his scrawny form, pulling his spindly legs high out of the mud like a disgruntled stork.

During the day, we kept to our separate quarters, Lena and I, each in our rooms, the living rooms an uneasy no man's land. In the evenings we ate with Rikh, a silent, awkward meal where all the proprieties were observed and we ate unhappily together. Suleiman was the only one who seemed unbothered by it all.

For a few days, the rain was unceasing. The road and garden were now flooded, cars safely up on bricks, jeeps the only vehicles that could cope with the churning mud and water that used to be a road, and I began to long for Abdi.

The nights were a particular torment. Rikh and I still slept in the same bed. We had to. There were only two bedrooms. But now he retired long after I had put the light out, slipping unobtrusively into bed to sleep with his back turned to me until the morning. I lay awake for hours listening to the rain, falling with a metallic clatter on the iron roof of the shed. I tried to speak to him, whispering his name in the dark, but he would not answer.

Lena now decided everything—from the food we ate to when we would change the linen. She even paid the servants. A task formerly mine. Rikh gave her money every month. He told me coldly, face averted, that he would put a small amount into my bank account each month "for your expenses." It was very much less than before, but it didn't really matter. There was nothing to spend it on now. I hardly ever went out.

Within a few short days my changed circumstances became evident. Every move I made was questioned, every outing required an explanation.

"You're going out?" Always in tones of polite surprise.

"Where are you going?" If it was to the library or to the Naafi, there were two responses, either "I'll go with you" and she would rise from her chair, slowly and stiffly, with the air of Mary Stuart on her way to the block or she would smile brightly and say, "Suleiman can drive you. I don't need him this morning/afternoon." And there I would be, watched and monitored round the clock.

A proposed trip to the Bazaar was met with, "no, not alone, dear, Suleiman had better... such a rough place etc..." or a stroll in the evening would be refused with a gentle but firm "no dear, the weather..." or, if the weather were fine with a slight shudder "oh no, dear, not at night. It's not safe."

We lived in a cantonment. It was an armed camp for God's sake. One, that at least for me, was becoming a prison, as little by little, inch by inch, kindly but firmly, my few pathetic freedoms were removed.

I heard nothing from Abdi. I had not seen him since the night of the ball.

The days were difficult, but the nights were unbearable. Rikh now retired very late. I think he waited until he thought I was asleep, so that he could rule out any possibility of talking to me. Restless and wakeful, before I slept I paced the confines of my room, Sulieman on watch outside my window. I felt like a locked in alley cat, full of longing and desire. The front and back doors were locked, and only Rikh and Suleiman had the keys.

One cool and balmy night, the air refreshing and moist, the full moon shone down, casting bright beams across the room and I longed for Abdi so much, I felt ill. I was desperate for him, to touch and hold him, to feel his slight but sinewy arms around me, for the touch of his lips and the dry scent of his skin. Rikh was away that night on Ops. So I waited until the doors were locked and I thought everyone was asleep and I tip-toed into the kitchen. The window creaked as I opened it, but there was no sound from Lena and Suleiman would be at his post by our bedroom window on the other side of the house. I climbed out, creeping past the bins and the servants shed, down through the garden wet with the heavy dew and out of the back gate. I ran to the park, hoping he would be there, praying he would be waiting for me. He was not.

I felt sick. I had risked everything to see him. Perhaps he had given up. Perhaps like Rikh he thought I was too much trouble. I walked home in despair.

Then a few days later, as I waited anxiously for Lena to collect me from the library, I began to feel angry. I was creeping about like a naughty child. I was colluding with their treatment of me. And out of fear. Fear of what precisely? A telling off from Lena... Being sent away? I felt ashamed. How Yolanda would have despised me. For all my brave talk, what had I become? The girl who dared to be different, the girl who had married outside her race, what had become of her?

That night I went out. Again through the kitchen window, now scornful of discovery, and paradoxically making less noise. I walked straight to the gardens and he was there.

We fell into each others' arms. But afterwards, as he had made no suggestion of a plan for us to see each other again, I said mournfully,

"I hardly ever see you. Don't you love me anymore?"

He held my arms tightly, and said angrily, "I want you. But I can't have you. Here."

He let me go, roughly pushing me away from him. "I've been warned off. Fellow officer's wife and all that."

Then he looked at me, "If only you lived somewhere else. Then it could be so different."

He was testing me and we both knew it. I did not reply. I turned and walked away, back to my cage. But what a glimpse of freedom he had given me.

My deliverance came without warning. I went to see Mrs Pepe and was dropped off at her front gate by Suleiman. Before I left I had told Lena I would be out for about two hours.

I knocked and rang the bell and no-one came. Eventually, the bearer opened the door.

"Memsahib very sick, Memsahib. Looks very bad." He was wringing his hands.

"Have you sent for the doctor?"

He face creased with anguish, he shook his head. "No. She cannot breathe, Memsahib." I could hear it. A harsh, rasping struggle for air.

I pushed past him and went to the telephone in the hall.

"Where's the number?" He picked up her worn address book and, hands shaking, leafed through the pages. I rang the doctor's surgery and told the nurse she must send him right away. She didn't argue when I told her who it was for.

"Go and get Mr Pepe."

"I can't," he wailed, "he will be at the club. I can't go in there."

We both knew that was true. The rasping went on. I went into the living room. She was lying on the sofa, her wrap had fallen on the floor.

"For God's sake, go and get him. Tell someone to go in and make him come home. Right away."

I went back into the drawing room. I waited. I tried to make her as comfortable as I could, lifting her so that she was in a sitting position. I don't know if it made any difference. It may have made her worse. She could no longer speak, her frail chest heaving, every fibre of her caught up in a desperate fight to breathe. I tried to help. I smoothed her hair, I held her hand, I spoke to her. It did no good. She was beyond us now.

No-one came. Then the phone rang. I ignored it. I was scared to leave her. It rang for a while and then stopped. After a while it rang again. I started to ignore it, but then I thought it might be the doctor, so I left her and ran to answer it.

It was Lena.

"Ah, you're there." In pleasant, measured tones.

"Lena, it's Mrs Pepe... she..."

"Yes, I know, dear, but you've been gone nearly two hours..."

Had it been that long? How had she managed to endure for so long?

Enclosed in her suffering I had lost all sense of time.

I said, "Mrs Pepe is very ill. She can't..."

Lena replied, "I'll see you shortly. Come straight home." I put the phone down and went back to Mrs Pepe.

Shortly afterwards, I heard Suleiman arrive in the Jeep.

Then later on, the bearer came back. Mr Pepe was with him. There was still no sign of the doctor.

I was sitting beside her, holding her hand. Her breathing had eased, the rough rasping gone, her breath now a deep sighing that merged into the next.

Mr Pepe stood in the doorway, his face a graven image of grief as he watched his wife slipping away. He took her in his arms and with a voice that was soft and gentle, but never faltered, said,

"It's all right, my darling. It's all right for you to go." Tears ran down his cheeks and into the lines around his mouth.

He gave her up to die. To put an end to her suffering by ignoring his own.

That bright morning, as the sun streamed in through the drawn blinds, the servants gathered silently outside the door, marking their own ritual of passing and Mr Pepe showed me what love is.

I had never seen it before and I would never be the same again. I crept away, leaving them together.

I got into the jeep beside Suleiman and he drove me back to the house. I went into my room and shut the door.

I did not sleep that night. I sat up alone and Rikh did not join me. At one point during the night, Suleiman came in. He brought me tea.

I looked up at him and said, "Mrs Pepe..." I was suddenly choked with tears. I had known her for such a short time, but we had known each other so well.

Suleiman nodded and withdrew. I drank the tea. Some hours later he re-appeared with a light woollen blanket that he draped around me. He was not a kind man and he did not like me, but he knew grief when he saw it and he respected it.

Sitting in the armchair by the window, I kept my own vigil. I watched dawn break and knew that she was gone. For a while I sat as the sun rose lighting up the shadows on the deep emerald of the grass, then I packed my bag and I left. I never went back.

Chapter Eight

I went to the station. I walked straight past the barrier and boarded the only train that was waiting to depart. The Delhi-Lahore express. It seemed heaven sent.

I sat down in a first-class European carriage. Within a few minutes, doors were slammed, a whistle blew and the train slowly pulled out of the station. I still had not really thought about what I was doing.

The train gathered speed. The sun grew bright and I drew the blind. After a while, the ticket inspector appeared and asked for my ticket. I hadn't got one, so he wrote me a chit and told me to pay at the other end. I bought tea from the *cha wallah* and drank it.

On the journey, I had time to think. I realised that all the major changes in my life had been brought about by death; my step-father's death freed my mother and I from a life of domestic violence, Yolanda's death had made me leave London and thus begin my journey to India, and Mrs Pepe's death had caused me to leave Rikh.

I cried for Mrs Pepe. I had known her for such a short time, but I loved her. She was the only friend I had made in India. I felt very alone, but I consoled myself with the thought that this was the beginning of a new chapter, my life with Abdi in the real India. That things had to be broken, chances taken in order for change to happen. Change for the better. Although very sad, I felt more like myself than I had for weeks.

I was out of the playpen.

When the train arrived in Lahore, I paid my chit and walked across to the Braganza. It would be ruinously expensive, I knew that, but it was only for a few days, until Abdi came and things were sorted out, and besides, it was the only place I knew.

At reception I asked them to put a call through to the base at Ambala. I couldn't get hold of Abdi, so I left a message that he should contact me at the Braganza. Then I asked for the smallest single room they had. I got it. It was not much bigger than a cupboard and not a large one at that, but it was pretty and fresh, with a shared bathroom down the hall. It overlooked a courtyard and was over the kitchens, but there was plenty of life and bustle, cooks and cleaners coming and going, and I comforted myself that I wouldn't be there for long.

As the porter closed the door on me, I sat down on the

narrow bed and realised that for the first time in my life I was alone. I had never lived on my own before.

Cocooned by my mother and then by Rikh, I had always been guided, often controlled, but always protected. Now I was on my own. It was a sobering thought.

I waited to hear from Abdi, sure that he would be thrilled that I had left Rikh and that we would have a chance of happiness together. I even thought that his last words to me had been a goad, a provocation, a prompt to leave my loveless marriage.

I waited for three days. The first day I cried, grieving for Mrs Pepe and not a little afraid of the enormity of what I had done. That evening, I smartened myself up a bit and went for a walk. I got as far as the Mall, hoping I might meet one of the people I had met with Abdi at Faletti's. But the crowds on the street bustled past me. Everyone seemed to have somewhere to go and someone to be with. I saw no-one I knew. I returned to the Braganza, convincing myself that my sinking spirits were due to tiredness and promising myself a bath and an early night. I had eaten nothing that day. I had left no word for Rikh.

The next day, hunger and the maid wanting to clean the room drove me out and I went to the Standard where I squandered what seemed like a fortune on a full English breakfast, forcing myself to eat every morsel of food I was offered, working my way through cereal and fruit, eggs, bacon and sausage, with fried bread and tomatoes. Not a crumb of toast was wasted, every drop of coffee drunk. It was not difficult; it was delicious and I was starving. It kept me going the whole day.

I walked up and down the Mall. I didn't dare go into Faletti's.

By the end of the third day I was panicking. I had heard nothing from Abdi and the realisation that I lacked the resources—both personal and financial—to survive alone was no longer a shadow in the corner, but an Eiger in front of me. Why had he not called? Why had I just walked out, leaping into the unknown without a thought for the consequences?

Oddly enough, I did not even consider returning to Rikh. I knew that was over. But what I longed to do was go home. To hide in my grey, dingy city where every street held a memory of a past that had defined me. A testament to my survival. Most of all I longed for my mother. I spent hours picturing her face. When she saw me she would look worried, purse her lips and then cope. She would say, "Oh Jeannie," shaking her head. She would hold me in her diffident embrace and all the harm in the world would disappear. She could cope with anything. Even me. With her, I could cope. Without her, not at all, it seemed.

But I could not go home, however much I wanted to. There was a world at war between me and my mother. So I walked the streets of Lahore, a frightened stray in a city of strangers.

My practical problems engulfed me. If Abdi had abandoned me, how would I live? I couldn't stay in the

Braganza for long, even the box room stretched my limited funds. I would have to get a job. But where? The only job I had ever had at home was arranged for me by Yolanda and her family. The Waldorf took me on trust because Papa Barroni had vouched for me. How would I get a job here? I knew no-one. I could hardly go downstairs and offer to wash up. They would never accept a Memsahib in a menial role. Office jobs were all taken by Anglo Indians. I paced up and down my cell like room hoping to find a solution. I found none. My situation seemed hopeless. What could I do?

The following morning, after a sleepless night, I walked through Lawrence Gardens, intending to ask for Lal at the Gymkhana Club, but when I arrived and stood under the marble portico, I was so daunted by its grandeur, I walked away. It was unlikely he would be there anyway. He could be anywhere. He could even be dead. I walked back to the Braganza, dizzy with hunger and sick with despair.

Strait-jacketed in my misery, I walked straight past him.

A taunting voice said, "Well, well, look who's here! The worm finally turned." Abdi was back.

I stared at him dumbly. "A very lonely worm."

He embraced me, "Not any more. I'm here now." It struck me he was enjoying this. I should have hated him, but I was so grateful to see him, I could have cried. Actually, I think I did. He sat me down and ordered coffee, and hearing that I had had nothing to eat, he ordered breakfast and we snapped smartly back into our allotted roles. The helpless and the capable, the powerful and powerless. That was how he liked it.

He poured my coffee and buttered a roll for me. "Couldn't leave the base 'til now."

I should have said, "You couldn't telephone?" But I was weak with relief and too besotted with him to question anything he did.

While I ate, he told me that Rikh had explained my absence as a "family visit." What a joke. Appearances kept up at all costs, even though everyone knew it was a lie.

I must have pulled a face because he said, "I don't think anyone expects you back."

"Rouge on a corpse." I muttered whilst chewing my bread.

"What?"

"You know exactly what I mean."

He smiled at me. "Yes. I suppose I do."

He took me upstairs and roared with laughter at my single bed.

"Oh no," he said, "this won't do at all." He looked around him, then stretched out both arms. He could almost touch the opposite walls and Abdi was not a big man.

"What is this dump? The servants' quarters?"

Tutting and shaking his head, he went downstairs. Within a few minutes, he reappeared with a porter, who hurriedly packed my few belongings and we were installed in a lovely room, with a bath, overlooking the garden. It may even have been the one we had before.

"It's paid up for the next month," he announced. It didn't occur to me to ask what happened after that.

He stayed with me for most of that time. Not all of it. There were times when he would announce, "duty calls" and then he would disappear, back into his family like a fox going to ground. He would stay away for a few days and nights and then reappear as abruptly as he had left, with a vaguely triumphant air. I now imagine it was because he had got money out of them, but I was too naïve to see it then.

It was a strange time. Unreal, full of denial and the distraction of treats and superficial joys. I still hadn't spoken to Rikh or even considered what I was doing with my life. Encouraged by Abdi, who never seemed to think about the future, or indeed even the present in any great depth. He simply went from pleasure to pleasure like a bee after pollen. Alighting on one, sucking it dry and winging off to the next. It was infectious. Together, we abdicated all adult responsibility.

I now think that this was a kind of delayed adolescence for me, the youth I had never had. My youth in London had been a solemn affair. I had had to work very hard pass my exams early in order to earn a wage and help my widowed mother. Then, although Yolanda had immense *joie de vivre*, we were serious in our desire to change the world and right the manifest wrongs we saw around us in the Thirties. Then came Rikh and the India League. Poor Rikh, always right, never fun. Then the war. My youth had been full of worthy intellectual pursuits and high-minded political action. Very few laughs, very little fun.

It was entirely different with Abdi. This was an idle life. He swiftly pooh-poohed any mention of a job for me. "No need" he declared. He threw money around like water and, in that respect, I was enough of a parched plant to lap it up.

I was very concerned at first about the length of his leave from the base, anxiously remembering Lena's warning about Rikh.

During the second week, I asked him about it.

"I'm on leave."

"Yes. I know but how can you get so much leave?" Rikh had never had any, to my knowledge, except a few days to pack up before leaving England and, recently, his desperate flight to Lena.

He shrugged.

"Well, as you know, I'm not the world's greatest pilot," he began cagily. I recalled his earlier crash.

"A few weeks ago, I got the chance to fly again and I made a bit of a hash of it. Just... a heavy landing, you know..."

I didn't. Rikh was a very good pilot. Nothing like this ever happened to him.

"Undercarriage collapsed. Well, smashed to bits actually." He pointed to his leg and grimaced.

"Were you hurt?" I had seen no sign of it, but he nodded stoically.

"Was the crash very bad?"

"Not really. Just a prang."

"But bad enough to injure you?"

"Not quite. I tripped, getting out of the plane."

I laughed.

"It's not funny. I could have broken my ankle." I assumed a serious expression, with difficulty.

"It hurts," he said plaintively. And after this conversation, but not before, he walked with a slight limp, when he remembered.

"Upside is, my doc here will write to the MO and drag it out for me."

I looked puzzled. I wasn't used to serving officers malingering.

"It's win, win, treasure. I don't wreck any more of their planes and I can be here with you. We can have a good time."

"That's lovely, but... a sprained ankle... not much of an excuse for not going to war, is it?"

"You'd rather I went back?" He looked at me sternly. "England's loss is your gain, I'd say. Anyway, beggars can't be choosers."

That was true enough.

"Don't look a gift horse in the mouth. Didn't your mother ever tell you that?"

She had. But I couldn't let him get away with everything.

"You're full of platitudes today."

He nodded with an aggrieved and martyred air. "It's the pain. Dulls the brain."

With that he got up, wincing, and we went downstairs in the lift. Then he commandeered a taxi to take us a few yards to the restaurant. We had walked the day before. Then, waiting at the bar, he was the life and soul of the party, greeting his numerous friends and acquaintances with a joke and a smile and walked without a hint of a limp across the room to our table. He was such a rogue.

But he was good to me on that leave.

A few days later Abdi took off to see his family, and I telephoned Rikh. After Abdi's talk about the base, it had been weighing on my conscience. It was so utterly craven to leave as I had done without a word, like a thief in the night. So that evening I plucked up the courage and dialled the number that used to be mine.

I rang late in the evening, at about ten o'clock. A time when I hoped he would be in and Lena would be in bed. Usually, she retired early. Lena answered the phone.

"Oh," she said when she heard my voice. She sounded surprised, more flustered than hostile. Worried that my hurricane Mary presence, even at one remove, would wreck the neat salvage job she was trying to perform on her brother's life. There was a long silence.

In the end I broke it.

"Will you not let me speak to him?" I was losing my nerve already.

I should have known better. "Of course, I will." Rectitude was everything to both of them. They could be cold and unfeeling, but rarely unfair. He came to the phone.

"Nita?" I was surprised how emotional I felt at the sound of his voice.

For a few seconds, I could not speak.

"I presume you are all right?"

"Yes."

"And with Abdullah?"

"Yes." There seemed little point in denial. He sighed. Did he hope I had gone away alone and come to my senses?

"Well," there was a long pause. "Then I must assume you do not want to come back." How could he even countenance the thought of it? Now, I think the man was a saint. But it's a chilly prospect, marriage to a saint.

"Oh Rikh," I was crying, "we'd destroy each other."

"Yes." His voice was full of regret.

"I'm sorry about your friend. I know you were very fond of her." The tears would not stop. If only we could have been this good when we were together.

"Well," he said softly, "I suppose at some time we will have to consider a divorce."

Then he said, "in due course. There's no rush."

"Goodbye, Rikh. God bless." Without thinking, my mother's goodnight benison slipped out.

"You too." He put down the phone. And on that oddly religious note, our marriage was over.

I still feel angry at Rikh and Lena's flat-footed attempts to control me, but I now see that they were floundering too. They couldn't cope. Neither could I. Their draconian restraint resulted only in my full out rebellion. My selfish embracing of a life lived only for pleasure. I know now what I knew then. That Rikh and I could not have stayed together. For me to grow up, I had to leave him. That if I had stayed, my childish destructiveness would only have grown worse. I knew all this, but I also knew he deserved a better wife.

Chapter Nine

The next morning Abdi came back. Early. He burst into our room and jumped onto the bed.

"Wake up, sleepy head! I've been up for hours."

I sat up, bleary eyed with sleep. I tried to embrace him.

He pushed me away. "Not now. Get up. I'm bored. Let's go and find some people."

So we did. Most mornings found us in the Standard or the Imperial Coffee House where we drank coffee, glanced at the papers and table-hopped, chatting to one acquaintance after another, exchanging gossip gleaned from the night before, making plans for the night to come. Coffee would spill over into lunch and like a babbling stream, gathering volume as we went, we would all go—a whole group by now—on to Stiffles or Lorangs for lunch and repeat the same thing until definite plans had been made. We would then retreat back to the quiet and cool of the Braganza, to rest before joining the evening fray.

Abdi was determined that his leave should be a whirlwind of constant pleasure—a non-stop round of dinners and balls, cocktails and lunches, picnics and excursions. There was music and dancing late into the night. Hearts were broken and soon mended, loves begun and ended with the same casual ease. They were revels of, to me, unparalleled luxury, but like Gatsby's they all had a slightly fevered air—as if we knew somewhere that it could not last, that when the war was over, and by now we knew it soon would be, things would be very different. So there was a note of transience, almost of frenzy, a clutching at the fading comet of Empire, a 'gathering of rosebuds while ye may'.

Abdi introduced me to a dizzying number of people, but of them all, I took most pleasure in the company of Imran and Ethel, an English woman with curls like Shirley Temple, who had a failing marriage to a senior ICS officer and like me, was an armchair intellectual. She would not go so far as to oppose the Raj except in conversational terms, so she was a timid rebel, and an ineffective one at that. She was rather despised by those of us who had seen 'active service' in the struggle, like Vicky and Imran and me, but she was bright and funny and she had a bruised sensibility that was deeply endearing.

Imran, who had no job except spending the large fortune his family of minor aristocrats had allotted him, read extensively and always lent me books. Under his guidance and at his insistence, I re-read Jane Austen and Trollope.

He showed me that observation could be trenchant without being cruel and provided a welcome counterweight to Abdi's giddy flight through the social whirl.

I saw Vicky again, but only briefly. At a ball at Faletti's one night, dressed in a sari that looked silver when it caught the light but deep midnight blue otherwise, a dress symbolic of her, I observed, dazzling but with depth. Abdi grimaced when I said that.

"Bit fanciful, don't you think?" he said with a sardonic smile, but Imran squeezed my arm and I knew that he not only understood, but agreed. She saw me and smiled and after a short while, came over to our table with Feroz. Vicky introduced us.

"Oh I remember you," he assured me. I smiled at him, politely doubtful. He was so impressive with his understated arrogance and regal bearing that I felt completely intimidated. I was about to waffle, which I always tended to do when awkward but he wouldn't let me.

"I remember Krishna telling me how a little office girl became our guardian angel," he reminisced to the others at the table," during a police raid, she kept our secrets safe in her handbag, eluding the police by riding round London on a double-decker bus."

We all laughed and exchanged pleasantries. Vicky

invited me to their home for drinks one evening, and by the time they left us, swooping away like exotic birds to alight on other tables, I was delighted by their friendship.

But the evenings I liked best were those when we all repaired to the Braganza in a convoy of *tongas* to sit at the tables on the lawn, as the silent stern-faced waiters, clad in white tunics and *pugrees*, kept us supplied with a constant supply of drinks and snacks and cigarettes. We would sit talking and drinking until dawn. I remember the sound of the distant piano in the bar, the whispered asides and laughter, and the beauty of the night. The cool air scented with night flowering jasmine and the flickering of the tiny candles on each table, pin points of earthly light that echoed the panoply of stars overhead.

In the course of this relentless social round two things were dawning on me. One was that my great love was an incorrigible flirt and the other was the extremely limited nature of my wardrobe. The two things were linked somehow. Both had the same effect on me. They made me anxious and insecure.

Abdi introduced me to "all his lady loves" as he called them. They were part of our social group and they were all European, nearly well-spoken and very glamorous. Imran rather despised them—calling them "the undertow of the fishing fleet"—noting with distaste that he would respect their hankering after what he called "Bohemia" more had they left their husbands before taking up with Abdi. He smiled kindly at me as he said it, so I was reassured that he didn't mean me, but not too much since he easily could have. "If the cap fits" and so on. I also wondered if Abdi's attraction for married women let him off the hook, as it limited their involvement rather neatly, preventing him from any real encumbrance. They were the kind of people, Imran said, who would push the boundaries but never cross them. Well, I said, that lets me out, I've crossed all mine and burnt the bridges behind me. He laughed at my mixed metaphor and patted my hand.

But one morning Abdi and I woke up late and were rushing to get ready to meet 'the gang' at the Elphinstone for lunch. Despite being autumn, it was warm and the sun was high in the sky, promising even greater heat to come. I got out my red suit and sighed at the thought of wearing it yet again. It was lovely, I had brought it from London where it had cost me what had seemed a king's ransom. It was a Paris model or at least a damn good copy of one. Abdi loved it. He said it was "Parisian," which was his highest form of praise. He had been to Paris before the war and there the "effortless elegance of the ladies" had made a huge impression on him. He called them "matchless," sometimes even "peerless." He had called me that, once or twice, but only when I was wearing my chiffon dress or this red suit.

This morning I was dithering around in my slip, dreading the moment when I would have to put it on and feel the wool against my skin. It was too hot for wool, but nothing else was nice enough.

He was sitting on the bed, his hair still damp from the bath, smoking a cigarette. He looked me up and down as I stepped into the skirt, pursed his lips and said, "Again?"

He had a way of looking at me, a cool, impartial stare, the slight raising of an eyebrow, that seemed to confirm all my insecurities, convincing me that my clothes were all wrong, my feet too big and my stomach sticking out.

I felt angry and a bit tearful.

"I wasn't always like this." I kicked my slippers under the bed.

"Like what?" He was buffing nails now, my Narcissus.

"Shabby." That was how he had made me feel.

"I had lovely things in London. You don't need to be rich to dress well in London."

He looked at me in horror, the damp curls clinging to his forehead, his child's eyes open wide.

Then he said accusingly, "What a cad you must think me."

I hadn't a clue what he was on about. I hadn't been thinking of him at all.

I felt a bit worried. When striking a serious note, it was quite easy to get it wrong with Abdi. I looked at him, wondering what was coming next.

"We'll go to Ram's first. Come on. Get dressed."

He took me to Kirpa Ram & Bros., the department store on the Mall and bought me a beautiful white silk blouse. It was lovely, nice enough to wear without a jacket so at least the top half of me didn't boil.

That afternoon he had what he described as an "appointment." I never knew what these appointments were, whether they were family or business based or if he were seeing one of his old flames in secret. You could never tell with him. Certainly, he was still attracted to his former loves, he flirted with them shamelessly, and one in particular, a plumpish blonde called Jean Frances, he would actually embrace every time they met. They would talk in half sentences and laugh at unspoken jokes, touching each other with a casual warmth that spoke of real intimacy. It hurt me, but I learned to ignore it, because he always came home with me, as it were. At least at that stage.

So, I was having tea on the lawn at the Braganza on my own and attempting to read 'Barchester Towers.' I was desperately trying to drum up an intelligent opinion of it to relay to Imran later, when Eva Maria marched across the grass with her purposeful stride and sat down opposite me.

"Abdi has put you in my hands," she said pouring herself a cup of tea without being asked. I must have looked as flummoxed as I felt because she went on,

"A new wardrobe, he said." She took the last cucumber sandwich and ate it with relish.

"Don't look so alarmed. We'll have fun."

She had brought a copy of French Vogue with her, a few months old, and began to rifle through it. After careful scrutiny, she showed me the fashions she thought would suit me.

"Plain simple lines, jewel colours, beautiful fabrics. No bows and ribbons." Clearly she would brook no argument, or even discussion from me. She looked at me with her steely gaze as if she knew exactly what I looked like in my smalls and then she softened.

"By the time, I've finished with you you'll be the most elegant woman in Lahore."

She was as good as her word.

Eva Maria took me in hand. She transformed me. It was a comprehensive change; a metamorphosis, in fact. She took a London office girl who became a frugal officer's wife and turned her into a beautifully dressed, groomed lady of leisure. When it was all over, I didn't even recognise myself.

Eva Maria was a seriously elegant woman herself, always well and appropriately dressed, with an unerring eye for what would suit me. "Flaunt the assets, hide the flaws" as she put it.

She chose my new wardrobe with a discrimination and expertise that made me wonder if she had ever worked in the rag trade in her Lewisham days. She picked through pattern and fabric, amending designs to enhance, quizzing the poor *dherzi* at every turn until the poor man was on the point of tears. She also haggled about the price of everything, making sure Abdi got value for his money. For it was made clear from the outset that Abdi was paying for all of this largesse. When I tried to ask him if I could contribute, even in a minor way, he shook me off, he would have none of it. I was to be remade in the form of his desire; I did not argue. It felt like all my Christmases had come at once.

A few mornings after our tea on the lawn, Eva Maria called for me. She spirited me away, informing Abdi that he would not see me until late afternoon. Then she took me in a *tonga* to the Anarkali Bazaar. Anarkali in those days was the most magnificent bazaar in all of India, encompassing a mile long conglomerate of smaller bazaars. It was a shopper's paradise. Within the walled city there were other smaller bazaars that specialised in particular trades or crafts. The Sua Bazaar was famous for goldsmiths and jewellers, Kinari for gold and silver thread embroidery, Baza Hatta was the stronghold of cloth merchants and Juti bazaar sold shoes. Each one of them was larger than the whole bazaar in Ambala. But none of them compared to Anarkali.

We entered Anarkali at Lohari Gate whose portals were graced by two markets, flowers on one side and fruit on the other. A Gog and Magog of produce, in glorious profusion, arranged in decorative baskets that rose to a height of nearly twenty feet. The scent and colour of the flowers and fruit was overwhelming. I thought of my mother—her love for pineapple, the only exotic fruit she had ever seen. I remembered her delight when I had brought her one and wished I could bring her here. It was a cornucopia indeed

I wanted to get down and see more of these wonders, but Eva Maria wouldn't allow it.

"No time for sight-seeing. We have business to attend to." After a brief haggle, where I fear she fleeced the poor *tonga wallah*, we descended into the bazaar, where she took me to a series of material shops that left me staggered by the scope of their stock.

She took me into the dark, shady interior of the Karachi Cloth House, where she made the assistant show us bolts of cloth in all colours. A sea of shimmering silk was soon billowing out around us. She draped it over me as if I were a tailor's dummy. Rejecting most of what was offered her, pulling a face, feeling the cloth between her fingers and stoking it against her powdered face and mine, she finally pronounced on what would suit and then went into a muttered debate with the vendor as she showed him the photographs she wanted the *dherzi* to copy, discussing the cut and quantity we would need. I followed her around like a dazed puppy, stupefied by the munificence around me.

The same performance was repeated at The Bombay Cloth House and Dunichand and Sons. We bought miles of fabric, each parcel wrapped neatly in brown paper and tied with string. At one point as she was draping me in a burnt orange silk that I would never have chosen but which, in fact, suited me very well, I came out of my trance and remarked,

"Golly, bit different from home. No rationing here."

She turned and smiled at me for the first time. A conspiratorial grin.

"No. You can fall on your feet here, if you've a mind."

Then she turned back to the hapless assistant and knocked more off the price.

By the time she had finished with me and the shopping and fittings were over, everything in my wardrobe was new, from lace underwear to gold kid evening shoes; dresses in silk and satin and fine lawn cotton, skirts and blouses, scarves and stockings by the dozen, even a pair of tailored linen trousers that made me feel like Katherine Hepburn. All in deep, rich colours that glowed and shimmered with restrained tastefulness.

She also made me buy shoes with heels, which I had avoided for years because neither Rikh nor Abdi were particularly tall. She told me off for not daring to stand out from the crowd.

"You're tall. Don't hide it, stooping like that because you're with a shrimp like Abdi, stand up straight and flaunt it. Don't be afraid to use your assets."

She took me to her hairdresser on the Mall. A man called Victor, an assumed name for snob value I imagined since he was an Indian who proudly informed me he was trained in England, but he was a master of his craft, who brought about a transformation similar to Madame Andrea in London, cutting my now shapeless and straggling locks into a chic bob. Eva Maria wouldn't let me have a perm.

"No. No frizz. Waves." And she made me buy spiky metal clips which you had to fasten in when your hair was wet and then it dried in crisp waves.

"They look more like weapons," I remarked fearfully.

"They feel like it too. For God's sake don't rest your head against anything while they're in, or they'll stab you."

"Are they really necessary?" I was never very brave about these things.

"For you, yes. Your hair is straight and fine and if you don't want to look like you've just been let out of the institution, you'll use them. Every time you wash your hair."

She laughed at my daunted face. "Courage, baby. You have to suffer to be beautiful. We're not done yet."

Then she chivvied me on to an extraordinary chemist where we bought enough cosmetics for a West End show. When I demurred, she countered that nature was not to be trusted, but Max Factor was. There was no arguing with that.

She was a tornado of a woman, sweeping everything up in her path, brooking no dissent, but at the end of it all, when the final fittings were over and the whole lot had been delivered to the Braganza, she banished Abdi for the afternoon and made me try it all on. Everything—ranged in outfits for each occasion, from silk slips to evening bags.

When the fashion parade was over, we sat together on the sofa and she poured us a stiff drink. Then raising her glass she said with a triumphant air,

"My, my, Mrs Rikh, you do scrub up nice!"

She had been inexhaustible, domineering and unrelenting. She had not considered my wishes and feelings at all, but she had dragged me up by my bootstraps and turned me into what she called "a stunner." It was all her work.

Abdi was delighted by this transformation. He made me try everything on again that evening and pronounced it was all "peerless." I said I hoped so because it must have cost a fortune.

He shook his head. "Not with her at the purse strings. She's the most penny pinching woman in Lahore. She makes grown men cry. She's famous for it."

He winked at me. "I'm not a complete fool," he said, pulling me down onto the bed.

Chapter Ten

The war was over. I read the long awaited news in the paper over breakfast, then walked out into the hotel gardens to be alone. Seeing the grainy pictures of rapturous crowds outside Buckingham Palace, I wondered if my mother was among them. I searched for her face but did not find her. In my present life of almost obscene privilege, I thought of my ruined city, my London, battered and bruised but not broken, and although I hated any notion of jingoism, I knew exactly what that flag-waving crowd had endured and the price they had paid for their joy.

I banished Abdi from our room and wrote a long letter to Mother. I had actually written to her very little since leaving England, not confident that any letter, even in the service bag, would ever reach her, but now things were bound to improve. Up to now I had confined myself to platitudes, not wanting to worry her when she could not contact me, but now I told her everything. That I had left Rikh; she and Yolanda had been right, the difference in our ages had meant that the marriage did not last and the importing of his sister, I did not say why, into our home, had been the final straw. I finished by saying that I was very happy with a man I truly loved, who was kind and generous to me and that India delighted me as I had hoped it would. That my life was now very pleasant and I was having a good time. That much was true anyway. I finished on an all-singing, all-dancing riff of happiness that was like the resounding finale of a Hollywood musical. And about as real.

When I joined Abdi at Lorangs, he and all the chums were making plans for the evening. A gala victory ball was to be held at Nedous Hotel and the world and his wife were to be in attendance. There was an atmosphere of fete that day, a feeling heightened when I saw Imran.

"Well done, Britannia," he said, giving me a rare embrace. I gave him a quizzical look.

He smiled which was rare for him. "Now, at last, we can get our independence."

I hugged him back, as he quoted Wordsworth, "Bliss it was in that dawn to be alive, but to be young was very heaven."

And it was and we were. For a brief moment. War had not vanquished us as we had feared it would. We felt elation that we had survived, that we had defeated Fascism and its hateful ideology, and a better world was, at last, within our grasp.

As we were getting ready for the ball, Abdi had champagne brought to the room. I raised my glass in a toast, "Yolanda."

"Who's she?"

I had never told him. She was far too precious to be bandied about for Abdi's jaded appreciation.

"The brightest and best. *Ave atque vale*."

"What the hell's that?"

"Latin."

"Of course. I remember."

I went into the bathroom smiling. He probably thought Yolanda was one of those ancient Roman seers whose works he had slumbered through at school.

I pulled out all the stops that night, sporting my new finery. An emerald silk gown, with a sweetheart bodice and peplum. He loved me in that dress. I took so long getting ready that Abdi, always easily bored, went on ahead to have drinks before the ball.

"I'll meet you there."

By the time I was ready, the streets were choked with cars, *tongas* and rickshaws. Every hotel and restaurant was having a gala evening it seemed. All of Lahore, both European and Indian alike, was out and about that night. It took forever to get the short distance from one block to the next. In the end, anxious because I was now very late, I paid the *tonga wallah* and got down to walk the remaining distance.

At the junction of McLeod Road, opposite the High Court, an impromptu demonstration was taking place. I walked straight into it. Banners were waved, a man in a congress cap stood on a makeshift crate and addressed the crowd. He said, "Brothers! No Empire in history ever disbanded itself! India must prepare herself for a mass battle for freedom. Let us unite against British oppression and become free citizens in our own land."

The crowd roared its approval, chanting *"Hindustan Zindabad."* I walked through the crowd smiling, in entire agreement. One man blocked my way and frowned at me sternly, "Quit India!" he demanded. I didn't feel threatened at all. In fact, I could have hugged him.

"Hindustan Zindabad," the words came easily to me. I had chanted them often enough in Trafalgar Square. *"Hind swaraj,"* I added for good measure.

He looked bemused, but stood aside to let me pass. I was delighted. Euphoric. That night I walked on air. Hitler and his vile Reich had gone, the Japanese were defeated utterly, the full horror of Hiroshima did not come out until later. I was young, in that beautiful city and in love. India would be free. What could go wrong? The entire world was a lovely place to me that night. Perhaps it was the champagne.

When I arrived at Nedous, Abdi greeted me approvingly. "You look..."

"Peerless?" a gentle mockery, "or dare I hope for matchless?" He laughed, but I noted that he was sitting at a table with Eva Maria, where he was eyeing up two very pretty girls, sitting alone at the next table. Sitting with him, I thought, if I had arrived any later. Abdi was hopeless. His eye didn't so much wander as was never still. He was always on the trawl for some new attraction. But tonight, I refused to let it worry me. There was a bigger picture, a greater cause for joy in the world. Tonight, I decided, I would abandon fear.

It was a lovely evening. A gala indeed. The cocktails flowed, the band played, we danced with stranger and friend alike, all of us, for that brief moment, united and glad.

While Abdi was away from the table, Eva Maria gave me a cooler appraisal. One devoid of sexual attraction. She noted every detail then gave me a nod of approval.

"Good," she said, "You used the clips." My hair for once had done what I wanted it to.

"Yup. I put them in and it was absolute torture."

"Excellent. You look... classy. A consort for a king." I laughed aloud at such uncharacteristic extravagance. I wondered how many gin slings she had had.

I danced a lot that night. My beautiful dress and smiling happiness made me the belle of the ball. I was in great demand. They were practically queuing up to dance with me. From ageing, portly Majors in uniforms studded with medals to svelte, young Sikhs in evening dress and coloured turbans, every man there wanted a dance with me, it seemed. At first, I demurred, thinking that Abdi would object, but he and Eva Maria waved me on, smiling like a pair of approving parents. Or so I thought. More probably, he had designs on the girls at the next table and didn't want me to cramp his style.

Nedous was wonderful that night. Everything from the streamers, to the flowers on the table, was perfect. At one point I went to the Ladies powder room to repair the damage. As I put on more lipstick I noticed the cloakroom attendant, an old lady in a faded sari. She was sitting in a chair in the corner, fast asleep. A middle-aged woman in ill-fitting mauve chiffon elbowed me aside.

"Wake up!" She clapped her hands loudly. The old woman woke with a start and looked anxiously around her, as if not sure where she was.

"Really, these people!" Mauve Chiffon stared at her reflection in the mirror and smoothed down her corrugated hair. "Most idle souls on earth!" She glared at the old woman, looked pointedly at her, and then reached for the saucer on which were a few pitiful coins. She opened her sequinned bag and emptied the coins into it. Then she said, "service must be given before it is rewarded."

With a sour, colluding smile to me she swept out. The old woman looked about to cry.

"I am so sorry, Memsahib. I have been here since eight o'clock this morning." It was now about two o'clock the following morning. She misinterpreted my expression because I have never hated anyone as much as I hated that woman in her mauve chiffon, a fetid relic of a world already dead, or felt so deeply ashamed of my countrymen.

"Rancid old bitch," I couldn't help myself. The old woman began to cry. She must have thought I meant her.

I opened my bag and took out my purse. It only had a few rupees in it. I never carried much money and I had paid the *tonga wallah*. But I handed it to her. She refused to take it, horrified.

"No, no Memsahib."

"Yes," I said and I placed it carefully on her saucer and marched purposefully to the door. As I opened it, I turned and saw her open the purse with a look of wonder.

"It all belongs to you, anyway. *Hindustan zindabad*." She must have thought I was drunk.

Much later, at the end of the evening, Abdi asked me for some change to tip the doorman who had gone in search of a taxi for us. I told him I hadn't got any. Then I told him why. To my astonishment he looked cross.

He sighed, "What did you do that for? What good did you think it would do?"

I was still flush with my success at the ball and I wondered if his crossness was because of that.

"Globally, not much. But it might give her a better time. For a while, anyway."

"A very short while. If anyone finds out, they'll probably kill her."

I thought that was just stupid. "Don't be so absurd. It was less than ten bob."

"Oh, they'd do it for a lot less, believe me. Next time you get a charitable impulse, Memsahib mine, resist it. For all our sakes."

He shook his head, then caught sight of his reflection in the mirror. Clearly, he liked what he saw. He was a very good-looking man, my Abdi, but he was also very vain. One time when he hogged the full length mirror in our room, I had dubbed him Narcissus. He asked me who that was and was pleased as punch when I told him the son of a Greek god. He liked that and referred to it often between ourselves, unaware of his avatar's fate.

In the taxi he said, "You were a great success tonight."

I asked him if he had minded. "Not at all. Why should no-one else want what I have?"

It struck me that he had not minded other men wanting me, in fact, he had actively encouraged it.

The next morning, as we were finishing breakfast, Abdi dropped his napkin among the toast crumbs, smeared marmalade and empty coffee cups, then stood up, ground his cigarette out on his bread plate and announced, "I'm off. Duty calls."

I didn't take much notice. If I had I would have imagined he was going back to his family for a few days, but I was deep in the morning paper. As soon as the war ended, Wavell had released those activists from the "Quit India" movement that were still in jail. He convened the Simla

Conference, inviting all parties, to discuss proposals for an Interim Government, paving the way for Independence.

Imran had been telling me all about it the night before, as one of his cousins was a delegate. He said it was becoming "crystal clear" that, while most of the Congress Party had been in jail, Jinnah had used their absence to consolidate his position among moderate Muslims and alienate them from the Congress Party. Imran said Jinnah now had widespread backing and had pronounced gloomily that the Pakistan we hoped "can and will never happen" now looked possible. Feroz and Vicky were right, he said.

I had tried to interest Abdi in all this, it was his future after all, but he disdained all politics with what I thought was a "let them eat cake" attitude and went away to talk to someone else.

"When will you be back?" I asked him now, lifting my head from the paper.

He shrugged, "don't know, Toots. Bye."

And with that, he was gone. I didn't love it, but this time, I wasn't in a flat spin. I was certain he would be back soon.

I went back to our room and got ready to go out. Over coffee later in the morning, Eva Maria said,

"Where's Abdi?" I think she missed her morning dose of gossip from the night before.

"He's gone away. Only for a few days."

"Are you sure?" She looked at me with her rather chilling stare.

"Of course," I announced confidently, "he'll be back soon." I was looking round to see if Imran had arrived yet.

"Mm, maybe." She didn't sound sure. I felt an icy splinter of fear.

"Do you think he's gone for good?" I could barely get the words out.

"No," she said with her cynical smile, "you're not that lucky."

She was an odd one, Eva Maria, we had little in common, not even liking at that point, but she seemed to have taken me under her wing and during the time that Abdi was away, it was she who made sure that I had company. On the rare evening when I was not invited out or had decided to stay in and have an early night, she would telephone the hotel and inform me I would be joining her and whoever else was with her at such and such a place and she would send a *tonga* in half an hour to collect me. Although I occasionally felt irritated by such high-handed chivying, I went along with it. It was better than being alone and she was not one to be crossed either.

I still thought of Rikh often. Wondering how he was and if, now that the war was over, he would resign his commission in the Royal Air Force and immerse himself in the struggle for independence, but I didn't like to call and ask him. I knew I had relinquished any right to be informed of what he was doing.

A few days later I received a rather cryptic phone call from Abdi informing me that he was on the base at Ambala, arranging his discharge on the grounds of being unfit for service. Flat feet, he proclaimed. They had always looked fine to me. In fact, he had rather a high instep. Laughingly, I asked if anyone had even looked at his feet.

"Certainly not," he replied. "What a ghastly idea." It occurred to me that for a man who was so promiscuous, he was oddly coy about anyone seeing his body. Anyone he was not in bed with, that is. Then, he could strip off like grease lightning.

I told him he was a fearful liar. "You don't know the half of it," he replied. I told him I loved him anyway. He said goodbye warmly enough, but he gave me no idea of when he would be back.

So I settled down into a bachelor existence, sure it would be short-lived. I made the usual round of drinks and dinners, luncheons and outings. Eva Maria made sure I was never really alone, but the social round was never as much fun as it was with Abdi. I missed his mocking commentary on all we met and did; his ability to turn a prosaic afternoon tea into a party, his ardent love-making and his mischievous laughter.

I spent a lot of time with Imran. We both loved browsing in bookshops. Uttar Chand Kapur in the bazaar was our favourite and we passed many a happy hour there, selecting the volumes Imran wanted to buy – he bought books by the boxful – seated on bales of old newspapers, tied up with string, leafing through their wonderful and eclectic collection while the overhead fan groaned as it churned the dusty air.

We would read and then sit up late at night discussing the books he had chosen. One night, after Eva Maria had declared we had "bored everyone away, including me," and we were alone, he asked gently,

"Why did you leave your home?" We both knew he meant my husband.

I sighed, "It was never really my home."

"Yes," now a little impatient at my lack of candour, his face slightly averted, "But why Abdi?"

I was about to reply that we had fallen in love, but even then, I didn't quite dare speak for Abdi.

"I fell in love," I replied.

A fleeting smile rewarded my reluctant honesty. "He's not half the man you deserve."

I was tired enough to look crestfallen. He patted my hand. "But then, my dear, they never are."

I knew that Imran had a partner. It was common knowledge. A man he had lived with for years who was kept discretely in the background. I longed to meet him, I knew the person who could capture Imran's lasting affection would be a rare and fascinating man, but it was not permitted.

As was often the case in those days, among men who are now called 'gay', the man who shared Imran's life, remained shut away, like a guilty secret, unable to be introduced even to his closest friends. It always seemed to me terribly wrong.

Lahore was known at that time as the 'Paris of India'. Imran was even prouder of his home town than Abdi and he used to say that he who has not seen Lahore, has not been born. I could only agree, transported as I was into this new kaleidoscope of a world, vibrant, sensual and enriching.

They were great shoppers, the Lahorias, and prices were ridiculously low. Ethel and I spent days prowling round the bazaar, seeking out treasures at bargain prices. I acquired a collection of silk *dupattas* in the glowing jewel colours Eva Maria was so fond of and I draped them around our room at the Braganza, their vivid hues an enduring pleasure. I bought incense and small brass bowls for candles and flowers, and to the disdain of the Anglophile Braganza, turned our room from a transient, impersonal space, suitable for almost anyone, to my own oasis, my refuge.

But to buy anything in Lahore you had to haggle. I found that very alien at first, embarrassing even. It felt wrong to me to quibble about annas when the vendors were so comparatively poor and I lived a life of complete opulence. But, Abdi had been right when he told me that for them it was a way of life, a time honoured exchange they expected and enjoyed. He said they would feel cheated without it, a dish without relish was how he put it. So under Imran's patient tutelage I learned to haggle a bit, although I think I was mostly humoured and never achieved the kind of significant bargain that Imran and Abdi took for granted.

In the general store—Jagat Singh Kwatra and Inayatullah, it was rather improbably called, that stocked everything from Tootal ties to Huntly and Palmers biscuits, we even found Abernathy biscuits, my old favourites. I pounced on them like a bird of prey and made sure I always had a secret store in the drawer of my bedside table. My solitary vice. Like Proust's madeleines, their crisp, buttery taste brought back to me the comfort of home and the smell of my mother's kitchen.

During Abdi's absence, Imran and Ethel were my daytime companions. The evenings were taken up by Eva Maria and her more sophisticated social whirl. She made it obvious that it was somehow expected of me and I did not demur.

I met Vicky occasionally. Once, quite unexpectedly, in the HMV record shop on the Mall. I used to go in there in my rare moments of solitude and listen to the records. I never bought any—I didn't have a gramophone, but they were very forbearing, letting me listen to anything and everything from Beethoven to Benny Goodman. She was in one of the booths, listening to a Haydn Symphony and she beckoned me in and we listened together. I shared her joy in music, but alas, none of her skill.

Chapter Eleven

Abdi was gone for much longer that time, but I assumed that it was simply taking a while for the red tape involved in his discharge to be dealt with so I didn't worry unduly.

Until one night when I returned to the Braganza having spent a very enjoyable evening with the usual crowd, dining and dancing at Faletti's and rather shamelessly flirting with a tall, handsome Sikh who reminded me a little of Lal. He made me laugh and he complimented me outrageously. He called me "the most beautiful woman he had ever met." Even when you know it is absolute nonsense, it is still very agreeable to be told that.

So I walked across the lobby, flushed with flattery and a little too much wine, when the hotel manager, Mr De Souza, who like Mr and Mrs Pepe was Goan of Portuguese descent, came out of his office and asked if he could have a word with me. He then invited me to step into his office for a moment.

I was surprised by this request and even more when I realised that he had clearly been waiting for my return. He was a softly spoken man with impeccable manners.

He began pleasantly enough.

"I am so sorry to trouble you, especially at this hour, Mrs Rikh, and I am certain that this is just an oversight but..."

I hadn't a clue what he was talking about and my expression must have reflected this because he went on, "I am afraid that the account has been allowed to reach such a level that I felt I must bring the matter to your attention."

I was so shocked I didn't know what to say. I opened my mouth and then closed it. Words wouldn't come.

"It is long overdue," he added gently as he handed me a white envelope. It was not sealed. I nodded and took it from him. He ushered me out of his office wishing me a very good night.

When I was safe in our room, I opened the envelope. In it was our outstanding account. It was astronomical. The charges for our room and board were bad enough, but they were to be expected. What shook me rigid was the small fortune Abdi had racked up in extras—the reckoning for all those wonderful evenings when he had invited everyone to join us and regaled them with drinks and coffee and food until the early hours, the late suppers and early breakfasts and all the libations that had gone with them. All those had been charged to him and we would now have to pay for it.

I went into a flat spin. The amount we owed was larger

than the total amount in my bank account. I could not have settled that bill however much I wanted to. I spent the night in a complete panic. I knew exactly from my experience at the Waldorf in London how these things were dealt with and how the guests who behaved like this were viewed. Flushed with shame, I wondered if they thought he'd deliberately taken off to try and wriggle out of paying, knowing full well that Mr De Souza would be more reluctant to get tough with me than with him. I felt completely mortified.

I didn't sleep at all that night. In the morning I went straight downstairs to reception and rang Abdi at the base. He was not there and no-one knew where he was and when or if he would be back. I felt sick.

I then asked if I could see Mr De Souza. I was ushered straight into his office. He was seated at his desk, going through the hotel ledgers. He took off his half-moon glasses and wished me good morning.

I began by apologising. He looked sternly at me for a moment, no doubt assessing my sincerity. I told him that I expected Abdi back any day now and whilst I was so sorry that I was not in a position to settle the bill in full, I could certainly pay a small amount of it on account and was happy to do so right away. I had my cheque book in my hand. A hand that was shaking.

He sized me up in a glance. Then shook his head and smiled wanly, "no, no, Mrs Rikh, that will not be necessary. As a rule, it is not our policy to extend unlimited credit indefinitely, but, in this case, I am sure our friend will soon return and all will be settled forthwith."

He rose. The audience was over. Stammering my thanks, I left him. Walking across the lobby that suddenly seemed huge, sure everyone in it knew and was looking at me, I made my way to the Standard. My hands were sweating, but even in the bright sunlight, I felt cold. I kept seeing Eva Maria's expression when I had told her Abdi would be back soon. "Maybe," she'd said. She clearly hadn't believed a word of it. Had she seen it all before?

My head was waging a total war with my heart. What was right in front of me was what my heart refused to consider. He loved me. He had to. We were soul mates. This was just a mistake, an oversight as Mr De Souza had said. Abdi was certainly heedless, feckless even, but he would never do this to me. Never.

I went into the Standard to our usual table. I greeted everyone with a smile that made my cheeks ache and asked Eva Maria if I could have a quiet word with her. She nodded, got up and led me to a table at the back of the restaurant. We sat in silence as the waiter brought our coffee.

"What's up?" She lit one of her permanent cigarettes with the stub of the previous one, then looked me straight in the eye.

"Abdi's left me with the bill for the Braganza. It's massive."

She pulled a shred of tobacco off her lower lip. "It would be."

"I haven't got the money to pay it." She nodded, unsurprised.

"I can't get hold of him. I don't know when he'll be back."

I felt humiliated, almost tearful, but it was somehow a relief to confide in her. Her steady gaze was cool, her sympathy not effusive, but still oddly reassuring. I felt there was little she could not cope with.

She poured our coffee. "Don't panic. They'll wait. They know he's good for it."

Then she put her head on one side as if weighing me up, "But, if you are ever really stuck..." she paused and blew a perfect smoke ring, "there is a way... for a girl like you... to make money."

"A job?" I was eager, no desperate. To stand on my own two feet financially, to be independent, everything I had taken for granted since I left school, seemed like paradise now.

She smiled dismissively, "Not exactly." Then with an almost imperceptible movement, she shook her head.

"Do you think he'll come back?" It was a plea from the heart. Almost a wail.

She laughed. It was a harsh, grating sound. "Yes. Unfortunately, I do."

I didn't know what to make of her. But I had few real

friends here and she was rapidly becoming one. We drank our coffee in silence and then went back to the others.

He came back. Not that day or the next, but about ten days after my frantic call to the base. Ten long, anxious days during which I felt as if I were being keelhauled by waves of anger, fear, and blind panic. I sought Eva Maria's company, although I liked her much less than Imran and Ethel, she was the only person I knew there who could even begin to calm me down. Her cool, jaundiced manner was soothing, a protection against the storm of my emotions.

When I returned to the Braganza, I took to dashing across the foyer, trying to avoid catching anyone's eye in reception, rushing to get to the lift before anyone could call me to account and ask me why the bill was still unpaid. I heard nothing from him.

Then one morning, just as before, there he was, as if he had never been away, sitting in the foyer, looking as fresh and clean as a child groomed for a special outing. Grey flannel and a white silk shirt. Clean shaven, clear skinned, his dark eyes huge in that delicately sculptured face, his clothes immaculate, he really was a very good looking man. I instantly felt hot, bothered and tousled, although I had only just finished getting ready to go out.

"Why didn't you call me? " I was angry this time, but as always when angry with him on the verge of tears.

"What on earth are you in such a tizz about?" he said, not unkindly.

"Where the hell have you been?" I hated it and I knew he would hate it more, this sounding like an irate wife, but I couldn't help it.

His face closed shut, like a slammed door. "Something came up."

"We haven't paid the bill... Mr De Souza gave me the account... it's massive... I couldn't pay it... I haven't got enough money..." I was blustering and bobbing, like a rowing boat in a gale.

He stared at me in polite amazement. "Is that all?" he asked.

Then as I geared up for more, he said, "well," cutting me off in full flow, "I'm here now." And almost resentfully he walked across the foyer and disappeared into Mr De Souza's office. I drank what was left of his coffee.

After what seemed like an insultingly short time, they both emerged, smiling and shaking hands. He rejoined me.

"All settled. Storm in a teacup." It hadn't felt like that to me.

I put the cup down. My hands were shaking. "Silly girl," he took my arm and led me upstairs to our bedroom.

He looked around at my new décor. "Gone native?"

"Don't you like it?"

"Very much. I am one, remember?"

Later, he said, "What we have...," as he embraced me, his mouth seeking mine, "must be..." he ran his hands down my body and I shivered with pleasure, "delight or nothing at all."

I wanted him too much to argue. And besides, fundamentally, I did not disagree. I was all for delight. There had been far too little of that in my life.

He was a very skilled lover and he knew what gave me pleasure. But he held me at a pitch of needing, never quite letting me go, never quite satisfying. In a constant state of arousal, always wanting more.

So again, despite everything my head was telling me, I ignored it, taking my lead from him, skimming across the surface of my life, like a stone skittering across a pond, never daring to sound the depths beneath.

He had said what we were about was delight and this time he set about providing it. No-one could do it better. We made love often, and during this time, perhaps the only time, with something approaching tenderness. For once, he was gentle, almost kind and he did not canvas other women. We reached a sensual delight, a silent ecstasy that was oddly innocent.

Although he was a confirmed party animal, loving nothing more than an appreciative audience for his titbits of scurrilous gossip and rather cruel wit, he made time during this stay to be alone with me when we were not in bed. He took me for picnics in Jilani park and we sat on the grass, drinking wine from a flask and basking in the dappled sunlight that filtered through the leaves of the trees above us. We even ate alone on some evenings, unprecedented for him, in candlelit booths in the

Standard, curtains drawn, sharing our food as we shared our bed.

One morning he borrowed Imran's car, a pre-war Ford convertible. The weather was cooler now and I remember the sensation of the wind in my hair as we drove out into the country. The Punjab—land of rolling wheat fields and fast flowing rivers. At one point we came to a standstill as a boy who could not have been more than twelve, barefoot and white robed, shepherded his flock of goats across the road to seek fresh pasture. The twentieth-century with its mad progress, machinery and armaments, faded away, as the child ushered his animals to safety. They were unwilling and wanted to roam in different directions, but with the patience of the East, so incomprehensible to the West, he succeeded at last by taking his time. And I thought it wonderful that I, an English woman in silk stockings and lipstick, seated in a car that roared and spluttered and smelled of oil, should be brought to a halt by a pastoral vision as old as time. This was Gandhi's India, a land of infinite horizons.

Abdi was impatient, he banged the steering wheel with his hand and swore, but the child took no notice at all and I marvelled at his wisdom.

Rikh had always told me that Divali was a magical time. But our first Divali had been on the base where we watched the celebrations from a sedate distance and I felt like a child excluded from a party.

Id had come and gone in one of Abdi's absences—I

imagine he was with his family—but I never really knew. He was always very unforthcoming about his whereabouts and he didn't like to talk about his religion. I had asked him often, in that Muslim town, about the glorious mosques around us, their history and their tradition, but he always rebuffed my interest. He had a love-hate attitude to his religion. It made him uncomfortable and he didn't like to be reminded of it. I felt much the same about my own. Since Yolanda's death, I had struggled to believe in a benevolent deity. In fact, when I thought about it at all, which was rare, I decided I loathed God for the suffering he either inflicted or was prepared to stomach. I found religion very hard to swallow, so I didn't push it with Abdi.

But Divali was different. A festival of lights, celebrated by Hindus and Sikhs alike; it had a joyous, inclusive feel to it. As if a great party was going on and we were all welcome.

It was also the festival of Laxmi, the goddess of wealth, and the market stalls were piled high with sweets, loaded with honey and sugar, and great mounds of flowers. The streets were full of people, dressed in their brightly coloured best, bustling from friends to family and back again, bearing gifts to bring sweetness and good fortune in the year to come.

The city was transformed. Earthenware oil lamps, like little cups, were placed around the exterior of the houses, forming garlands of gentle light. A million tiny lamps lit up the ghostly outline of that dark, Moghul city.

Fireworks were let off as soon as it was dusk, and for a whole week the air smelled of smoke, as the multi-coloured flowers of light formed and faded away in the night sky. Everyone had parties. Indeed, I think that was the first time I ever went to Eva Maria's house.

She lived in a palatial bungalow near the Civil Lines, not far from the river. We arrived late to join a crowd of men and women in evening dress drinking ruinously expensive whisky and eating tinned cocktail sausages on little sticks, a great delicacy in those days. The party was in full swing in all the reception rooms and had spilled out into the garden. Everyone was talking and laughing, strangers were introduced and were soon on first name terms. Assignations were made and couples sauntered out into the dark, hidden in the leafy depths of the garden, their presence only visible by the glowing ends of their cigarettes. Everyone smoked in those days.

A small group of Indian musicians sat on the floor in one of the rooms and serenaded us with the low, insistent beat of the *tabla* and the soft wail of the sitar. Servants dressed in white with scarlet *pugrees*, circulated in house and garden, serving drinks and food from silver salvers.

There were fireworks later on. An impressive display of rockets, star bursts and Catherine wheels. The Indian men present were delighted by them. At one point, I remember, they were running up and down the garden, laughing and throwing lit fireworks into the darkness, cavorting like schoolboys. Eva Maria, the perfect hostess, always making sure the food was handed round and the drinks flowed, rolled her eyes at me in passing.

"Why are all men such children?" she remarked. Abdi was not immune. Despite his initial scorn, he was soon in the thick of it, darting here and there, inciting mirth and having fun. The lord of misrule.

Long past midnight, I went for a walk alone in the now deserted garden. The smoke from the fireworks had wafted away. The stars were so bright, the sky now so clear, you felt you could fall into its inky depths. A last rocket blazed its lonely path across the darkness and then was gone.

Abdi appeared from behind a tree. I laughed and told him he looked like Pan.

He wrinkled his nose.

"Saucepan or *paan?*"

"Neither. A God. Lord of misrule and the lawless dark." I was a bit drunk.

"I remind you of him? Another God?" He hadn't forgotten Narcissus. Even in the dark I could tell he was thrilled.

"Yes. You do." I didn't like to remind him that Narcissus drowned in his own vanity and Pan was half a goat.

"You've had one hell of an education."

I had. I thought then of the long afternoons, learning Greek and Latin, at the Godolphin and Latimer School where I had been a scholarship girl, and the plain old maids, desiccated and unloved, in worsted and tweed, who had taught us. I thought of their great knowledge and passion for their subjects, which had to be everything to them, taking the place of lover and child. Vestal Virgins devoted to learning. Silently, I remembered and honoured them, but I was glad that my mother's poverty had decreed that I could never become one of them.

We walked home that night. Most of the lamps had burnt out, but a few still flickered, casting their dying light on the marble outlines of that ancient city. Its beauty staggered me, as did the beauty of the man who walked beside me. For a brief moment they were both mine. *Et in Arcadia ego.*

One evening, shortly after Divali, I was dressing for dinner at Faletti's when Abdi stopped me as I was about to step into my black crepe evening dress.

"No. Not that one." He walked across to the wardrobe and surveyed its contents. Thanks to his largesse, there was plenty to choose from.

"This," he pulled out my orange shot silk and looked at it with approval.

"Wear this tonight."

It was a lovely dress and the fabric was beautiful, but I hardly ever wore it as it was quite revealing and I preferred less vibrant colours. I was not as conservative as I had been in London where everything I wore, except for my red suit, tended to be monochrome, but I still fought shy of the vivid colours that most Indians loved and tended to stick to blues and greens rather than yellow and orange.

But I put it on, always anxious to please him and appear as attractive as I could in his eyes.

He was in a good mood that night. Talking and laughing, full of jokes and innuendoes, his eyes glowing with mischief, like a cat in the dark, relaxed but vigilant. We had a pleasant if rather sedate dinner with the usual group of friends, but over coffee and brandy in the lounge, Abdi became restless. Suddenly, he stood up, took my hand and pulled me to my feet and said, "Come on. I want to show you this." He looked at me quizzically. "And perhaps you to them," he added elliptically.

"Where are we going?" This was the first I had heard of us going anywhere.

He looked at Eva Maria. It was a conspiratorial look, as if they both knew something the rest of us did not.

"You think it's time?" she asked languidly. He nodded and she smiled her doubting, mocking smile and got up as if on cue, throwing her fox fur jauntily over one shoulder like a hunter shouldering his rifle.

Most of the group wanted to stay put, so Eva Maria and her new constant companion, a Brigadier in the British Army whose name was Whyte—but known to all as Chalkie—got up and followed her with the good-natured lope of a well-trained Labrador.

We piled into a taxi. Abdi sat in front to instruct the driver and the three of us crammed in the back, with Chalkie in the middle at his own insistence.

"I got lucky tonight," he beamed, pressing his leg against

mine. Then he winked at me, his broad, fleshy face flushed with whisky and anticipation. We set off in the direction of the old town. We drove through Taksali Gate and inched our way down the narrow streets that even at that hour were choked with rickshaws, stalls, carts, people of all kinds and ages, *pi dogs*, stray mongrel dogs, and the occasional cow meandering along, getting in everyone's way, but stopped by no-one. Car horns blared non-stop and drivers leaned out of their windows to yell at the extraordinary miscellany of obstacles placed in their way. I remember the shrill sound of dance music from an old radio by an open window. The cacophony of sounds and sights of India. I loved it. It seemed incredible to me that less than ten minutes away was the cocooned splendour of Faletti's where we had been sitting, serenaded by a string quartet, being served freshly ground coffee (still a treat after all those wartime years of bottled coffee extract) and Napoleon brandy, the gentlemen with their cigars and the ladies in copies of Paris fashions and Chanel No 5. It was terribly popular then that perfume, although I still preferred Arpège, when I could get it.

Abdi had brought me some scent—a small, black glass vial with a chasséed silver lid, containing an Indian perfume. It was very different to our floral colognes, being oily and sticky to the touch. It smelled of musk with a distant note of aromatic spices—cardamom and cloves perhaps? To be honest, I didn't like it much. I found it cloying, but he thought it sexy, so I wore it in the evenings when he was with me, cursing when the oil stained my fine new clothes.

The car stopped outside the open door of a rather ramshackle house. Curtains were drawn across every window, but we could hear music coming from inside. At the entrance we were greeted by a fattish man, in slightly grubby white *kurtas* and a splendidly garish gold brocade waistcoat. It was undone, which was just as well because most of his diamond buttons were missing.

He greeted Abdi as if he were his long lost brother and helped Eva Maria and I out of the car, with elaborate courtesy, leaving poor old Chalkie to scramble out by himself.

He then placed a string of flowers around each of our wrists, with the lordly air of a man distributing Cartier bracelets. I must have looked bemused because he smiled at me and said, "Don't worry, Memsahib, these are free."

He led us up a narrow flight of stairs into a large empty room, dimly lit by small lamps in each corner. The carpeted floor was covered in white sheets with cushions and bolsters strewn around. The others sat down on the floor, leaning against the cushions. They all seemed to know the score, so I followed suit.

Then the man walked into the centre of the room. Abdi whispered in my ear that he was Fazal, the ace pimp of Lahore, and before I could comment, Fazal began to speak. First in Urdu and then in English. A non-stop litany of sale.

"We have all new girls—freshly arrived from Chamba!" He announced triumphantly. Chamba was an area famed for the beauty of its women. His hair was sleek with oil and his eyes rimmed with kohl. Now and then he would toss his head, a practised gesture he was certain was alluring.

Two girls walked half-heartedly round the room. They were plump and very made up, dressed in full skirts and tiny fitted tops, their heads covered with silk gauze veils. Chalkie perked up and grinned brightly at them.

Abdi was not impressed. "They're not new at all," he told Fazal. "She's been in Lahore longer than I have." She didn't look that old. In fact, she looked considerably younger than I was. They walked around in a desultory fashion and then disappeared behind a beaded curtain.

Fazal resumed. "My girls make very good wives," for some reason he looked at me when he said that, "excellent mistress... Superb in all matters of sexual congress," he assured Chalkie. Then he raised one arm and snapped his fingers.

Three different girls entered in a line, then walked around the room. They were much better looking than the previous bunch. One girl, with her oiled black hair and delicate face, had the serene beauty of an Indian carving. Her yellow silk sari was wound tightly around her curvaceous body. These girls had a graceful sexiness that was the antithesis of the pre-war tarts in Piccadilly. The goods were not so much thrust in your face, but rather hinted at. The thin silk of their garments covered but did not conceal what lay beneath. Their hands and feet were decorated with henna, painted on in intricate patterns.

Two musicians followed them in, took up their place in the corner of the room and began to play. Slowly flexing their bare feet, the girls began to dance.

Fazal pointed out one girl dressed in purple silk covered with gold spangles.

"Her sister—almost her twin—was chosen by scout for His Highness Maharajah of Patiala," he announced proudly. Abdi had told me that Patiala was notorious for his promiscuity and extensive harem. Fazal went on, "Only most beautiful girls go there. She now resides in his palace in lap of luxury," he intoned rather mournfully. I wondered if he regretted the loss of her earnings or merely wished he could join her.

The purple silk girl looked across at Abdi, then turned away. The musicians by now had really got going and the third girl cast her beguiling glances at Abdi and Chalkie. Then she sang. Abdi whispered that these girls were not just tarts, but courtesans, who could run a salon in the French way and were accomplished singers and dancers.

The purple silk girl stood in front of Abdi and danced, as if only for him. Twisting and twirling, her shimmering skirts flying, the silver bells on her anklets a soft accompaniment. Her body was supple and graceful and she was not shy in displaying its charms. I felt a bit awkward.

Fazal resumed his pitch, "we have rooms available here

for your love nest. Running water, clean sheets, everything you desire catered for."

"Or we can now accommodate you in your hotel. Or even your home. We will travel to the Civil Lines where in shining silk and resplendent jewels girl will enchant you with her provocative dance and enthral you with her song."

Chalkie, pink and perspiring, looked as if he were about to faint with delight. Eva Maria glared at Fazal. Whatever he was on about, she didn't like it.

A brass tray was passed round by an old woman. She offered *paan* and little cakes. Abdi placed a silver rupee on the tray. I took a cake and bit into it. It was very sweet and dry, a bit musty, which was odd because Indian sweets usually tasted very fresh.

The girl in purple silk drew nearer. When she got close, with her veil tossed aside, I could see that she was very beautiful. She was now almost touching Abdi, her body a siren call to his. I could also smell her perfume. Sweet and heavy. The same as mine. I had no doubt that she had been his lover. Perhaps still was. I looked at her and she caught my eye, then looked away and finished her dance, so close to him that her skirt trailed across his lap. He pressed it to his cheek, closed his eyes and inhaled her perfume. Then she walked away, pausing in the doorway to look back at him with the most naked invitation I had ever seen. Did she expect him to follow her?

I was shocked, but I knew that if I showed it in any way

Abdi would despise me. He had wanted me to see this. This was yet another of his tests, one I had to pass. To fail would only drive him away. Perhaps back into the dancing girl's arms.

I felt very hot, sick and suddenly a little dizzy. I wondered too late what had been in that cake. I looked across at Abdi, his dark eyes shining, and I knew he wanted her. I said softly, "She is very lovely." It hurt me to say it. He looked back at me and smiled, "You could do this too."

I thought he meant just for him. I beamed back at him, flattered and encouraged. Imagination flying, carried away on a tidal wave of hope, seeing us as a modern couple, a marriage of free spirits, at liberty to roam but choosing to remain.

In my defence, it was the first time I was ever stoned. On the other hand, I was always imbecilic with hope even when stone cold sober.

I burbled on happily in this vein in the rickshaw going back to the Braganza. Abdi didn't respond, but I was too far gone to make anything of it.

The next day he was very quiet, preoccupied. I caught him looking at me once or twice and had the vague impression I had disappointed him. I couldn't think how. I asked him if anything was wrong, but he just shrugged and said, "things to do." Shortly after that he went out.

He returned late in the afternoon. He was tired and slept awhile, then took me out to dinner at Stiffles. The usual crowd was not there and I wondered if he had chosen it deliberately so that we could be alone. We ate and then returned to the Braganza, sitting on the lawn, having coffee in the starlit dark.

We were quiet that night, but I thought happy. We went to bed early. We did not make love. He said he was too tired, but then he went to his jacket pocket and pulled out a small package wrapped in pink silk.

Inside was a pair of gold, filigree earrings he had bought for me in the Sua Bazaar. They were quite beautiful. On one a gold crescent moon dangled from a tiny chain, and from the other a cluster of little golden stars. He said,

"You want the moon and stars. I can only give you these."

I was enchanted by them. They were so exquisite, the craftsmanship so fine, I loved them more than I ever could any diamond. I put them on. I told him he was my moon and stars. He smiled and said that was what he was afraid of.

But I laughed and embraced him, sure he was just being Abdi, certain that I could conquer his diffidence with my love.

Chapter Twelve

The next morning he was gone. He did not even say goodbye. When I awoke—late—whatever was in that cake had made me completely stupefied—he had already left. That, alone, did not make me panic. He often came and went without warning, always dancing to his own tune, never explaining or informing me of his intended arrivals and departures.

But this time was different. This time he had taken his clothes with him. He had never done that before.

He was gone for a long time. After a month, I was anxious. After two months, I was really scared. He had never stayed away that long before. Mr de Souza again presented me with our bill, this time with an additional cause for alarm. The previous bill, which Abdi had assured me was "all settled" had, in fact, only been paid in part, so what was now outstanding was the current one plus the arrears from the last one. All of it long overdue.

Heart pounding, hands sweating, I rang the base, who crisply informed me that, as Flying Officer Abdullah Kasim was now officially discharged, they had no knowledge of his whereabouts.

I swallowed my pride and made a dismal round of his many friends and acquaintances. Those I knew, anyway, asking if they had any news of him. They all laughed and smiled, shrugged their shoulders and said no they hadn't but "you know Abdi... he comes and goes... who knows why or where." Indeed. I smiled my best fixed grin and thanked them. They tried to reassure me, "don't worry, he's bound to turn up, one of these days, like the proverbial bad penny," and again "you know Abdi..."ours is not to reason why." I wondered bleakly if they knew the rest of that quotation. Either way, it didn't bode well.

Then one morning I was having coffee at the Standard with Ethel, when Jean Francis came over to our table.

"I heard you're looking for Abdi." I was too desperate to dissemble.

"Yes. I am."

"Well, you're not the only one." She had a painful smile just like mine. Her red lipstick was too dark. It made her teeth look yellow.

"Do you have any news of him?" I coughed, trying to get rid of the lump in my throat and only succeeded in making myself feel sick.

"Yeah," with reluctant sympathy, "s'only gossip, but it's

reliable. Friend of mine saw him last week at the Charleville."

I looked blank. "He's gone to Mussoorie." A charming hill station he had told me about often. The Charleville Hotel was famous as a place of assignation. He had promised to take me there.

She looked at me pointedly. "He wasn't alone."

Like Eva Maria, she looked posh but her vowels weren't. My misery was complete. I bowed my head, to hide the tears that were not very far away.

She stood there, awkwardly, shifting her handbag from one arm to the other.

"Look... I'm sorry... but I thought you should know..." She walked away. We hated each other, but she wasn't a bad sort. God only knows the dance he had led her. Very similar to the one he had led me, I imagine.

I continued on with the usual round, the mirth and platitudes increasingly turning to ashes in my mouth, getting a bit panicky when the bill for dinner or lunch came, but only occasionally having to pay my shout. My friends, particularly Ethel and Imran, were generous, but I was beginning to feel awkward. Especially, when Imran confided in me that his "so-called friends" were always trying to touch him for money because they knew he was rich. We were having one of our solitary, late night heart to hearts on the lawn at the Braganza, when the darkness and the absence of others seemed to invite confession. He bewailed the fact that he always paid for everybody, not because he begrudged it, but because it made him doubt their friendship. He worried that his friends "only saw him as a meal ticket." He told me a long, wounded tale of how one of his dearest friends had taken advantage of him in this way, stringing him along cynically, offering "the carrot of friendship to make donkey cough up" was how he put it. He felt used and abused and with reason. I knew then that I could never ask him for money.

My situation seemed hopeless. Until one evening in the bar at Faletti's, waiting for Eva Maria to show up, I overheard a conversation between two profligate Indian princelings, who I knew by reputation but not in person. Like Algernon in 'The Importance of Being Ernest' they were bewailing their lack of "ready money."

"On my uppers, old chap." The Prince downed his whisky and called for more. They brought him a bottle.

"And likely so to remain 'til next quarter day." They made me smile. Their voices were pure Oxbridge and reminded me of Lal.

His companion piped up, "What about the family?"

"Raided lock, stock and barrel. Many times. No, old chum, that cupboard's well and truly bare."

His friend downed his drink in silent sympathy. Then had an idea, "What about Fazal?"

"Fazal? Which one?"

"Hira Mandi one. He's always good for a loan. He'll charge like an angry rhino, but he always coughs up."

I could have kissed him. Eva Maria arrived shortly after,

but this wastrel prince had given me an idea. I knew Fazal, or rather Abdi did, and he would be sure to give me a loan, knowing that Abdi would repay it on his return. He might drive a hard bargain, but at least he was not a complete stranger.

I knew I was clutching at straws but I also knew that 'needs must'. In hard times in London in the Thirties, everyone who was not a Rothschild lived on tick or the 'never never' as we called it. It was a way of life. Nobody liked it, but it was a means of getting by. Sometimes the only means. Every Tuesday or Wednesday, there would be a procession of women, in carpet slippers, their coats on over their pinnies, trailing resignedly up to Notting Hill where the pawnbroker was, hocking their meagre possessions—wedding rings, odd bits of jewellery, I even saw one carrying a gramophone once, to be redeemed the following pay day.

We were not above it ourselves. Even Mother, despite her rigorous budgeting and Calvinist horror of debt, was not immune. She would pronounce, "No, Jeannie, if we can't pay for it, we won't have it. It's as simple as that," but during the lean times after my step-father's death and before I started work, she would occasionally have to tramp up the hill and pawn her wedding ring. I shrugged it off at the time. Her marriage had been a disaster, the ring can't have meant much to her, I thought with the blindness of childhood. But I did notice that she always redeemed it. Her finger was never without it for long. Was it her badge of respectability? It mattered then. We both knew the stigma of illegitimacy and the price we had paid for it.

However, it was different now, it didn't matter to me. So, the next morning I went hot-footing it to the bazaar to see Fazal.

I took a *tonga* to Hira Mandi. The *tonga wallah* shook his head when I told him where I wanted to go and said, "No, Memsahib, that place is not good. It is not for you."

I told him it was and that I wanted to see Fazal. He looked a bit alarmed then and, turning away from me, drove there in complete silence. I always tried to use the same *tonga* when I could. I liked this *tonga wallah*. He was older than the others and had told me all about his family, which was very numerous and utterly dependent on him, especially his no-good brother, a "*goonda*", thug, he called him, and the difficulty of making ends meet. We had very different ends, he and I, but the difficulty seemed much the same. I missed his chatter this morning, but I was determined to see this through, however unpleasant it might be, and resolve my problems.

A Pathan was guarding Fazal's premises. There was no other term for it. He was impassable. Tall and well built, he took up the entire doorway, blocking all entry. He stared at me, his face completely immobile. He could have been carved from stone. I told him I had come to see Fazal, who knew me. He stood aside and silently pointed to a stout wooden door, studded with rusty looking nails. I had not seen it the night we went there. I imagine it must have been wide open then.

I went through the door. The old woman who had passed around the bhang cakes appeared. She looked even ropier by daylight. She scuttled along a corridor lined with closed doors and boxes, some empty, just rubbish really, some still sealed. I had no idea what they contained. The girls from the previous evening were nowhere to be seen. She took me through a bead curtain to the back stairs. They were narrow and incredibly steep. Not very clean. She was surprisingly nimble for someone who looked so decrepit. I wondered if she was actually much younger than she looked.

She left me outside another closed door. I knocked.

"*Ander aana!*" Come in.

I walked in. Fazal in the morning was a very different animal. His avuncular bonhomie, his florid expansiveness all gone. Now, he was grey-skinned and beady eyed. Show-time was over.

He was hunched over an elaborately carved but very dusty desk and he wore a tight Astrakhan coat over his *kurtas*. His greasy locks were held off his face by a diamanté Alice band. It looked really daft. Girly. I was very glad of that band. It stopped me being terrified of him. He looked at me in silence, waiting for me to explain why I was there.

I began bravely enough "I was hoping you... I was led to believe... you could help me."

Wrong choice of word. His face closed up like a fan. He looked at me suspiciously.

"How may I help you, Memsahib?" He didn't sound very inviting. In fact, he was positively frosty.

I persisted. I had no other choice.

"I was told... by a mutual friend... (praying he wouldn't ask me who) that you could perhaps assist me with a loan?"

His face softened. "Yes. You can have a loan. I will give you a good rate, a special rate. How much do you want?"

His tone was much friendlier. I relaxed a bit. I mentioned the sum I had worked out would cover most of the bill at the Braganza and leave me a little over for day to day expenses until Abdi should return.

He shook his head, sorrowfully. "This is not a paltry sum."

"I know. It is a lot of money. It's just that I am in a jam—a temporary fix. My friend had to go away at short notice. But he'll be back. Soon. I give you my word it will be repaid in full immediately on his return." It never took much for me to come off the rails.

He looked politely doubtful. I put my Bulova watch that I had bought with my first earnings from the Waldorf and the little silver bracelet that Mrs Pepe had given me on the desk and pushed them towards him. He was not impressed.

Then he walked over to the door, opened it and yelled, "*Chai lao.*" Bring tea. Then back to me.

"I will need more than that."

I gave him my wedding ring. "It's solid gold," I said. He nodded as he examined it.

"You have asked me for a lot of money…"

It was no use pretending. "Look, Mr Fazal, I am desperate. I haven't got anything else."

He looked me up and down as if assessing my worth. I wondered if he was thinking of selling me to the Maharajah of Patiala. At that moment, I'd have considered it.

"You are not a good risk, Memsahib, but Fazal has a gentle heart," as if on cue the Pathan from the doorway entered the room, carrying a tray with two glasses of tea on it. He must have been listening at the door. I noticed he was armed. A rather nasty curved dagger was thrust through his belt.

"I understand your predicament… so, you will pay me five hundred rupees every month. Without fail. Interest will only be eight percent."

"Per annum?"

He smiled as if I had said something really amusing. "No, no, no. Eight percent per month."

Even I could work out that that was nearly one hundred percent per annum.

He pushed a glass of tea across the desk. I must have looked as if I needed it. Then he opened a drawer and swept the watch, bracelet and ring into it. He pulled out a huge wad of grubby notes and began to count them.

"I will need also two signed blank cheques and your copy chit from the Braganza."

I knew I was being completely stitched up, but I consoled myself with the thought that Abdi would soon be back and he would know how to sort it all out. Fazal could clean out my bank account, I thought as I signed the cheques, but then I remembered how little there was in it.

I handed them over and he gave me the money. Then he took my hand. His hands were very small and a bit clammy. He held my hand for too long, patting it as if I were a child. Then he ushered me past the Pathan and down the stairs. In the doorway he smiled, baring his betel-stained teeth. In the bright daylight, his eyes screwed up against the sun, he looked sinister, like an old vampire. He said. "I will see you again, Memsahib."

I walked away, determined not to look back.

The further I got from Fazal, the better I felt. I walked back towards the Mall, eager to meet my friends for coffee and lunch without having to feel like a scrounger. Now I didn't have to panic at the sight of a restaurant tab, I could pay for myself. I felt self-sufficient, strong. I elbowed aside all misgiving. I was pleased with myself. I had not gone looking for a rescue. I had grasped the nettle, dealt with it myself and solved the problem. Temporarily, at least. Or so I told myself.

The feeling was transient. It barely lasted through the coffee. I sat with Ethel and Eva Maria at the Standard and suggested we go on to Stiffles for lunch. My treat, I announced grandly. Eva Maria waited until Ethel went to the Ladies. Then she pounced.

"You solved your money problems, then. How?" She was never one to beat around the bush. I didn't answer, but busied myself powdering my nose. I held my compact up so she could not look me in the eye.

"Imran stumped up, did he?"

"No." Pride stung me into replying. My downfall. "I don't sponge off my friends. I borrowed it."

She looked hard at me. I couldn't go on powdering my nose forever.

"Please tell me you haven't borrowed it from some crook in the Bazaar."

"No. I borrowed it from Fazal."

"Jesus Christ!" She was shocked and that was rare for Eva Maria.

"You bloody little fool. Straight from the frying pan into an inferno."

She had never spoken to me like that. I could feel my short-lived confidence draining away.

"Is Fazal very tough?"

"No. He doesn't have to be. His pet Pathan is. Welsh on a payment and he'll cut your throat."

I laughed uneasily.

"You think I'm joking? It's happened before. Last spring actually. She was a nice girl."

I stopped smiling. She lit a cigarette and handed it to me. Then lighting her own, "Now, this is what we are going to do. I will front you the money to pay him back. Right away. Before you get too deep in his clutches. He'll bleed you white and spit out the pips."

It was a mixed metaphor, but I got the drift.

"You and I can come to an arrangement... We'll discuss it later."

She picked up her bag and walked resolutely to the door. Leaving me to pay and explain hurriedly to a bemused Ethel that something had come up.

There were never any arguments with Eva Maria. It was her way or no way at all. So although I felt belittled and a bit affronted, there was no doubting her superior knowledge of how to steer through the rapids. She was a survivor, hard-boiled and resilient, but she clearly had a heart of gold. I could only marvel at her kindness. And be grateful for it. It was only later that I learned how much this gratitude would cost.

As ever, with her, everything was done with despatch. We went straight to her bank, The Standard Chartered, then on to Fazal's. She paid him in full and when he demanded quite a bit more for loss of interest, she didn't argue but just paid up.

This was totally out of character. When paying for my "trousseau" as she had called it, she had haggled with the best of them. In fact, she was the best of them. She must have been really afraid of that Pathan and she would never have been afraid without reason. Fear was not in her nature. The cheques were not presented, but I never saw my watch, bracelet or wedding ring again.

She didn't waste much time. Back in the Standard, she took me to a booth at the back of the restaurant and drew the curtains.

I didn't beat around the bush either. I asked her what arrangement she wanted to come to about repayment and said that I was certain Abdi would be back soon. I said I was terribly grateful to her and I was sure that he would be too.

"I'm not." She pulled down a diamond bracelet over her wrist. She had kept it hidden by her jacket sleeve until that point. "However, there is a way for a girl like you..."

She twisted the bracelet round to show it to greater advantage. It was a beautiful piece, studded with diamonds in an Art Deco geometric pattern that caught and reflected the light.

"You could help me out..." We were both mesmerised by this bracelet. She twisted it again, this time the depths of its' cool white facets prismed, casting flares of purple and gold. There was a large ruby at the centre of it.

"Pigeon's blood, they call it, from Burma. All the best ones are." She took it off and laid it across my wrist, then looked up at me and grinned. "Not such a bad life is it?" You could see her point. It looked like something Wallace Simpson, the Duchess of Windsor, would have worn. She took it back, then looked at me steadily, waiting.

Finally, the penny dropped. Far too late. Eva Maria—

her palatial home, her furs and jewels, her opulent lifestyle—the absence of any permanent partner or obvious source of income—yet clearly an abundance of both. The rotating cast of men.

"You mean be a whore?" I was so shocked I just came out with it.

"Well, you could have put it with a bit more finesse, but if you want to call a spade a bloody shovel, yes."

"I couldn't do that."

"You already have."

I looked at her in horror, my sense of self plummeting.

"Do you work for a living or do you take money from the men you sleep with?"

"I love them." It seemed the only answer.

"More fool you. Hasn't exactly worked out to your advantage, has it?"

I could not argue with that. But all the time during this conversation I felt as if my life had shifted and was becoming something I no longer recognised.

"All married women are whores. They're just stuck with one man. Now, this way, my way, you can repay me, have a very nice life and only a few companions."

She lit another of her eternal cigarettes. The sudden brightness of the match, against the deep curtained shadows of the booth, made her face look old, raddled. She blew out the light.

"I will choose very carefully for you, Nita, you can rely on me for that."

She was already calculating what she could charge. She saw the expression on my face and in a low, caressing tone said, "don't be scared, little one, you could go far. And if, in the cold light of day, you decide you don't like anyone of 'em, you won't have to see him ever again."

She sat back. "Think about it. You'll never have to wash their socks, take their orders or put up with their families. It's give and take—you minister to their needs for a very short time, and they provide for yours for a lot longer."

Put like that, it didn't sound so bad.

"Anyway, luvvie," the voice was back in Lewisham now. During the conversation it had bounced between the broad Cockney vowels of the East End and the strangulated elocution of the suburbs.

"You haven't really got a choice, have you? I need that money back and I need it soon. So, if you can think of another way…"

We both knew very well I could not… She smiled. "Good. Leave it with me." She left the booth, leaving me reeling in the dark.

True to form, she didn't waste any time. The following day after lunch, she waylaid me on my way to the Ladies.

"See you at mine. Nine o'clock tonight. Best bib and tucker." I must have looked daunted because she patted my arm, "Don't worry. I'll be there. In any case, this one's an angel. My *tonga wallah* will collect you. Don't be late."

No backing out there then.

She got me through the evening in a haze of alcohol. I

don't know what she put in her gin slings, but they could fell an ox. By the time she introduced me to my first client, I could hardly stand. Conversation was going to be a challenge.

Happily, he didn't want much talking. He was young and good-looking, oddly nervous. I wondered if it was his first time. It was the done thing in those days. Young men were sent discretely to whores to "break the seal." It was a horrid expression.

Eva Maria frogmarched me into one of her ballroom sized bedrooms. Well, she had to because what with the nerves and the alcohol, I certainly could not walk reliably. She sat me down on the bed.

"This won't take long," she said. She made it sound like a visit to the doctor.

He walked in and smiled shyly at me. I wondered how my life could have reached this nadir. Then he gulped, his Adam's apple bobbing in his long thin neck. He was very young. I smiled back, trying not to fall backwards.

He said "Hello, my name is Cyril. I'm minor Patiala." I gathered from that that he was one of the junior princes. The Maharajah had been so profligate with his seed, Abdi had told me, he had hundreds of children, all living in the palace, all lavishly provided for and well-educated by their promiscuous papa. Many of them had British names. He also told me that they posed such a problem to the Raj in terms of inheritance that the British had graded them, so that when the time came their legacies could be processed in an orderly and lawful fashion.

I told him my name. He didn't waste any more time talking, having announced his provenance, but lurched into the matter in hand. He hurled himself at me. I fell back on the bed. I wanted to laugh. It was like a bloody French farce.

But it was no laughing matter to Cyril. Once engaged, Cyril was serious. He had the driving ardour of a child, part desperate, part dutiful. He tore the dress off my shoulders and fondled me so roughly, my breasts hurt. He ground his pelvis into mine as if he wanted to crush it. It was like being attacked by a bone grinder. I put up with it for as long as I could.

"Ow! Stop it! You're hurting me." He stopped at once, and pulled away, looking appalled, his dark eyes huge in his still childlike face.

"I'm so sorry... I... don't..."

I didn't know which one of us was more pitiful. The inept child or his drunken tart.

Then he tried again. All I can say is if his father was a polished seducer, his son had inherited none of his skill. Perhaps that came with experience. Remembering my own encounters with strangers in the Blitz, I came to his rescue. As gently as I could, I tried to show him what to do.

In the end, he performed the act of love with a shaky proficiency. It was all over very quickly. As soon as it was finished, he pulled out of me and lay on his back, staring up at the ceiling, aghast at his success.

He said, "Thank you." As if I had given him a cup of tea. I sat up and reached for my cigarettes. I lit one and passed it to him. He smiled at me, the beatific grin of a contented child.

He was so pleased with himself. He smoked the cigarette solemnly, in silence, then got up and began to dress. He had a nice body. Tall, slender, athletic.

"That was... first class. Excellent," he pronounced. "Eva Maria said she'd sort me out." He walked over to the mantelpiece. It was made of carved marble. He reached into his trouser pocket and tucked a fat wad of notes behind a small silver vase. I watched him as he finished dressing and combed his hair. Then he turned to me and said,

"Thank you. It was wonderful." His face glowed like a medieval saint. Clearly, the whole business had been a revelation to him.

He walked to the door, then turning said politely, "I hope I see you again." Then he left. I burst into tears. I don't know what I was crying for. Me? Him? Lost love?

Lost life?

I squashed my face into the pillow and howled. The door opened.

"Blimey. Bad as that?" Eva Maria. She sat down on the bed.

"He didn't hurt you, did he?" I laughed at that and the

laughter in my throat got choked up with the sobs and I coughed, unable to breathe. She dragged me up to a sitting position and thumped my back.

"Choke up chicken." My mother used to say that. Gradually the sobs subsided.

She looked at me. I must have looked a sight. More Medusa than Aphrodite. Hair on end, mascara running in rivulets down my face, lipstick smeared across my mouth.

She looked down grimly, "You've ruined that pillowcase." I had too. It was covered in make-up and sodden with tears. "It's silk" she said, walking over to the mantelpiece.

"Sorry."

"Don't make a habit of it or we'll have to put the price up." She was counting the money. She put most of it in her pocket and held the rest out to me.

"Here you are. The wages of sin." I took it. It was a sizeable amount.

"The wages of sin are death." I might have been drunk, but I remembered that quote all right.

"Yeah," she sighed heavily, sitting on the bed beside me. "I used to be devout. Seriously religious. I even toyed with the idea of becoming a nun."

I couldn't believe my ears. "You're kidding?"

"No, I'm not." She lit herself one of my fags. "Another one?"

"Yeah." I smoked as that sank in. "What stopped you?"

She laughed and then coughed her racking smoker's

cough. "Came to my senses. Now." We were back to business. She got up and started to fold the sheet back.

"Wasn't so bad, was it?"

No. It wasn't bad. It was just wrong—deeply, alienating—utterly wrong, but bad, no, not really.

She stood up. "Good. Cos he wants to see you again." I stared at her in disbelief.

"Told you. He's a sweetie, isn't he? Sort yourself out and come downstairs. I've got supper for you."

She was never one to disobey, so I did.

And that was when I entered another world. A world where I had no bearings. I felt like Alice, tumbling down her well. All I had to do to survive was abdicate all sense of myself. So I just stumbled on, blindly, and survived. I wouldn't admit it, but inside I knew Abdi would never come back now.

So I painted on a smile when I left my room in the Braganza, the silk-draped refuge I had created for another man, but the smile was not connected to my brain. I wiped it off with the lipstick when I was alone again.

I felt no real connection with anything—neither my past nor recent life—London, Rikh, the India League—it all seemed part of a sepia toned past that eluded me. It felt as if I carried around someone else's memories.

Perhaps I didn't want to connect with it. Perhaps I knew too well that those I had loved the most—Yolanda and my mother—would despise me now. But they were not here. One was dead and the other was three thousand miles away. They were not here and neither was I, in any real sense. I laughed and chatted—good humoured, superficial, inconsequential, but none of it meant anything at all.

Imran wasn't fooled. He tried to talk to me several times, but I always fobbed him off, I was too tired, or on my way out. In the end, late one evening, over coffee with the others, he just looked across at me and said, "You're very unhappy, aren't you?"

I was so far gone, I actually wondered what he meant. I wasn't unhappy, I wasn't anything. I certainly didn't want to go into it. He told me I should find out what my real feelings were. I told him I couldn't imagine anything worse. I didn't want to know what my real feelings were. I wanted to avoid them at all costs. They had failed me so utterly, I wanted never to feel anything again.

I had loved Abdi. He was always a monster and I knew it, but I felt we were lovers, partners in a true sense, and he did not. He had not loved me nor wanted my love. It bored him. He had only wanted to possess me for a while. I was a peculiar trophy, his very own tame Memsahib, and he soon tired of it. So, no more feelings for me. They had done me no good at all.

Eva Maria's philosophy of pleasant, fleeting sex—sometimes enjoyable, always profitable—seemed as good a way of surviving as any other. I had to get money from somewhere. I was towed a long in her wake—without thought or will and I did not care.

I took the crumbs that fell from her table. It was only feelings and memory that tripped you up, dragging you back into a world that was only pain. I wanted none of that.

I wanted to wake up each morning and with a new day—unconnected to idiot hope or longing—make a new person just for that day. A person I could jettison at the end of it. A disposable person for a disposable life. Soon used, soon over. And then begin again.

For a while it almost worked. My numbness became a carapace, my indifference my armour.

Chapter Thirteen

Eva Maria had a troupe of Indian musicians. They played in her house several times a week. There were just four of them—three men who played sitar, *tabla*, and harmonium and a woman who sang. She had a glorious voice, rich and soaring, full of expression. I had not particularly liked Indian music until that time. I had only really heard Bazaar music which was shrill and tinny, but this was very different. She sang *ghazals*, traditional love poems set to music, full of love and longing. The musicians played hidden away in a shadowy recess, providing a strangely lyrical counterpoint to the rest of that house. The music was complex and intricate, and it was a joy, striking a note of serene beauty in the circus that went on all around them.

I saw his hands before I saw his face. He was seated on one of the low sofas with his back to me. But then he leaned forward and stretched out his hand to take the drink offered to him and that was enough. I knew that hand. The long, tapering fingers, the prominent knuckles and bony wrists. The skin that covered it was rough and dry, flecked with freckles and ginger hair. I knew it very well.

His name was Derek and he was a doctor. I had known him in London where he was my friend Yolanda's great love. He had filled her life with joy, expanding her horizons in the way she had mine. They had been a strong and vibrant couple, united in their desire to make a better world. Together they had seemed to complete and fulfil each other, and I had never seen her so happy. But then, the last time I saw her, he had broken her heart. I never knew why. Suddenly, she was anxious and afraid, unsure of everything except her desire to keep her unborn child. His. The one she was determined he would know nothing about. She told me she wanted her child, but not a husband. Certainly not Derek. He must have hurt her very much for her to feel that.

She made me promise not to tell anyone. She invoked our childhood bond, when as two outcasts at school, we had formed a friendship 'contra mundem' that lasted until her death.

I didn't press her for an explanation that night, sure we would meet again at work the next day, sure that this was only one of many conversations we would have. I told her I would go with her when she told her parents, who as devout Catholics, would feel nothing but disapproval and shame. I wanted her to know that whatever she decided her future would be, I would always stand beside her.

We parted in a rush to get home before the bombs started falling. I made it back, she did not. Seeing him again, reminded me how raw the pain of her loss still was. Just by being there, he evoked her. Her aloof smile, her crumpled cigarettes, her deep, gravelly laugh.

Pole-axed by memory, I stood stock still in the doorway. Until Eva Maria came bustling up, took me by the arm and marched me in, whispering under her breath,

"Your next client. Nice man. English doctor. He could be a regular for you."

That he could never be. Unstoppable, she steamrollered on.

"Derek, this is Nita." She presented me with a flourish, like a dealer with a new deck of cards. He turned to face me. We stood in silence.

"I'm sure you two will get along."

"Yes," he said. I said nothing. My throat felt as if I had swallowed broken glass.

She led us into a room and left us. I sat on the bed and he walked to the window. Probably wishing he could jump out of it. I know I did.

Eventually he turned to face me.

"However did you end up here?" It was a reasonable enough question.

"I could ask the same of you."

He smiled ruefully, a smile that died before it reached the corners of his mouth.

"I have always used whores." So that was what had broken her heart.

"I was brought up like that." I didn't feel that was any excuse and it must have shown in my face because he became defensive.

"It never meant anything." It did to her.

"I always loved her best." I was sure that was true. But for her, too many casual betrayals, the airy acceptance that he had hurt her and would again, the realisation that he had trashed the love she valued most "for nothing," that was what had broken her.

There was nothing small about Yolanda. She never grasped the mean-spirited wilfulness of weak people. Like Derek and me.

There was another long and awkward silence. Then, "were you very desperate for money?"

"Yes." I didn't want to tell him about Abdi. He could surmise the train wreck of my life without me spelling it out, I decided.

"What happened with Rikh?" I remembered that he had liked Rikh. They had got on very well.

"It didn't work out." I didn't want to do chapter and verse on that one either. The disparity between my life now with all its sordid capering and the idealism of my London youth was too great. Measuring the distance tore me apart.

"She always said it wouldn't last," he said gently. She had too. And although I said nothing, frozen by a flood of memory and loss, inside I was howling, like an animal in pain. Who was I howling for now? Derek or Rikh, with their dogged determination to shoehorn the women in their lives into a size they could handle, Yolanda—all her bright promise lost, or me?

He was speaking again. He had to repeat it. "Could you not ask Rikh...?"

"No." Another silence. He then told me that, after the Blitz, he had volunteered for the Army Medical Corps, that he had served in Imphal and later at the big military hospital in Poona. He said that he imagined he would be sent home soon, but added bleakly that he would try and resist that one because now there was nothing for him to go home for. Then he reached into the top pocket of his shirt and pulled out a wad of notes. He pushed it across the bed towards me.

"NO." I practically threw it back at him.

"I didn't mean that we should... I just thought... a loan from a friend..." he was rushing to save my face.

"I don't want it."

"Do you want me to try and find you a job?" That was different. A proper job, a normal life. Can Alice come back through the Looking Glass, I wondered?

He went on, "I can't promise anything, but I could try. Perhaps a clerical job in the hospital?"

I stared at him dumbly, wondering if I could ever return

to a life that depended not on fawning for favour, but what my mother would have called "an honest day's work for a fair day's pay." It seemed like a distant dream, more unreal than any far pavilion or palace.

He walked slowly round the room, taking in the marble fireplace, the Persian rugs and the heavy satin drapes.

"It wouldn't run to anything like this... I can't promise, but I could try."

I nodded. "I'm at the Braganza... for the time being."

He nodded back. "I'll be in touch." We didn't speak again. After a little while, he left.

I sat in the room alone for a long time. At one point Eva Maria came in. She was very disappointed, she said. He was one of her "Old Faithfuls" and she had hoped he would become one of mine.

"No," I said sharply. That surprised her. Usually, I left the decisions to her.

"He didn't hurt you, did he?" She was always on the lookout for that. I told her it wasn't me he had hurt. She looked at me long and hard and then fixed me a stiff drink. I drank it down, gratefully. Wisely, she left me alone. She asked few questions as a rule and I am sure would have answered even less.

Later, I went downstairs and sat in a quiet corner, listening to the musicians. As the singer's voice rose and fell, soft and clear, singing of her doomed love in an ecstasy of distress, she seemed to be speaking for all of us. Our longing for love, and the terrible power of our dreams.

I drank a lot that night. First at Eva Maria's and then back at the Braganza on my own. I wanted to drink myself into oblivion, to the point where I couldn't feel anything anymore.

At about three o'clock in the morning, I started being sick. Once I started I could not stop.

The next morning he came to see me. He came up to my room, where I was lying on the bed, hoping to die. He looked askance at my silk-draped love nest, but said nothing.

"I'm sorry about last night." I couldn't work out what he had to be sorry for. But by then I felt so awful, I couldn't have worked out my own name.

"It was such a shock... Seeing you there..." Indeed. I could barely speak. As soon as I tried to raise my head, the room reeled. I decided not to bother.

He looked at me dispassionately. "You feel like hell, don't you?" Miserably, I nodded. Bad mistake. I retched weakly.

He ordered coffee and bread and butter to be sent up. Then he gave me two aspirins, which I managed to get down. It wasn't easy. The aspirins seemed to float on the water I was trying to swallow and kept bobbing back, like buoys. In the end, I swallowed them, but as soon as the coffee arrived, the smell alone made me retch. Shakily, I stumbled into the bathroom and tried to be sick. There was nothing to bring up but a bitter frothy bile. Just like Cornelius, I thought.

Derek came in and heroically held my head while I tried to vomit up my entire stomach. It went on for ages. Then he helped me back to the bed.

"Any diarrhoea?" he asked cheerfully. I shook my head.

Then he said. "Do you mind if I examine you?" Frankly at that point, I wouldn't have cared if he'd cut my head off. In fact, I would have been grateful. In any case, he was a doctor. Perhaps he could give me something to make it all stop. Anything.

Slowly and calmly, he palpated my abdomen. At one point he frowned and prodded and pushed one area again. Then he pulled my robe down and the sheet up and patted my arm with an awkward smile.

He stood up. "I'll see you again soon." I leapt to the wrong conclusion. I must have looked appalled because he said very gently, "You'll have to see someone, Nita."

"Why? Am I ill?"

"No. But you are pregnant."

I stared at him in horror. I had missed a few periods, but women often did when under pressure. In the Waldorf during the bombing, Yolanda, Betty in reception, and I used to laugh about it. Gerry's Gift, we called it. A reprieve from the curse. It happened to a lot of women. I just assumed this was the same. Temporary, unimportant. It hadn't signified anything then except strain. There had been plenty of that in my life recently.

"Are you sure?"

He nodded again. "Yes. You'll have to start thinking

about what you want to do. But don't take too long. I think you're already ten or eleven weeks."

I felt as if I was falling. Falling through everything my life had been, falling down into a very dark well, my mother's life.

He left and shut the door firmly behind him.

Later that day, I pulled myself together, went out into the glaring sunlight and presented myself at the Services Hospital, which as a serving officer's wife I was still entitled to use.

The Doctor who examined me was kindly enough. He confirmed Derek's diagnosis, informed me that I was fit and well and would have to attend the hospital for regular check-ups from now on. When I told him I felt awful and was being sick all the time, he became impatient and said it was normal, that pregnancy was not an illness and that I should buck up and get on with it.

I walked back through Jilani Park, which was opposite the hospital. It had been our favourite park, perhaps because it was less formal than the others, more rustic in feel. Abdi and I often had our picnics there, lying in the shade of the tall trees, talking and laughing. Abdi imparting the latest piece of gossip as we walked through the long grass. I thought how fitting it was that our child would be born within sight of that place.

I walked for hours that afternoon, past the tomb of Anarkali, jewel of Akbar's harem, buried alive for bestowing a smile on his son. A Persian verse is inscribed on the wall: "Could I but behold the face of my beloved once more." It seemed horribly apt. I walked on.

The bazaar looked very different to me that day. Suddenly, it seemed very alien. Garish and tawdry, the lights unbearably bright, the music loud and discordant, the hawkers insistent, bullying. Hands clutched at me, trying to pull me into their shops, shrill voices rang in my ear. What had seemed charming and exotic now seemed intrusive, devouring. I wanted them all to go away, to leave me alone. It was like being trapped on a merry-go-round. I soon lost my bearings. The narrow winding alleys became a maze.

A *bundawallah* beat his drum and two tortured looking monkeys, dressed in tatty costumes, cavorted in an obscene courtship dance. Their capering a parody of Abdi and me. Gratification without joy, need without love. Was that all I had been to him?

I walked for hours, trying to find my way home. At one point I passed a shabby looking bear, old and dirty, who danced on ulcerated feet. He lumbered around in circles, without reason or direction, in a world of pain that mirrored my own.

At last, I found a rickshaw. He took me back to the Braganza. As I walked across the endless foyer my head hurt and I felt sick again. Strange how quickly paradise can become a nightmare, I thought.

That night I ignored Eva Maria's summons. I stayed in my room and wrote a long letter to Abdi. I told him I was pregnant and desperately needed his help. I told him that we needed to talk—so that we could decide together what to do.

I laid my cards on the table. I told him I was sick, afraid and lonelier than I had ever been in my life. That I was reluctant to consider aborting our child, even if it were possible, not on moral grounds—I have always believed absolutely in a woman's right to choose—but merely because the selfishness of that idea somehow repelled me. In my case it would only be killing for convenience. I said that we had made a new life, a person, without thinking or caring, but I balked at the idea of disposing of it like so much detritus. Perhaps I was my mother's child, after all.

I did not tell him about Eva Maria. I left that to her. I did wonder if they had met, without telling me.

I ended my letter by saying that, although I did not know where he was, I knew from his absence that I had no claim on him. He had made that clear. But I did tell him that despite all that, I still loved him. I just wanted to see him again and talk to him.

I made two copies of the letter. I sent one to the base at Ambala, marked 'please forward' and the other to his home in Lahore, which I delivered by hand. A servant took the letter from me and then shut the door. No-one spoke to me.

I walked back to the Braganza. In front of the station, across the way from the hotel, was a family of beggars. I saw them every day. There was a boy of about eight and a girl who can have been no more than five. Their mother, with a baby at her breast, sat on her haunches in the gutter a little distance away, watching them. The boy was clearly the main breadwinner and took his responsibilities very seriously. He was an ugly child, whose exaggerated gestures, as he jabbed his fingers to his mouth and rolled his eyes with stagey suffering, did little to enhance his money making skills. He made great efforts, but earned very little. His sister did better. She had the capricious, intermittent charm of childhood—sometimes a sweet, gentle smile, sometimes a blank stare, but she was more real in her exchanges than he and she earned a lot more. There was a desperate, angry edge to his gurning and grovelling, which repelled.

As I slowly walked across the square, he approached me with his usual routine. A complete hat and cane number of cries and grimaces. I remember that day he was trying to sell me a flower, which was already wilting in the heat. He knew it too, looking at it with concern as if it had somehow let him down, by withering before its time.

I thought he is just like me—trying to flog a dead flower, to palm himself off on people who do not want him. Endlessly ingratiating, knowing it would fail. I reached into my bag and gave him some change. It was not a lot, but as I put the coins into that dirty little hand, he gave me a smile of such radiance, I stopped dead in my tracks. Innocence had not been stamped out of that child, merely buried beneath his burdens. He ran to his mother and gave her the money. She smiled wearily and raised her hand in thanks. I knew they would eat that night and perhaps tomorrow. The boy ran off, relieved of his need to earn. The palash trees were shedding their blossoms. He picked up a bloom and threw it high into the air, running and jumping to catch it, laughing and shouting to his sister to join in. Then, turning, he saw me still watching him and he waved. He waved to me every day after that, although I gave him no more money.

I don't know if it was the dawning of the maternal in me, but I have rarely loved anyone as I loved that unknown child, whose joy could not be crushed by the misery of his life. He, alone at that time of my life, gave me hope. For me, he was India.

I didn't tell Eva Maria. I didn't have to. The sickness went on... and on. What the doctor at the hospital had blithely dismissed as 'morning sickness' and with a cheery smile 'all perfectly normal'—went on all day and all night. I don't know why people said it was restricted to the mornings. Mine never stopped. So I lurked in my room, not daring to be too far away from my bathroom.

When I failed to turn up for the usual coffee at the Standard for the third day running, Imran sent some flowers with a sweet note that said, "We have all missed you. Hoping all is well."

Eva Maria just showed up early one morning. She came straight up to my room unannounced and rapped softly on the door. Thinking it was my morning tea, my *chota hazri*, I opened it.

She looked at me sternly. "Where have you been? We had a deal."

I tried to reply, but had to dash to the bathroom to be sick. When I came back, she was sitting down at the table and smoking one of her interminable cigarettes. The smoke made me gag. She took no notice.

"I've ordered coffee for me and tea for you." I nodded, feeling wretched, swallowing hard to get rid of the bitter tasting bile in my mouth. My throat was sore from repeated retching.

She sighed, "Well, Nita, you do seem to have rather a talent for frying pan into fire."

I couldn't argue with that. Then in horribly matter of fact tones, "How far gone are you?"

Miserably, I told her what Derek had told me.

"You should probably get rid of it."

"No!" I was surprised by the vehemence of my reply.

She took a long drag of her cigarette. The stub glowed. "Might be your best course of action." She looked round the room, taking in the silken drapes and the incense holders. It was a tart's parlour all right.

"Not exactly ideal for a baby, is it?"

I stared at her. In the chaos and hysteria of my thoughts, I hadn't got as far as accommodation.

She went on, "Hotels, especially like this one, do not

usually favour the pram in the hall... even when there's a father."

Although, as ever, I had to have my head dragged out of the sand, when forced to confront the truth, I could not deny it. I contemplated my future. It didn't look very bright.

Then, most surprisingly, "I got rid of mine. I sacrificed my babies on the altar of common sense." Here she inhaled as if it hurt," I have never ceased to regret it."

We sat in silence. Then she stubbed her cigarette out and lit another. "So, I won't blame you if you don't."

Without looking at me, she stretched out her hand and took mine. She squeezed it hard and then dropped it as if it burnt her.

And I nearly laughed aloud—because with that brief gesture, the Belgian from Lewisham, the would-be nun who ran a brothel, was awfully like my mother.

Abdi did not reply to my letter. I'm not sure if I expected him to. I hoped he would but was not really surprised when he did not. As the weeks went on and his child grew within me, I gave up hope. Pathetically, I still longed for him. I could banish him from my thoughts by day, but at night he turned up in my dreams. In them, always, he came back. The terrible tenacity of hope.

Chapter Fourteen

Derek was as good as his word. He got me a job in the Services hospital—in the Admin wing, filing. Exactly where I had started off at the Waldorf, shuffling around huge mounds of paper, but although these were patient records, the minutiae of lives, it seemed to me as if I had come full circle. Right back to where I had started. What a game of 'Snakes and Ladders' life is.

Neither the work nor the hours were arduous. It was only a part-time job, three afternoons a week and the pay was pitiful, but perhaps I was spoilt and, in any case, it was something.

Eva Maria also preoccupied herself with my income, but she was more ambitious, or more focused on money, anyway.

"I'll sort you out," she declared determinedly, "now... who do I know..."she pursed her lips and frowned and

I knew she was mentally rifling through her vast acquaintance of men she could make money from.

Tentatively, I suggested Cyril, the Junior Patiala. "No, he's hopeless. He'd fall in love or run a mile."

So that was the end of him as far as she was concerned. I let her lead me because I had proved over and over again that my attempts to direct my life had, so far, only ended in disaster and also because I was terribly lonely.

Ethel had disowned me as soon as she knew. I told her I was pregnant, feeling nothing but distaste for half-dropped hints and veiled truths, dreading the day when my increasing shape would reveal my condition all too plainly. You can only hide an expanding waistline for so long. So I came straight out with it and she was horrified. A daughter of the Raj, she played with the idea of being different, but it was only ever a cocktail hour diversion. Her liberal views were not a code to live by, just a conversational gambit to astonish her friends. She was a timid, conventional soul at heart.

Like all good cowards, at the time she voiced a tepid sympathy. But thereafter, she was more and more absent, as smiling she walked away, declining all invitations to meet, becoming involved with other friends at the periphery of my group. As I got further embedded in Eva Maria's twilight world, several of my so-called friends began to avoid me. A delightful fling with Bohemia would not stretch to the acceptance of whore with a bastard child, it seemed.

Imran was altogether different. As a Muslim and a homosexual, an abandoned pregnant woman might well have been anathema to him. But he would allow none of that. When I told him, he looked concerned and straight away offered me the safe haven of his family home in the Punjab. He told me he would arrange an apartment for me there and make sure the child and I were looked after. I cried when he told me that. Not because I would ever allow him to provide for me, but because he was, at that time, the only friend who cared enough to offer. He was also the only one other than me who had even begun to grasp that what began as an inconvenience, a source of social embarrassment, was, in fact, a life—and would become a person with feelings and a future.

I think it was about then that, trying to find an anecdote that would take my mind off my problems, he told me something that intrigued me. It appeared that at about the same time that I joined Rikh in the India League in London, Jinnah had attended a black tie dinner at the Waldorf Hotel, where I worked. It was there that Rahmat Ali, his host, over oysters and Chablis, asked him to be the leader of a separatist Muslim movement with a view to the creation of a sovereign state of Pakistan. Apparently, Jinnah turned him down flat, telling him that the whole notion of Pakistan was an 'impossible dream.' Right under our very noses, while I was doing the filing in my cupboard of an office, fending off the advances of the General Manager or dancing with Freddy from Accounts at the

Tango Teas, a few yards away a man was pondering the fate of millions of people, of whom I would be one.

Imran said it was only the decisive victory of the Congress Party in the elections of 1937 that we had celebrated with such glee in the League, and their subsequent refusal to share power with the Muslim League in the provinces, that had convinced Jinnah that Muslims would never get a fair deal in an India governed by the Congress Party.

Imran was a very good friend to me. On a personal level he was sensitive and kind, and on an intellectual level, whatever he thought of the mess that was now my life, he always treated me as an equal. If only.

However, his increasing involvement in politics meant that now he was often absent from Lahore. He travelled the country, organising and attending meetings as, like King Canute, he tried to hold back the engulfing wave of the Muslim League and their dream of a sovereign state. He worked tirelessly to try and bridge the divide, to join the severed threads of independence, in the form of an increasingly autocratic and inflexible Jinnah and a frazzled and despairing Nehru, both of whom were his friends.

Eva Maria came up with two men. They were much older than me, "sugar daddies" I suppose they would be called now. She told me they were "less active," and only really wanted a presentable and charming companion. Someone to talk to, confide in and regale with tales of a licentious youth we both suspected were largely fictional.

The first was a General in the Army who had a wife and four grown-up children in East Sussex. Somewhere near Hastings, I believe. He took me to dinner and escorted me to the balls and soirées he felt he should attend, happy to introduce me as Mrs Rikh, "Husband a serving officer. Air Force" and cloak me with a respectability I no longer had. He was a pleasant enough companion in public, well-mannered and attentive, but the private face was very different. And I did wonder what she was like, his wife, Jilly, who would far rather stay in rain-soaked Sussex with her farm and her horses than live a life of ease with her husband in India. I pictured her in headscarf and jodhpurs, capable and imperturbable, out in all weathers, with greying hair and prematurely wrinkled skin.

Then I began to show and my General dumped me. Rather unceremoniously for someone who made such a fuss about manners. He ummed and aahed and drank several large Scotches, then he screwed up his face alarmingly and growled, "It's the look of the thing, don't you see." I saw. I saw that he was terrified anyone would think the child was his. I also saw that he was quite strait-laced for someone who kept a whore and required a great deal of imaginative and not very pleasant incentives to achieve release. Verbal abuse and spanking with a hairbrush did the trick as a rule. Then he would groan, "Oh... Nanny..." and it would be over, while I struggled not to laugh. She must have been one hell of a nanny if merely the thought of her and her belabouring could yield such results after fifty years. When he dumped me, I felt a bit cross with him for being such an old hypocrite, but not very because what had seemed perverse at first very quickly became humdrum, rather dull. I also felt that I understood Jilly. He was a bit heartless, my General.

The second was an elderly Nawab who had been to Marlborough and was very fond of the Brontës. Jane Eyre was his particular favourite and we spent hours discussing the influence of the Yorkshire moors and the cruelty of Mrs Reed. He was also fascinated by Cathy and Heathcliff. He wondered if two people could love and hate each other at the same time. I put him straight on that one. Entirely possible, I assured him. He could not believe love could desire the destruction of the beloved. I did. Ain't I the living proof of it, I nearly said, but knowing that such a bald confession would horrify him, I hinted instead that my own experience had not been so different. He changed the subject and we went in to dinner.

He was a kind and civilised man. He averted his eyes from my burgeoning bulk, which I tried to camouflage with ever more voluminous *dupattas* and saris. Indian dress is much more forgiving than European but, in the end, there is only so much you can hide with a draped scarf. It soon was very obvious and he did ask me once if I had plans for the future. I replied no, merely fears. He became very kind after that. He never referred to it directly, but he continued to seek my company and tactfully and discretely, he paid for it.

He was much older than I was. I now think he must have been about seventy, although his slim figure, perfectly cut suits and carefully dyed hair made him look much younger. We became friends. He asked me about London, which he had known as a schoolboy and young man in the days before the First World War. His father used to take a suite at the Savoy, he said, and he had been taken to the theatre where the sight of Lily Langtry in a box had thrilled him. He bought a postcard of her which he kept for many years. The Jersey lily, he called her.

He asked me about my husband. I didn't say much, except that we had met in London and had worked for the India League. He pronounced Krishna Menon 'a great rogue', I felt comfortable enough to disagree, saying I knew Krishna was a great man. He smiled and said he suspected the two often went together. I told him my husband had deserved a better wife and at that he opened up to me, telling me about his wife. His had been an arranged, dynastic marriage, he said. His wife had given him three sons and had died giving birth to the fourth. His eldest son now 'called the shots' he called it, in their small principality in Montgomery and he was content to let him do so.

He took a rather melancholic view of Independence, saying that he felt the Princes' days were done, and although he knew a separate India and Pakistan were inevitable, he feared their creation would be 'cataclysmic'. How right he was. He said when the time came he would leave his house near Lawrence Gardens and return to take his place by his sons' side, in this new Pakistan—a new order he felt no love for—to 'face the music and take whatever may come.'

I told him I was sorry that he felt that way, saying that we had always hoped Independence would bring freedom to many and he said that he thought that would be the case, and that the few, like him, who had lived so well at their expense would no longer. He said it was historical justice and, in the scheme of things, not a bad thing at all. He also said he knew he was an anachronism.

We used to sit and talk by the hour. Later, he spoke again of his wife. He showed me a yellowing photograph of a beautiful girl in a sari, whose perfect features and dark, dreaming eyes were trapped in a monogrammed, leather frame. He said he had not known that she was a person with a rare capacity for love, that because of his background he had taken her youth and beauty utterly for granted, but what worried him more, as an old man, was that he had not realised that she had been devoted to him. He said that was rare in an arranged marriage, or perhaps in any marriage at all, and he had not loved her as she deserved to be.

It seemed my confession had set him free. I said I could not live with my husband, although he was a good man.

"They are sometimes the hardest," he said, "a devoted partner only exposes our own shortcomings and shows us how far we fall short." Indeed.

Then he smiled, "Whereas, on the other hand, a rogue..."

"Is often no partner at all."

He patted my hand and we talked of other things. We were worlds apart—he and I; he an aristocrat with his elaborate courtesy and old fashioned notions, acutely aware that he would and should have no place in the modern world. And I, who had smashed the old order by my very being and always tried to break every rule I encountered, even when it broke me with it. His detached wisdom made me consider how my often childish iconoclasm had created very little, despite the scope of my dreams. My utopian vision of a modern couple, sexually free, an alliance of choice, had led me to live a life that was hideously predictable, first a dependent wife then a pregnant whore, reliant on the random handouts of men.

Gently, and by example, by being so far out of my frame, he made me think, my Nawab. He was a decent and honourable man, a rare bird in my life, and despite all our differences, I was proud to call him my friend. He made me realise that smashing up the old order was not enough, that care and insight would have to be put into the creation of a new one, and that we would not do this by stamping our feet and wishing for it, but slowly and painfully with our lives. We were on the cusp of huge social change and it was a frightening and lonely place to be. Yolanda would have understood.

While I was preoccupied with my own dilemma, the world

outside was changing fast. The old Empire, bankrupted by war, rushed to rid herself of those colonies who had long yearned to be free. Strikes and demonstrations were taking place all over the sub-continent and they were becoming increasingly violent. Muslim fears of becoming subsumed into second-class citizens in a Hindu dominated India had been fanned to a fever pitch of paranoia by the League. Churchill was quick to use this to British advantage. Always a bitter opponent of even the slightest degree of autonomy for India, he felt a weakened and divided India with an unworkable 'moth-eaten' Pakistan, stranded on two sides of the new republic, would be far more susceptible to British influence, and with the post-war emergence of Russia as a super-power, which he had accurately predicted very early on, he was felt it was essential for Britain to maintain a foothold in the area. He met Jinnah secretly in London. Divide and rule. Plus ça change... even with a new Labour government.

It all began rather sedately. People were seen wearing badges with a picture of Jinnah on them in the streets of Lahore. Not many at first. But they became more and more. New slogans were shouted in the impromptu demonstrations and meetings on street corners, "*Quaid-i-Azam Zindabad*", Long live the Quaid, i.e. Jinnah and then, more ominously, "*Bann key rahey ha Pakistan*", Pakistan will be established.

Still we hoped compromise could be reached, that the towering figure of Mahatma Gandhi would prevail and reconcile the two opposing sides. However, in February '46 elections took place in the Punjab and the Muslim League won the greatest number of seats, but not an outright majority. A Coalition Government of the Punjab was formed under Hayat Khan Tiwana, whose party had been routed in the election. It was doomed to fail from the start. The Coalition aimed to represent everyone, but pleased no-one and was never accepted as a legitimate legislative body. Continued demonstrations by the League with increasing counter-demonstrations from both Hindus and Sikhs ramped up the tension.

Both Vicky and Imran went on these demonstrations. I begged to go with them. I had fought for freedom for India; I had always believed in its cause passionately and I longed to participate. But they refused point blank to let me join. Vicky kindly told me that these things so often degenerate into a bun fight and in my condition I was too vulnerable. I wanted to go, but they would not hear of it. Perhaps they were right. On one occasion they were roughed up and came home with cuts and bruises, and on another they were rounded up by the police, manhandled onto trucks and dumped miles outside of town to make their own way back on foot in all that heat. I could not have managed that. So I was reduced to the position of a helpless bystander as I watched the city I loved change from a cosmopolitan haven to a hornets' nest of civil hatred.

On my way back from the hospital late one afternoon I

ran into one of these impromptu demonstrations. A man was standing on a crate, addressing the crowd, urging them to fight for Hindustan. I couldn't have agreed more, but then I heard him say a phrase which chilled me to the bone. I was all for *"Hindustan Zindabad"*, but this was different. He shouted *"Pakistan Murdabad."* One man's voice became a chant and then a roar as the crowd screamed its approval in a great wave of sound. They shouted "Death to Pakistan." I was surrounded by a sea of men, yelling and filled with hatred, all shaking their fists. I faltered, the only way ahead was through the crowd.

For the first time I was frightened by my own side. Their faces distorted with rage, they embraced the notion of death for their opponents. This was not the India we had fought for. Gandhi had been our prophet of non-violence and he had brought an empire to its knees without killing anyone. I wondered how Rikh would feel if he could see this and was glad that he had not.

The man beside me looked at me and said "Go home, Memsahib. This is not your fight." And I could have wept because it was, but not this. We had embraced Gandhi's vision of an India, a place where all her many peoples could live in peace and freedom with religious and racial tolerance for all. That was not what these men wanted. A shot was being fired across the bows. Two nations, whose very existence was loathed by the other, were preparing to fight. They both wanted their own hegemony and they were prepared to kill to get it. I had seen war. I had lived through the bombing of London. I'd seen the damage and the injury and grief, but this was different. This would be civil war. The battles would not be fought by two opposing nations, but by brothers and people who had lived together for centuries. They would tear each other apart, destroying everything they had and had been. It was an awesome and vile prospect. I went quickly back to my room and stayed there. For a long time, I could not stop shaking. I had seen the future in the face of that man and it was full of hate.

Shortly afterwards, the Nawab was called back to Montgomery. A mob had turned on the Sikhs in one of his villages and burned down their homes and their temple. Eleven men were killed. The Nawab went to help his son and try to restore peace. He did not return.

At our last meeting he had been sad and distracted. His parting words to me were, "The fall of empire engenders anarchy, with sudden violence in its wake. Make sure you are not caught up in it." He kissed my cheek and was gone. I missed his friendship and his wisdom very much.

Chapter Fifteen

As Blanche DuBois remarked, 'I have always depended on the kindness of strangers.' That was certainly true of me. As my pregnancy went on I had to give up my job at the hospital. That was the custom in those days, but I became more and more worried about my lack of money and security. The small sums I earned only provided a brief respite from my problems. I moved into a smaller room at the Braganza, which was still far too dear, but the hotel represented the only home I had known in Lahore and I was terrified of leaving it. How would Abdi find me if I left, I agonised, refusing to face the fact that he had made no effort to find me at all and I could easily have left a forwarding address. I was full of fear and misgivings and the constant twists and turns of the political situation, with everything still in flux, did not help. The future seemed to slip and falter in front of me, a sliding, amorphous cloud, which threatened a gathering storm, both personally and politically.

I refused to even consider going home. I probably could have done at that time, although with injured troops and those waiting for home leave and demobilisation, I would have been pretty far down anyone's list. But I would not even think of it. The thought of facing my mother, of running home with my tail between my legs, was one I recoiled from. She would have worried and fretted and been distraught at the prospect of my fate so closely resembling hers. Then she would have done everything she could to help me and we would have been two infants—me and my child. No, I knew I had to stand on my own two feet and try and ensure that my child, unlike hers, knew her father's face. Who was I kidding? Only me. I wouldn't go because I still hoped to see him again.

Late one evening over drinks on the lawn Eva Maria smiled wryly and said, "By the way, he still wants to see you."

I forgot to breathe.

"Won't take no for an answer." Idiot hope surged through me.

"No. Not him. Cyril Patiala. I keep telling him it's no go, but he keeps asking for you."

I told her I wouldn't mind seeing him again, but how did she think he would react to the Bump? She shrugged and said it went against her better judgement, but we'd never know unless we gave it a whirl. In any case, he was driving her nuts, she said.

So she set up a meeting and I met him again later that week. We talked rather diffidently and he remarked that I seemed "not quite so tickety-boo today."

It may have been because I was sober, which I certainly had not been before. But I didn't want to disappoint him or string him along, so in the spirit of this new honesty, I told him I was a bit preoccupied because I had been obliged to change my accommodation.

He replied with ready sympathy, "shifting is never pleasant. Unless for good reason."

I couldn't argue with that. He chatted a little more, mainly about his new car, a Buick coupé of which he was inordinately proud. We chatted about this and that in a desultory fashion, and then he made a lunge for me. He squeezed me in a muscular bear hug and then pulled away. He had felt the Bump.

"Oh," he said, "I did not know you were..." he searched earnestly for a delicate enough expression, "... anticipating."

"Dreading is more like it." This was becoming my mantra. He nodded knowledgeably,

"First time is always fearful for ladies." Then horrified he might be wrong, "it is first time?"

"God, yes."

Then he asked me very politely what my plans were. I replied that I had no plans, and with a bravado I did not feel, I added that I would have to make it up as I went along and take what comes.

He sat on the edge of the bed, leaning on his hands and looking concerned. He was absurdly young. He was silent for a while, deep in thought and then he cleared his throat and said,

"If you are... uncertain as to future arrangements, you could come to my father's house. He has many ladies there."

I stared at him aghast. "As my... er... you have right of entrance."

Shocked, I replied rudely. "I don't want to be part of a harem."

He looked at me blankly, unable to understand my incomprehensible attitude. "There are many babies there. We will look after you," here he swallowed bravely, "... and child."

His careless generosity confused me. I didn't know whether to laugh or cry. Instead I choked as I wondered what Fazal would have made of his offer. A fat fee, I have no doubt. Hiccupping, I tried to get back to some semblance of reality.

"But it's not your child."

I spoke gently, trying to offset my prior rudeness, but he was oblivious to both, it all just rolled over him and he smiled his broad, beatific smile and said, "No-one need know that."

For a moment I wondered if he liked the idea, if it would

enhance his reputation as a ladies' man. Making him seem more like his father. But then he squeezed my hand and I felt ashamed. I really didn't know what to make of Cyril. Was he immensely kind or just a bit dim? I was never sure. Or was he just so heedlessly rich that what would have been a big gesture from another was very little to him?

I refused as graciously as I could. Imperturbable as ever, he took it all in his stride and asked me if I would like to play cards. I agreed. It seemed the least I could do. So we played rummy, which he was surprisingly good at, winning most of the games, and shuffling and dealing the cards with panache, as proud of himself as any schoolboy in the playground. He told me it was only a case of memory, apparently he could remember all the cards we had discarded and so gage the odds. Then he announced it was getting late and he should run along. He kissed me chastely on the cheek and left an envelope full of money on the mantelpiece. I felt badly about taking it, but Eva Maria told me not to be so silly. It was the last I would get out of him, she declared somewhat grimly.

She was entirely wrong. About a week later, he asked to see me. He took me to dinner at Nedous, then on dancing to Mendoza's Band at Faletti's, where his presence caused a great stir. Well, he was very handsome and he was royal, if junior. I wondered what they made of his pregnant partner though. A few of our fellow dancers looked very askance at me. But he treated me throughout with an ostentatious courtesy, careful to let others see that I was with him. It strikes me now that it was utterly deliberate. I don't remember what I thought then. Not much, I imagine, thought didn't feature much on my horizon in those days, it was crowded out by fear and denial.

We had, in fact, a very pleasant evening, dining well and dancing, and though he was no great brain, he was an agreeable and amusing companion and I forgot all my cares for a while.

He took me for a drive through Lahore, whose main purpose seemed to be to show off his car and then dropped me off at the Braganza. He kissed me good night and said, "Chin up. Good luck." I took that to mean he was saying goodbye. He pressed a small envelope into my hand and with a squeal of his white wall tyres roared off into the night. My surmise was correct. I never saw him again.

When I got to my room I opened the envelope. To my disappointment, it did not contain money but two dusty looking stones. They were small and cloudy and looked very unimpressive, certainly nothing to shout about.

Next morning at coffee, Eva Maria asked me how the evening had gone. I told her very pleasantly, but he had not given me any money. She sighed and shrugged her shoulders in a resigned sort of way. Then I fished the envelope out of my bag and handed it to her.

"He did give me these. Very sweet of him. Moonstones, I think."

She took one out and held it up to the light. "How many have you got?"

"Erm... two." She screwed up her eyes and peered at the stone.

"I think it was awfully nice of him." Then more defensively, "I like moonstones."

She laughed. "You silly cow." I was rather offended.

"They're diamonds."

"They can't be. They don't sparkle."

Then slowly and patiently, she replied, "No, not yet. Because they're not cut. They'll sparkle like Grieg lights when they are." She put the one she had examined back in the envelope. "This one'll take your eye out."

I think my mouth actually fell open. She grinned broadly. "Shall we have a drink? Your treat. I think your money problems are over."

And so they were. Thanks to the random kindness of a boy I barely knew, and certainly had no claim on, the rest of my pregnancy was passed in comfort and ease. Eva Maria sold the diamonds for me. I was a little surprised at first that they fetched a much smaller sum than I had imagined, but she assured me that that was the going rate for uncut gems, that most of the value of a diamond lay in the skill of the cutter to bring out the brilliance and I had, at that stage, no reason to doubt her or to think she would sell me short.

I now believe that it was entirely in her nature to do just that, especially as my ill-timed pregnancy had reduced her income, but then I was merely grateful for her help and her friendship—which was unfailing. Obviously, I was no longer part of her nocturnal activities, but she insisted on including me at all the coffee mornings, lunches, drinks et al. She was the only person at that time who stood between me and utter loneliness and she was a bright, if acerbic companion. She dragged me off shopping again, this time to get things for the baby—a subject I had given no thought to. The amount of stuff a baby apparently required staggered me. It seemed more like kitting out a safari than the everyday needs of a tiny child. Crib, linen, pram, little dresses (worn by both boys and girls in those days) and a mountain of terry towelling nappies were the minimum according to her. I didn't demure. I wanted this child—so unplanned and unwished for, abandoned by one parent even before birth, to have everything it might need.

It was while we were on one of her marathon shopping trips that I first felt the Bump move. I had been to the hospital that morning for a routine check-up, and after being assured all was going along very well, went back into town to meet Eva Maria for lunch. It was baking hot, the relentless sun shone and, after eating, I wanted nothing more than to go and lie down in my cool room, where the gentle, rhythmic whirring of the fan would soon lull me to sleep. Eva Maria would have none of it. Anyway, while we were standing in Kirpa Rams waiting for the assistant to show us yet another pram —we wanted one which was small and compact, not common at that time—I felt a fluttering in my stomach which became a lurch and then a very definite kick. A person was growing inside me and it seemed that he or she had very definite ideas about transport. I stopped dead, in mid-sentence, transfixed by wonder at the everyday miracle that was taking place in my body.

After that, the Bump became a person. A separate being with pronounced likes—being warm, rest and a cool bath, and dislikes—noise and cold, who reacted to each of them. A car backfiring made her jump. If I cried when I thought of Abdi she became agitated and would kick and wriggle. The first tentative, butterfly flutterings became more muscular as she grew bigger, defined kicks and jabs were felt. And, as the pregnancy wore on, a tiny heel or hand could be seen under my skin as she sought to sound the confines of her world. Then the Bump became a she. She was a girl. I was sure of it. Rubbish, said Eva Maria, pooh-poohing the idea with scorn. You can't possibly tell she said. I could. I knew she was a girl from the moment I felt her first kick. God knows how, but I was sufficiently sure never to even consider boys' names.

As the summer wore on, I became bigger and more tired. The monsoon came and went, but this year only lasted for a very short time, and then the heat returned and it became more and more uncomfortable. I began to take my daily walk earlier and earlier in the morning to avoid the dusty pavements and the merciless sun that glittered and glinted like a blade. For the first time in my life, I woke early and took my walk between six and seven before breakfast. Bump was an early riser too, twisting and swimming inside me and the rhythm of our slow, morning walk seemed to sooth her.

I used to walk to the Mall. There I would window-shop and dawdle, watching the town come to life around me. India rises early, at that time the stalls were being filled with produce just brought in from the outlying countryside and the fleshy orange of mango and papaya, the bright jewel red of split pomegranates and the cool green of watermelons were a lovely and refreshing sight. *Cha wallahs* were brewing their aromatic tea, I would always pause to buy some, loving the cardamom scented, milky drink and then I would walk on past the street vendors laying out their myriad wares to the more refined splendours of the Mall, where I would gaze hungrily in the shop windows, longing for the fashions I could no longer wear.

I stepped off the curb without really looking. You didn't have to. There was never much traffic at that hour. A few handcarts and bicycles mostly. The Raj rose later than the rest of India. Or at least would not be seen in public at that hour, requiring a bit more time to keep up appearances. Smiling at the thought of all the faded Memsahibs still abed with their *chota hazri*, their thinning hair tortured into curls beneath their hair nets, perusing the Times of India and working out their menus for the Bearer, I was thrilled that I was no longer part of that safe, but stunted little world. I stepped out and was brought up short by a passing *tonga*. It went past at a brisk trot and there were two people seated in it. That was unusual at that hour. The odd *tonga* that you did see at that time was invariably empty. I had not seen it coming. So I stepped back, missed the curb and gave myself and the Bump a vicious jolt. She kicked hard in protest and I paused, winded. Then I looked up. I saw a man and a woman talking and laughing and there was just something about that man that could only have been him. The angle of his head as he leaned in to her, the arm lightly placed around her shoulders, the sudden bark of laughter, the careless intimacy. He was here. In Lahore with another woman.

I felt sick. She was not a member of his family. She was European and she was nobody I knew. I walked quickly back to the Braganza. Calm down, I told myself sternly, as my heart raced and my hands began to sweat. Probably he has just arrived. He would come to see me very shortly. Who was I trying to kid? They were returning from a night out, just as he and I always had. Hatred and jealousy burned through me. I loathed her for having everything I once had. Wanting him again, despite my advanced pregnancy, my bloated body yearned for him. It only took a glimpse of that rotten, elfin face with its fine bone structure and long, slender neck. Hating him, loving him, sick with the maelstrom of feelings he always aroused in me. Desperate for his touch, his smell, wanting to kiss and caress him and rake my nails across his smug, smiling face, to leave him as scarred as he had me.

I went back to my room and stayed there. Terrified to stray in case he came and I missed him. I waited all day. He never came.

I cried for a long time that night. For my lost, unworthy love, my nemesis. The Greeks would have loved Abdi. They could have invented him.

Bump protested at first—the sobbing must have felt like an earthquake to her. The shelter that was her world no longer certain or safe. Then she curled into a tight, frightened ball and kicked no more. When the tears dried up, I thought of my mother. How much she had loved and sacrificed for me. How she had defended and sheltered me. I marvelled that such a young girl, in London without family or friends, could ever have found such strength. Throughout my childhood, it never occurred to me to doubt her. She never gave me cause to. I measured myself against her and was frightened by how much I fell short.

When I awoke the next morning I was angry. Abdi was clearly in Lahore and must have received one of my letters. Then the possibility that they may not have been passed on to him occurred to me. The post in India could be unreliable and the fact that he had so resolutely kept me away from his family could only mean that they were hostile to me. I supposed you couldn't really blame them—a pregnant Memsahib, separated from her husband, with no fortune, family or influential friends would hardly be an attractive prospect to them.

I made up my mind I had to see him. I dressed with care,

paying attention to my make-up and hair, and covering my bulk as best I could with the voluminous silk *dupatta* I had bought in the bazaar in Ambala on our first meeting. I did the rounds of all his favourite morning haunts, hoping to find him at breakfast with his latest love.

He was nowhere to be seen. I even went to a few of the shops that he frequented, A. N. John, his barber, and on down the Mall to the Luxmi Building and his beloved Ranken & Co, past the Elphinstone Hotel and Kandawala Motors as far as Stiffles and Lorangs where we had so often dined. Retracing our old steps, I realised he would not be there and that the only way to be sure of seeing him would be to go to his home. If he were out perhaps I could speak to his mother. Whatever she might feel about me, I reasoned, she might at least have some interest in her grandchild.

I felt shaky and scared, sick and a bit sweaty, but determined to see this thing through, if only for Bump's sake. She had a right to know her father after all. Nobody knew better than I the desolate void of not knowing who you are, where you came from, who you might be like. No. She deserved better. I walked determinedly on through Lawrence Gardens to the broad, tree lined avenue where Abdi's family home was. It was a lovely white stucco house, in the colonial style, large and spacious, surrounded by a broad verandah leading on to the gardens. A gracious and civilised home. The *Chokidar* who guarded the gate asked me what my business was. I told him I was there to see Abdi.

He nodded and let me into the gardens, then went into the house to inquire. I stood in the shade of a banyan tree and waited. It was very hot. After a few minutes, he came down the steps frowning and beckoned me to follow him. He said the *Begum* would see me. He led me into a cool, dark hall, with a marble floor and a few antique Indian chairs. Then he left me. The blinds were down and the furniture and fittings of dark wood, so it was not easy to see in there. However, I could see that the few Persian rugs on the floor were beautiful, old and very valuable. I waited.

Eventually a woman came down the stairs, wearing the traditional *salwar kameez*, her head covered in a chiffon scarf edged with a wide gold-thread border. She wore a huge emerald ring on her index finger.

A bearer, dressed in a severe black and red uniform with a starched *puggree* fanned out in crisp pleats like a peacock's tail, accompanied her. They did not look friendly.

She walked towards me, but stopped a distance away, as if not wanting to come too close. I asked her if she was Abdi's mother. She looked a little like him, but not much. Her eyes were like his, large and fine, but her other features were broader and coarser, and the sharply aquiline nose gave her the look of a bird of prey. Her mouth was set in a straight, hard line. She bowed her head in assent.

I asked if they had received my letter. Again, the regal

inclination of the head, but no words. I wondered if she could speak English.

"I am... your son..." words failed me in the face of her implacable silence. My mother's training kicked in.

"How do you do? Er... My name is Juanita Rikh," I extended my hand with determined politeness. She did not take it.

"I am perfectly aware of who you are," she replied icily. Her English was excellent. She could have been one of the duchesses at the Waldorf.

"Then you must have received my letter," again the nod of assent, but no more. Clearly she was not going to help me out with this.

Floundering, I jumped straight in. "I have to see Abdi."

"My son will not see you." That sharp rejection hurt so much, that for a long time I remembered it as an actual, physical blow. A slap in the face. But it could not have been because she was never at any time close enough to touch me.

Crimson with anger and pain, I cried out, "he has to. This child is his."

She stared at me in impassive silence. I might as well have been reading out my laundry list. I was convinced she was keeping the letter from him.

"He has a right to know."

"What makes you think he does not?" She turned to her Bearer, pulling her scarf across her face.

"I do not know this woman. My son has not asked me to know her."

She turned her back on me and walked away down the hall and into a room on the right. Her voice with its perfect enunciation came wafting through the open door like a cold wind.

"Show her out." The Bearer closed the door behind her and escorted me off the premises, right to the front gate. He wasn't taking any chances.

Back on the road outside, my misery was complete. I had failed to protect my child. Because of me she too would be disowned, unwanted, never knowing who she really was. She would be told her father was a Muslim, that he was from Lahore, and that her eyes were like his, but what would that mean to her? He would never be anything but an absence in her life, a gaping wound she could never staunch. No-one knew this better than me and yet I had inflicted it all on her. In a vile, genetic pass-the-parcel, I had handed on the pain as if it were an heirloom.

I didn't want to see or talk to anyone. I stayed in my room. By choice. Eva Maria rang and I told her I was ill. She knew something was wrong, but this time she didn't pry. Perhaps he told her.

While I remained in stasis, India was in turmoil. In the end, it was Imran who roused me from my apathy.

He came to see me. He told me he had just returned from Calcutta. I stared at him blankly. Clearly, he expected a response because he asked me if I had seen a newspaper. I said no.

He sat down and ordered coffee. He looked exhausted. His clothes were crumpled and he was unshaven, which was unheard of for him. I asked him what was wrong and he just stared at me, for a moment speechless at my ignorance.

Then he told me. He said he and many others had been increasingly concerned at the inflammatory language used by Jinnah and his supporters in their newspaper, *Dawn*.

I shrugged and said that both Jinnah and Nehru were very fond of the purple phrase, but were far too pragmatic to let it affect their actual political message. Not anymore, he told me and quoted from Dawn's latest editorial, "The rape of the Muslim nation is about to begin in a more ruthless and criminal manner than Hitler and Mussolini ever dared in Europe."

That did shock me. "That's dreadful. He's threatening them with extinction," I blustered. Imran said he was so disturbed by the viciousness of this new rhetoric that he and several others had decided to attend the Direct Action day in Calcutta that Jinnah had called for to see what Suhrawardy, Chief Minister of Bengal, would say and to gage the mood of the crowd. Suhrwardy had declared Friday, the 16th August—an official holiday in Bengal—so that all who wished could attend the rally and was to address the crowd on the Maiden in person.

The coffee arrived and I poured Imran a cup. He drank

some and then went on. He told me that thugs had been bussed into Calcutta early that morning. They had rampaged through the city centre, burning and looting Hindu businesses and homes.

He took a deep breath and went on. Elsewhere, Hindu mobs had built barricades to prevent Muslim labourers from the jute mills across the Hooghly reaching the city. As they tried to cross the river, they were pelted with bricks and stones.

I asked him what the police or the army were doing. He replied that the police were expecting anti-British demonstrations like the ones the year before and so had taken steps to protect Europeans. They were the only group on this occasion who were ignored and therefore quite safe. The lone voice at the earlier demonstration I had witnessed in Lahore had been quite right. It was no longer our fight. But those at the eye of the storm, as Imran put it, were initially left completely undefended.

By early afternoon tens of thousands had reached the Maiden where the leaders of the Muslim League addressed the crowd. Although they urged them to return home peacefully, the crowd was, by now, in no mood to listen. Jinnah himself, had clearly expected trouble because he stayed away, safe in Bombay on the other side of the country. When the speeches were over, the crowd dispersed, burning and killing as they went and by four o'clock the police signalled to the army that they had lost control of the city.

At dusk, Imran said, there was a short but severe thunderstorm which cleared the streets. He and his companions hoped that that would be the end of it, particularly as it was Ramadan, and most Muslims would return home to break their fast.

So Imran's group went back to their hotel, the broken glass from ransacked shop windows crunching under their feet, had several stiff whiskies and thought it was all over. But, in the early hours of the morning, they got word that further gangs, now residents as well as bussed in thugs, wielding torches, machetes and guns, were swarming through the maze of narrow streets and alleys that formed the slums of Calcutta, where no police vehicle could follow them. Huge billowing clouds of smoke began to rise, engulfing the city.

By daybreak, Imran, pulling all the considerable strings at his disposal, was able to go with the Governor of Bengal, Sir Frederick Burrows and an army escort, to survey the damage.

He paused here and poured himself more coffee. His hands were shaking. He told me that it was only when dawn broke that the scale of the slaughter became apparent. He had walked down streets littered with the corpses of men, women and children, their bodies hacked and mutilated, charred and blackened. They lay where they had fallen, now only prey to the buzzards and *pi dogs* who feasted on their remains. He had seen buzzards so gorged with human flesh they could not fly and a dead baby, his head smashed to a bloody pulp, having his brains pecked out by a crow.

Burrows, a former grenadier guard and veteran of the trenches, commented that this carnage was worse than the Somme.

Imran said that the bloodshed, once started, could not be stopped. It raged on through Saturday and Sunday. Burrows now brought in the troops in vast numbers, but it was too late. No go areas had already been established.

Imran was devastated by what he called "this mindless orgy of killing." He had been threatened at knife point by Hindus, who refused to let him enter their enclave. He told me that barricades now divided faith from faith. He saw a mob beat a Hindu man to death while Muslim policemen stood by and would not intervene, despite Imran's pleas. He saw street after street, ruined and burnt out, shops, offices and homes destroyed and everywhere the corpses of men, women and children, hacked to death by their friends and neighbours. Thick black smoke hung over the city like a pall. It was a vision of hell, he said.

By the time he had finished we were both in tears. He said that Burrows had estimated around five thousand people had been murdered, in a sudden spasm of savagery, that had destroyed all our hopes and dreams for the future. Imran, his face now frozen and immobile, pronounced bleakly that "Now to every Hindu, a Muslim only looks like a killer, and vice versa."

We sat together in that verdant garden, surrounded by

constantly watered trees and flowers, a bright oasis in a desert of hate, silent and appalled. Imran was exhausted by reliving the horror he had described. He said at one point that our long cherished dream for a new world had degenerated into a blood soaked nightmare and I could only agree. In the end, he got up and went home. His shoulders hunched, his back bowed, his clothes creased and sweat stained, he bore little resemblance to the man I had first met.

I sat on alone for a long time after he left, trying to understand what he had told me.

I failed. In the end, it just seemed more senseless murder and hate. I had hoped we had seen enough of that in Europe to last forever, but it seemed not. India was rushing headlong to her own agony. And all our plans, our meetings and organising, our agendas and good intentions, even the towering intellects of Gandhi and Nehru, had been powerless to stop it.

I can't pretend to make sense of it, even now, and I don't pretend to have the clear eye of a historian. I do not have an accurate perception of this. Confused and tormented with my own considerable problems, I merely watched as these events took place all around me. But I was there. I had a ringside seat and that is all I can lay claim to. I have been a bystander at some of the most cataclysmic events of the twentieth- century. So that is the best I can offer. I don't have an overview but I am a witness, a voice.

Chapter Sixteen

It was very hot that summer. The unusually short monsoon had brought none of the usual relief. Every morning the sun rose and a wall of implacable heat rose with it. By July the temperature was in the nineties again.

I was very uncomfortable. I felt huge. When I dressed and put on my lipstick I felt like a ceremonial elephant, dressed up for a parade. Vast, lumbering, unwieldy. My ankles swelled. I was very glad Abdi could not see me now.

Imran came to see me sometimes, a loyal and steadfast friend. But he was often in Delhi now as Attlee's government together with the Viceroy, Lord Wavell, became increasingly concerned at the degree of violence in the riots and the hardening of attitudes between what were now clearly two bitterly opposing sides, Congress and the League. Despite British machinations and procrastinations, serious moves were at last being made towards Independence, and Imran began to take his place on the national stage. Lahore, as capital of the Punjab, the prize most desired by both parties, filled up with officials and civil servants at all levels. The Braganza became their headquarters.

One morning in the end of August, I woke early. I had been having what my doctor had described as Braxton-Hicks contractions. When I asked him what that was he replied airily, "Oh, a kind of dummy run. A rehearsal if you will," and went on writing his notes. They hurt like hell, and more alarmingly, as the time went on and the contractions became more and more intense, the Bump assumed a hard and almost square shape. "All normal," said the doctor. I wondered what it would take to arouse his concern. Death in a ditch, I imagined, and perhaps not even that. I now think that our polarised attitudes were predictable—he, with his encyclopaedic experience of childbirth, was rattled by very little and I, a first time mother, without an older woman to confide in, was rattled by everything. It all seemed very strange and frightening to me.

A monster of a Braxton Hicks woke me that morning, I groaned because I was still tired and it was very early, about five o'clock. Then I noticed the most unpleasant sensation, the bed was soaking wet. My waters had broken.

I sat on the edge of the bed as searing pain ran into my back. There was no mistaking this. The contractions got stronger and stronger and more and more frequent.

I dressed with difficulty. By now the pains were running into each other in a sort of crescendo. Then I got really scared because I was alone. I knew I had to get to the hospital, but the means of getting there eluded me. I rang Eva Maria. She was quite cross with me for waking her at first. She never got to sleep much before four, having to make sure all her 'guests' had left. But when she grasped what was actually going on, she told me she was on her way and to 'sit tight.' That made me smile because by that point sitting was not really an option, but then a sudden wave of pain engulfed me and I couldn't talk anymore. I put the phone down and wished my mother was here, longing for her soft Scots voice and cool, capable hands.

In a short while, Eva Maria arrived, immaculately but incongruously dressed in a black suit with a rather natty hat. She pounded on my door as if the place were on fire. It took me a while to get there and open it, but when I did she said, "good, you're dressed. Is your case packed?" Of course, it wasn't. It should have been. The hospital had given me a comprehensive list of things I should bring with me months ago. Eva Maria had personally stood over me and made sure that I had every single item on that list. Two nightdresses, cotton only, two flannels, slippers. But I had never packed the case, so she flapped about, opening drawers and finding very little beyond an old nightie I had brought from England that she glanced at with disgust and then thrust back into the drawer.

"Oh for God's sake, the kid will have left home before we find this lot. Put your shoes on."

She manoeuvred me into the lift; her neat, birdlike frame overwhelmed by my bulk. By this time, despite the pain, I was laughing. It was all too absurd. Crossing the lobby, I had to stop twice and hold on to the back of a chair, transfixed with pain, as the spruce and starched staff regarded me with appalled concern. I said to Eva Maria,

"Do Indian women manage this better?" I groaned, wishing I had one to ask for advice.

"Certainly quieter," she replied cheerfully, "but then they are probably gagged," as she bundled me into the back of a taxi. As sitting was by now out of the question, I straddled the seat as best I could on all fours. Eva Maria got in the front beside the driver and barked,

"Services Hospital!" and the taxi driver, who had no doubt seen it all before though in different circumstances, started the car leisurely as if he had all the time in the world, then drove off at a snail's pace.

"For God's sake, man, get a bloody move on!" Eva Maria kept looking back at me. I think she was rattled because her hat was crooked and she had abandoned all thoughts of diction. I just tried to keep breathing because by now the pain was unbearable.

When we reached the hospital, I was rushed straight to the delivery room where the real agony began. They put me on a bed and stuck my feet into metal stirrups.

On instruction from the midwife, a rather beefy, grey-haired British matron who clearly knew what she was about, I pushed and strained for all I was worth. It went on for hours. The pain was oceanic. I thought I was going to die.

At first, we were very well-mannered and English about the whole thing, both of us polite and restrained, but after a few hours, I was screaming and she was swearing.

It was all a bit much for Eva Maria. She had told me in the taxi that she had never attended a birth before. Only abortions. The driver had looked very disapproving at that and when we arrived demanded twice the usual fare. Obviously he thought harlots could pay. She threw some money at him and he drove away, quite happy to take his share of our ill-gotten gains.

Eventually, it got too much for Eva Maria. Announcing she was "just popping out for a fag" she left the room and did not come back. The nurse told me later that she had in fact waited outside, on a chair in the corridor. I thought she had gone home.

The day dragged on. It was baking in that airless room with only one tiny fan, whirring frantically on a table in the corner of the room. In the end there was only an endless cycle of pain, relieved momentarily when the gas and air and exhaustion kicked in.

My midwife held my hand, which was good of her, because when the pains came I held her so tightly I could hear her knuckles crunching. A young Anglo-Indian nurse, called Daphne, who was immaculate and beautiful in her white uniform, came to relieve her.

My midwife assured me she was only going for her supper and would be back soon. I hadn't even noticed that night had fallen and the natural light had been replaced by electricity. Nothing but the pain existed.

Daphne offered me a glass of water. I drank it down eagerly because I was very thirsty, but then threw up. After that, she moistened my lips with some wet cotton wool. She was patient and sweet, but she didn't seem to really know what she was doing and that made two of us, which was alarming.

After a while, the midwife came back, told Daphne there was steak and kidney for supper and she should get there quick while there was still some left. That made me gag again. Daphne left for supper. The pain and pushing went on.

Then the midwife stuck her head between my legs and emerged smiling.

"Nearly there," she said. Suddenly she looked like an angel. Calm, proficient and strong.

"Now, one big push," and with a hot, tearing sensation, she was born. Lily, my beautiful child.

She was a most beautiful baby. Cleverly, she managed to combine the best of her father and me. She looked like me, but her huge dark eyes and long, curling lashes were all his. Her hair curled like his too, falling naturally into soft waves.

Her beauty was commented on by everyone. The nurses at the hospital went crazy over her and even the doctor, who had seen thousands of babies and was apparently impressed by none, looked down at her as she slept in the crib beside my bed and said, "The shape of that child's head is... er... exquisite." I could only agree.

She was quite a big baby, weighing seven and a half pounds at birth, and God knows, she had felt like a whale coming out, but she was never a shapeless podge, like most babies. She had tiny but well-defined features and an adorable rosebud mouth. I was besotted with her. She was my darling and my delight.

She was also an easy baby, with clear preferences, some carried on from the womb. She liked to be held, but only by me; the nurses practically queued up to hold her, but she would wrinkle her little face with outrage if anyone else tried to pick her up. Then she would howl, rather loudly for such a little thing, but she would stop in midcry if I took her back. It was quite funny and all very simple. She hated loud noises, being cold and wanted to be fed and cuddled by me.

The night she was born the doctor examined her and she was pronounced fit and well. Then, despite my protests, she was taken to the nursery for the rest of the night. That was the norm, I was told firmly. "For one night only," my midwife said, "so make the most of it. It'll be the most sleep you'll get in six months." Then they installed me in a room of my own and tucked me in as if I were the infant.

Early the next morning, even before *chota hazri*, they brought her back to me. They had tried to give her a bottle feed, the nurse said, during the night but she wasn't having that. She spat out the teat and then choked, so they gave up. She put her to my breast and she knew exactly what to do. Apparently, some babies don't. She did. She sucked away, feeding easily and happily until she had had enough, then she turned her head aside and fell asleep. The nurse laughed and said if only they were all as good as that. She said Lily was a definite little character and she had taken quite a shine to her already. I was very glad to hear that because one of my fears was that some people would be nasty to her because she was half and half. The nurse was so nice that I confessed as much. She smiled and said, "Not me." Then she went on, " The black and white pups are always the best looking."

I should have been outraged by that phrase. Three commonly used words that revealed generations of prejudice. A view of the world Yolanda and I had longed to see destroyed forever. But I was too tired and too cowardly to argue. Instead, I smiled weakly and said nothing.

She smoothed the sheet down for me and turned to go. Then she said, "Oh, I nearly forgot. A woman came to see her last night."

I was puzzled and half-asleep. "Who?"

"Didn't give a name. Just came into the nursery and asked to see your baby. An older woman."

I smiled. Eva Maria. "I know. My friend who brought me in."

She nodded. "Maybe. She was veiled." I smiled broadly. That hat again. She had a new hat with a black lace veil she was very proud of. She'd seen a picture of Vivian Leigh in the paper wearing one and had it copied. It suited her very well although she looked nothing like Vivian Leigh.

I snuggled down to get some sleep. The nurse said they usually didn't allow visitors into the nursery, especially at that time of night, but the woman had been very insistent so they let her have a quick peek and then she had gone away. Definitely, Eva Maria I thought as I drifted off to sleep.

Imran came the next day. He brought us a beautiful cream embroidered shawl with a broad satin edge. It was a lovely gift. He also brought me newspapers and a little basket of perfect mangoes. He stayed and chatted for a little while, but then Lily woke and started to cry, she wanted feeding. Imran got up to go. The nurse came in and said, it was perfectly all right for the father to stay. I don't know which one of us was more embarrassed. We both went bright red, so I said he was absolutely not the father, but before I could say he was merely a friend, Imran had fled.

Eva Maria didn't come that day, but I wasn't surprised because she had been the night before.

The next morning while I was out of my room having a bath, a huge sheaf of flowers arrived. Narcissi—delicate, out of season, expensive. I knew exactly who they were from. Eva Maria must have told him. For a while I hoped he would come, indulging in tendrils of hope as fragile and transient as the flowers. But they soon faded, spring flowers in high summer, and he did not come.

That afternoon, Eva Maria did come. She raised her eyebrows at the flowers and asked if he had sent money. I said no and she snorted in disgust. She had obviously tried to push him into stumping up. Then she went to look at Lily. Holding her cigarette holder behind her back, she peered down at her.

"Pretty little thing. For a baby. She looks like you." Then she looked across at me and I wondered if she was calculating how long it would be before I could resume earning. At that point, Lily opened her eyes wide and stared impassively at Eva Maria.

Eva Maria shook her head, then turned away. "No doubt who her father is."

And I smiled but felt sad because it was unlikely she would ever see the eyes that were so like her own.

Chapter Seventeen

When did it all begin to go wrong? I can't be sure exactly. Perhaps from the moment we left the hospital. The first day I brought her back to the Braganza. The writing on the wall.

I remember our time in the hospital as one of happiness. We were both healthy and recovered quickly from the birth. And the hospital was such a closed world—a microcosm that aped the world outside, but had none of its tensions and cruelty.

Sickness and death happened there, but also care and healing. For Lily and I it was a milky cocoon, gentle and nurturing, a place of rigid routine—day and night punctuated by the unchanging ritual of baths and feeds, snatched sleep and wonder at my lovely child. I would spend hours just staring at her tiny hands with their shell-like nails, the deep gaze of her dark brown eyes, her velvet skin and soft, downy hair. I was drunk with her loveliness.

Here we were safe, mother and child only, no other criteria applied.

But in the outside world, the newspapers Imran had left with me described a very different place. A world that was descending again into hatred and madness. In the aftermath of what became known as the Calcutta Killings, and to avert further bloodshed, Wavell begged Nehru and Jinnah to work out a compromise.

What we did not know at the time, and was unknown to all but a very few, was that during that summer of 1946 a Dr Patel had developed a set of x-rays that confirmed his fears and proved his diagnosis. The so called 'bronchitis' that had dogged Jinnah for years was in fact tuberculosis and was so far advanced as to be incurable. He broke the news to his patient together with his estimate that Jinnah had no more than two years to live. He ordered him to rest and stop smoking and so slow down the progress of the disease. Jinnah redoubled his workload. Knowing he was working against time, he was determined to achieve his goal, his Pakistan, before he died. He did so with a zeal that proved both his courage and blind refusal to consider any compromise. The breakneck speed and intransigence of all parties meant that millions of men, women and children died with him. His motto was now, 'we shall have India divided or we shall have India destroyed'.

After a week I was allowed to take Lily home. Or what passed for our home. As I wheeled her proudly through the crowded foyer of the Braganza she began to cry.

Loudly. She was hungry. Everyone turned round and stared. I got to the lift as quickly as I could. But, unused to fitting a pram into a confined space, I couldn't seem to get the angle right. If the front went in, the handle jammed against the doors. A doorman came to help me. Together after not very gentle shoving and pushing, which only served to frighten Lily and increase the volume of her cries, we managed to get the damn thing in. Lily and I took refuge in our room. I left the pram in the corridor. But I was shaken. Here was none of the easy going acceptance that a child who was wet or hungry could be a bit of a nuisance until she was made comfortable again. The stares were not friendly.

The gimlet brigade, I called them that because they all seemed to have one permanently in their hands, were mostly men in military uniform or high-ranking civil servants, and they and their censorious wives thought the Braganza was no place for a baby. Theirs had all been hidden away in hill stations until it was time to send them 'back' to school. These children lived in a world of sunlight and flowers, with gardens to play in and adoring servants to look after them, pandering to their every whim until they were seven, when they were wrenched out of their gentle ayah's arms, and shipped off to a rain-soaked island they had never seen before called 'home.' They were then parked in a Dickensian preparatory school, like the one Rikh and I had been billeted in at Liverpool, prior to the real horror of public school. The harshness of it always appalled me, but they were little soldiers of the Raj and their training began early.

We settled in. Eva Maria had been right. It was not easy to care for a baby in one small room with a bathroom down the hall, and there was another problem. The money from the sale of Cyril's diamonds was running out. I had lived well during my pregnancy but not wisely, insisting on staying on at the Braganza where even the smallest room was expensive, and paying Mr de Sousa and Eva Maria back in full. Lily's layette had cost far more than I had imagined. I should have moved out, away from Lahore to a quiet place where I could bring up my child cheaply, but I was scared to be alone. Scared to start over in a new place where I knew no-one and couldn't speak the language, and even more frightened now that there were riots and angry demonstrations everywhere and an English woman and her half-caste child could well become the target of their wrath. Also I suspect now a more primal instinct was at work. I had made the Braganza my home, it was the only place I had lived in in Lahore, the place where I had briefly possessed my love and conceived my child. Here I had known my greatest moments of joy and despair. I was very loath to leave it. It was my bolt-hole and my refuge. I could not imagine life anywhere else. I refused to.

But as the weeks stretched into months, I came to hate it. Its ambience had changed completely. It was now stuffed to the gunnels with officials as the political situation worsened. Widespread violence had broken out in Bengal. Thousands of Hindus fled Muslim areas. In Noakhali Hindu women were raped and butchered along with their children or forced to convert to Islam at knife-point. Men were murdered with casual savagery. Gandhi went to the area and begged them to stop the killing.

Then came the backlash. Hindu mobs roamed the countryside in Bihar. Mosques were desecrated and burned down and it is estimated seven thousand Muslims were killed. Nehru visited the area at great personal risk and tried to reason with the crowd who chanted 'Jawaharlal Murdabad', death to Jawaharlal. He wrote that the picture was far worse than anyone had imagined: that there was a definite attempt on the part of the Hindu mobs to exterminate the Muslims. That men, women and children had been butchered en masse.

Although still far away, the whirlwind was rolling westward. It didn't encourage me to move into the country. I might be broke in Lahore, but I was at least safe. For the time being.

I began to struggle. I had no money and I saw no-one. Only Imran kept in touch. When he was in Lahore he always contacted me, but seeing him was difficult as I could not leave Lily and the places he frequented were not suitable for a baby. In fact, they did not admit children at all. Dogs yes, children no. So I was ever more alone. My world shrank until all I did was look after Lily. I fed her, loved her and bathed her. I even sang to her, remembering the old Scots songs my mother used to sing to me.

I washed her tiny garments again and again. She seemed perfectly happy. I took my meals in my room now. My one foray into the dining room had been a disaster. I could not leave her in the room alone so I took her with me. Despite the fact we were given the smallest table, tucked away at the back by the entrance to the kitchen, we still attracted a battery of stony stares as I wheeled her across the room. The maitre d' looked at us as if we smelled. I found that a bitter irony. I remembered his obsequious attention when Abdi had been with me.

"Madam is even more beautiful tonight," he would grin and grovel, pulling out my chair and shaking out my napkin, smothering me with attention. Not anymore. Madam was dismissed with a cursory nod in the direction of the worst table in the room and then ignored. The meal took hours to come and was stone cold when it did. Lily began to cry. Quietly, as if she too were daunted by the hostility in the room. A young waiter took pity on us. He picked her up gently, cradled her with a practiced air, smiled and said, "don't worry, Memsahib, we have plenty babies at home." He stayed holding her and rocking her gently until the head waiter came and shouted at him. That woke Lily with a start and she began to cry in earnest. She didn't stop then. I bolted what was left of my food and escaped upstairs as quickly as I could. As I wheeled her clumsily across that chilly expanse that seemed to grow larger with every step I took, I was in tears myself.

I suspect that the gimlet brigade with their Omo white offspring and attendant servants would just about have been acceptable in the dining room, but the sight of a single mother with her half-black child was a horror to them and they made that very plain.

My loneliness increased. Without an ayah, social activity was impossible. None of my old haunts were suitable for a child. I was an oddity, a Memsahib without servants, caught between two worlds. An outcast in one and a foreigner with incomprehensible mores in the other.

I was floundering. Often in tears, terrified of my life and the bleakness of our future. Bringing up a child on a pittance in the aftermath of a war. Full circle. But I never had my mother's grit, her granite soul that could withstand disaster. I now suspect I was also suffering from a swinging dose of antenatal depression, but we didn't call it that then. Perhaps if I had known other mothers, we would have shared our stories and supported each other, but I had no-one to commiserate with. I didn't know any other mothers.

I went for weeks without an adult conversation. No-one wanted to visit me in my hotel and sit, talking in whispers so as not to wake the baby, in a cramped and cluttered room festooned with drying nappies.

Vicky had tried. She came to visit me, bringing an exquisite embroidered dress for Lily and a silver apostle spoon. She sat and tried to talk to me as I fed and washed Lily. She even attempted to hold her, but Lily was by now only used to me. She wriggled and yelled in protest. Vicky handed her back to me and left soon after. She had tried to explain how things were outside my bubble. The mood in Lahore was becoming ugly, she said. She shared Imran's fear that the Punjab would become the 'powder keg.' In response to the appalling treatment of Muslims in Bihar, League militants were beginning to arm themselves. All India was awash with ordinance left over from the War and weapons were not difficult to acquire. Rifles and even machine guns were being sold openly in the bazaars and alleys of the old town. Vigilante gangs on both sides were amassing caches of these weapons and training to fight she told me. There was a growing fear that they would soon become too powerful to stop.

I listened in horror, but when Vicky asked me how I was managing, Lily let up such a roar of protest at her delayed feed, that Vicky left. In those days, when you breast fed your baby, you did so alone. After she had gone, I missed her very much. Her kindness, her refusal to treat me as an outcast, her memory of who I was.

The weather was now cooling down at last, so I used to take Lily out every morning and sit with her in Jilani park. I hoped we would see her father. We never did. But Lahore was full of beautiful parks and gardens in those days and I took her to all of them, hoping this would give her a sense of belonging. It was her town, her birthright, as London was mine, and I wanted her to possess it.

I struggled on for four months. Eva Maria had come to see us at first but had been driven away by too much baby, as she put it. I didn't really expect more of her, but I did miss her. Her acerbic comments and trenchant observations provided an adult relish my life now completely lacked. Although I adored Lily, it was becoming clear with every day that for me motherhood was not enough.

I was increasingly tired, anxious and desperately alone. When Lily slept the walls seemed to come in at me, emphasizing the cramped confines of my life. I was screaming with boredom and longing for contact. Anyone. Certainly none was available to me at the Braganza. A tentative smile or shy good morning was greeted with a blank stare or more often, an averted head. I longed for the careless and profuse contact of my old life, for the gossip at the Standard or the jokes and flirtation at Stiffles. I longed to dance and dress up again.

As ever, when Eva Maria did come, she came unannounced. I had no time to make myself presentable and always alone, I had stopped bothering. She found me with lank hair and no make-up, wearing an old cotton dress with a clean nappy over one shoulder and nappy pins stuck in the bodice.

She gave me a sharp look, moved a pile of baby things out of the way and sat down on the bed. In her tailored blue suit with red silk blouse and high-heeled sandals, she was an oasis of chic in a wasteland of bobbly white towelling and washed out cotton.

She said, "this isn't working, is it?"

Instantly, I felt sullen and tearful. "My mother did it. She kept me."

"Yes. And I take my hat off to her. But you're not your mother and she wasn't in India."

You couldn't argue with that. I had neither Mother's courage nor Mrs Lomasney. She had been my mother's employer, who became our protector. I said nothing. Eva Maria went on.

"This is no good. For you or her." She glanced across at Lily, fast asleep in the crib that was fast becoming too small, innocent and unaware that her fate was being decided.

"What she wants is a stable home, not a hotel room. How long can this go on for?"

I could not answer. My throat suddenly tight.

"She needs a parent who can secure her future."

"I am keeping her with me."

I was too tired and too worn down to wonder who she had been talking to.

"All right, but think of her. Is it the kindest thing to do? Or just the most selfish? What's best for her? In the long run?"

"But you told me you always regretted..."

"Yes, I did. And I shouldn't have. It was a knee-jerk

reaction, caused by my own experience. What do I know about keeping a baby? I didn't know how it would pan out. Now I've seen."

There was no mistaking what she was thinking. She took out her cigarettes and lit one for both of us. Then she stood up impatiently, "Have you got any hooch in this place?"

I had. I could not have lived without it. I got the bottle out of the cupboard and a tooth mug from the wash hand basin. We would have to share. She poured out a slug and drank it down, then did the same for me.

"Drink it." I did.

"This is tough. Don't make up your mind now. Think about it."

"I won't hand her over to strangers."

She looked at me hard and nodded. "Okay." Then, "you will always love her. But do you love her enough to do what's best for her? Even if it breaks your heart? Who comes first?"

I burst into tears. Unusually for her, she hugged me. For someone who was so cold, she had a surprisingly warm, firm embrace. I was weak and very lonely. She was the first adult I had had a conversation with in months.

"I could take her home."

"Yes, you could. But to what? A rerun of your childhood? From what you've told me, it wasn't exactly peachy, was it?"

No it wasn't. It was bloody awful. I said nothing.

"Nita, darling, very few men will take on a woman with a bastard child. And those that will, mostly ain't worth having."

I thought of my drunken, abusive step-father and shuddered. He had beaten me and made my mother's life hell. I didn't want that. Not for either of us.

Our situation at the Braganza quickly went from bad to worse. It was like being on a slope, as we slid further down, we accelerated.

The hostile stares were held for longer, crossing the foyer with the pram was like running a gauntlet of disapproval and dislike, the atmosphere so strong it felt tangible. The staff were now barely polite. Objections were made—the pram either in the foyer or the corridor upstairs was a particular point of contention. Complaints had been made that it "lowered the tone" and "looked bad." I said I would be perfectly happy to carry Lily while in the hotel, but obviously I needed the pram when we went out. I suggested that it could easily be kept in one of the small rooms by the entrance that the concierge used for luggage. I was told that was not possible. No-one said why. Then I was told that there had been complaints about her crying. This was petty and mean because she was a very easy baby and she did not cry much at all, but because of this we were no longer allowed to sit in the garden. There were also complaints about the amount of washing. I said I failed to see how that affected anyone but me, as I washed and dried her clothes in my room.

Lips were pursed and heads shaken. Then, one morning as I was wheeling her across the foyer on our way out, I was waylaid by Mr Henriques, Mr de Sousa's sidekick. He was a young man, whose slick and facile charm made him a great hit with the Memsahibs. He called me into his office and we had the usual pantomime as to where to park the pram. It was unacceptable in the foyer, but too large to be put in his room or outside the warren of offices that housed the management of the hotel. In the end, I took her out of the pram and held her in my arms. A bellhop was instructed to "lose the pram."

Lily slept angelically. Mr Henriques ushered me into his office. He asked me if I would like coffee. I said no. Then, with expressions of regret and much wringing of hands, he asked me to leave. He said with a sigh that it was "just too difficult." I wondered why. I pointed out that at the Waldorf in London where I had worked we would have been able to take one small infant in our stride. He nodded and said it was the "paraphernalia" which was the real problem. I said I thought that was absurd. Guests were arriving daily laden with golf clubs and cricket gear, tennis racquets and hockey sticks, to say nothing of polo kit and guns. All of which the concierge managed to accommodate with ease. His face relaxed. He had been drowning and I had thrown him a line. That was exactly it, Madam Rikh, he said. Grown up paraphernalia we can manage, he smiled at me, but Braganza cannot do babies. The clientèle object. The hand wringing began again.

Baby, and here he smiled at Lily as he prepared to chuck her out into the street, destroys our ambiance, he said.

We both knew this was rubbish. While I had been staying there with Abdi, a whole family of five had arrived from Simla and stayed for two months while being fitted out for a return to England. The children were aged from ten years to six months and had two ayahs and a governess in attendance. Nobody bothered about their effect on the ambiance or questioned their washing. They ran around the foyer and played in the gardens. The older two ate in the dining room. They were not conspicuously well behaved, but they were white.

He asked me how soon I could "make other arrangements. More suitable for baby."

All this was as if he were helping me out and all with the same unctuous smile. He was like the Cheshire Cat. His smile seemed spread around the room, like an oil stain.

I was shaking with fear and anger. We had nowhere to go and if I had to settle my bill at the Braganza, I would have very little money for anywhere else. The floor seemed to be giving way beneath me. Once again I was falling, falling down into my mother's life, back into my own origins. Having said his piece, which Mr de Sousa was obviously too cowardly to say to my face, Henriques regarded the job done and couldn't wait to get rid of me.

He said I should let him know when I had organised my removal. I did not reply. I demanded my pram back and it was brought straight away. The older porter looked at us sympathetically and insisted on wheeling it out and down the steps for me. He obviously knew exactly what was going on. I was clearly the talk of the whole place. He could also see the state I was in. He brought me one of the little gilt chairs from inside and put it as ceremoniously on the pavement as if he were attending a duchess at dinner, then said gently, "Sit, Memsahib, sit for a few minutes. Collect yourself." He went inside and brought me out a glass of water, which he served from a carafe on a tray. I thanked him and he smiled sadly at me. He nodded at Lily, "Very nice baby, Memsahib."

I burst into tears because he was the only person in that place, the place I had thought was my home, to have treated us with anything but abhorrence. He let me cry and then handed me a huge linen handkerchief. I dried my eyes and blew my nose. "Keep it," he said. I nodded, it wasn't in much of a state to be returned to him. It was so wet I could have wrung it out, I think. I got up and wheeled her away. The kindness of strangers, indeed.

I walked around all day long. Neither wanting nor daring to show my face back at the Braganza. I felt completely beaten. I had no money, no home, no friends I could go to. If I had felt alone before, it was nothing compared to this.

Half way through the afternoon, with aching feet and dry, stinging eyes, I passed the Anglican church of the Resurrection opposite the High Court at the far end of the Mall. I had been inside a couple of times before, though never for a full service, but its neo-Gothic lines and huge sandstone edifice offered shelter and sanctuary and I entered it gratefully. I left the pram outside, praying no-one would steal it. I took Lily inside with me.

I walked through the soaring vault of the aisle and felt comforted. At the altar a priest was kneeling in prayer. I sat down in a pew and watched him, wondering if faith could offer a way of life that hurt a little less than the one I had dreamed up. It hadn't served me so well after all. He got up and walked down the aisle towards me. He had a soft, wrinkled face that was covered in down, like an old peach. He looked kindly enough. I asked him if I could talk to him. He replied, "certainly, my child. Come with me." I followed him out of the church and into the vestry.

It was oddly Spartan for such a grand church. Just a whitewashed room with a table, four chairs and toppling piles of rather battered hymn books. The only adornment was a carved wooden crucifix. Christ on the cross.

He asked me how he could help me. I told him the whole story, rationalising he could hardly help if he didn't know the truth. I don't know what I expected. Some kind of romanticised Mary Magdalene scenario of the "I forgive your sins and I will help you" variety, I imagine. I was certainly desperate for solace. So, as he arranged the folds of his surplice neatly around his highly polished shoes, I blurted out the wretched milestones of my life. Rikh, my toxic love for Abdi and the child one parent did not want and the other could not provide for. I told the truth and did not gloss over anything. Relieved to have an adult listener at last, I did not pause to notice his response. I sailed on, failing to see the look of shock in the watery blue eyes and the mouth puckered in distaste. The increasingly icy stare.

In the end, my flood of narrative became a trickle and then dried up There was a long silence. He closed his eyes and inhaled deeply. Then he asked me how old I was.

I told him. He told me that I was still young, and that if I truly repented my life of sin and wickedness, here with a barely suppressed shudder, God, in his infinite mercy, would forgive me.

I had been hoping for more tangible help.

He went on. He told me that congress between the races was a sin that leads only to misery and vice. He advised me to search my heart and pray. He went on like this for what seemed like hours, churning out his prejudice like an organ grinder with a worn out song.

I asked him at one point what I should do. He didn't hesitate. Marry again, he said. Only this time, with your own kind. Embrace righteousness, he said, make a new life.

I asked what he thought I should do with Lily, the inconvenient remnant of the old one.

He waved his hand vaguely, unwilling to consider such a trifle. There are institutions, he said. I looked at him in horror, orphanages, he went on, some even run by the church. Now at last he looked at me and delivered the coup de grace, "for East is East," he intoned mournfully. I laughed aloud. I had begged for help and he had given me Kipling. Yolanda would have howled.

I took my child and walked out. Lily was still fast asleep. I walked out of that church that day and I have never entered another. I decided to stick with sin. That was the second time God had let me down. I would not bother Him again.

It was soon after that that she paid me a visit. That morning I was rushing to get Lily bathed, dressed and out through the lobby before anyone could intercept us and demand our plans for departure. After sleepless nights and circular, panic driven thinking, I had come up with nothing, veering between the comfort and defeat of going home to Mother and starting a brave new life somewhere else. I much preferred the latter, but had no idea how either could be achieved on my current bank balance. The only way I could eat now was to put everything on a tab I had no means of settling. I was at my wits end and dog tired. I spilled most of Lily's bath water on the floor and rushed her feed so that she was sick all down my shoulder. I didn't have time to change, so I dabbed at my dress with a flannel and hoped it wouldn't smell. In the middle of all this, the telephone rang. I swore, damning Messrs Henriques and de Sousa to the hell fire they believed in.

A male voice on the other end informed me that the *Begum* was waiting to see me. I hadn't a clue who he was. I knew who she was, but I was still completely at a loss. I had

had no contact with her since our only meeting when she had shown me the door. What did she want with me now? Why had Abdi not come?

I told her flunky to give me ten minutes and said I would meet her in the lobby. He practically snorted. A hotel lobby, he sniffed, making it sound like the gutter, was not suitable. The visit was of a personal nature, he said. I felt impatient and cross. Life was already unbearable. I couldn't see the purpose of this, except to cause me more pain. I was about to say that she and her son had had their fun. I did not want to be kicked around the block by Abdi's Mama again. I was about to say so when I remembered that as an elderly, high ranking Muslim woman, she probably spent most of her life in purdah. A public place was not an option for her, which was why in all my junketing around Lahore with Abdi, I had never laid eyes on her.

Sighing and with ill grace, I told him to give me ten minutes and then send her up to my room. He said he would and put the phone down. Then I tore round the room like a dervish, chucking things into cupboards and under the bed and moping up the spilt water.

I dragged a comb through my hair, straightened my creased and soiled dress and began to put a clean dress on Lily. She wasn't thrilled. She liked to play and take her time. She didn't like to rush. So she protested and grizzled as I thrust her arms into the little frock and buttoned it up the back. Then I held her. Just for a few minutes to soothe her. The *Begum* could wait. She wouldn't get much sense out of me if Lily was in full cry. I rocked her gently and she stopped struggling and kicking and sighed in relief. Then her eyes glazed over and she began to doze. She was a really good baby.

Then a brisk knock at the door. With Lily still in my arms, I opened it. For a moment she just stood there. Stern and implacable, she looked barely human. Swathed in layers of white silk and chiffon, with her veil drawn across her face, she seemed to me like a creature from a Gothic novel. Incorporeal and silent, wraithlike. I asked her to come in, then whipped a pile of clean nappies off the only chair and gestured for her to sit. I put Lily back in her crib. She stirred, but did not grumble.

The *Begum* uncovered her face and began to speak. Her manner was stiff, her voice clipped, but her eyes revealed another story. This woman was in turmoil.

"You cannot keep my grand-daughter here." She had a nerve. The barefaced cheek of it made me rude.

"You've changed your tune. Suddenly she's your grand-daughter?"

"I have seen her. I have no doubt who she is."

So, she was the veiled woman at the hospital. I knew Eva Maria must have told Abdi because of the flowers. He had gone running straight to Mummy. Suddenly, I felt afraid.

"She is very like him."

There was a long silence during which I could feel the sweat running down my back.

"If you let me take her, I can give her everything you cannot. Father, family and her rightful future."

Fear and hate made my chest so tight I could hardly breathe.

"I can give her a proper education. My son has told me you are an educated woman."

A blow on a wound that never healed. Why could he not have come himself?

"I will make her my heir. The fortune I inherited remains at my disposal. I will see you do not want for money."

"She's not for sale."

"You cannot keep her safe. Lahore is not for woman and children now. It will be a battleground. I can take her to my house in Murree. She will be safe there."

I glared at her, loathing her for everything she could give my child that I could not. Family, a future, and above all, a place of safety. She had stuck the knife in all right. Now she twisted it.

"Can you give her any of these? What can you give her?"

"My love."

She looked down at that.

"She will always have that."

"Then you would let me see her?" Could that work?

She shook her head. Now her voice was very soft. "No. Not at first. That would only confuse her when you were there and distress her when you were not." She smiled a gentle, bleak smile. "But later, when she is older and can understand, I will send for you. I give you my word."

I believed her. I wept. I could not cope. We had no future, but the enormity of giving her up was a nightmare I shrank from. I kept shaking my head, blinded with tears. I felt like a beaten animal. A hand was laid on my head, so fleeting and tentative, I wasn't sure it was there.

"Leave me alone."

She nodded. "I will hear from you."

I nodded and almost without sound, she left. Leaving Lily and I, alone together.

The next day, Mr Henriques came to see me. He glanced around the room, a look of disgust on his face at the plethora of baby 'kit' all around him. I had begun to supplement Lily's feeds with the bottle. She didn't approve but dealt with it well, drinking it down whilst looking at me reproachfully. But it all made for a lot more clutter. I hadn't expected anyone and the place was an absolute tip. He even had to step over a small pile of dirty clothes on the floor. He said he hoped our plans for removal were now in place. Then he said he had to warn me as well as the other guests, making it sound like a special favour in our case, that a Hindu mob was marching towards the old town, looting and burning as they went, chanting "Blood for blood." He said it was not safe to go out today. I looked at him in horror. The whirlwind had arrived. The beautiful, cosmopolitan city that Abdi had brought me to was vanishing, swept away by a vortex of hate. Sikhs, Hindus and Muslims, who had lived in this city in tolerance and harmony for generations, were now at each other's' throats, baying for blood.

All that day I held her close. During the night, I took her into bed with me.

A week later I gave her up. I knew that with Abdi's family she had a future and with me, only a past. A past that would turn her into a pariah, as I had been.

That morning she was on good form. Rolling over on her own as she lay on the bed, kicking her legs and burbling away. She was very proud of this rolling over business. I was terrified by it, afraid she would roll right off the bed, but each time she managed it, frowning slightly with her tongue sticking out a bit as if she were solving a particularly tricky problem, she would reward me with a triumphant, gummy grin. I played with her and held her tight, wanting to imprint myself on her, to show her that I would always be part of her as she was part of me. That wherever we were that would never change.

The *Begum* herself came to collect her. She arrived at the appointed time, attended by her bearer. I gave her a small bag with Lily's things in. I had dressed her in Vicky's dress and wrapped her in Imran's shawl. She looked very smart, with her still damp curls, as I handed her over to her grandmother. Unusually, she didn't protest, just looked at me as if wondering what I was doing. I kissed her cheek. Then she was gone.

It was Divali. The festival of lights that year was the

darkest time for me. I never told my mother. Neither of Lily's birth nor my abandonment of her. I was too ashamed. Shame kept me silent. Shame that, faced with the same Rubicon as she, I had funked it. She had risen to adversity with love and courage and I had failed. Failed to find a way to keep my child. Even dumb animals do better.

Loss would hit me later. For now, the shame was without limit. Before I had felt I was worthless. Now I knew I was.

That evening, Imran called for me. Eva Maria must have told him. She knew everything about everybody in this town.

He found me, dumb with despair, staring at the walls of my room, surrounded by what was left of Lily's things. The crib she was growing out of, the pram in the hall that had been so objected to, a few soiled clothes, there wasn't much. Imran took me to Vicky's.

That night she and Feroz ministered to me with infinite kindness. I doubt they approved of me, but they would never condemn. He tucked me up in his huge leather armchair, as gently and firmly as if I were an invalid, wrapping a cashmere rug around me. Was I shivering? Perhaps. I don't know.

Vicky brought me drinks. First hot, then cold, and food I could not eat. I could not speak or swallow. She tended to me as if I were her child, trying to coax me to take something. I could not respond. All I could think of was the child I had abandoned. My body ached for her. The feel of her mouth as she tugged greedily at my breast, the touch of her tiny hands, so like my own, with their surprisingly firm grip. The smell of her skin. I wondered where she was and who she was with. Would they comfort and hold her? I was tormented by the knowledge that she would feel frightened and lost. If she cried, would she cry alone? I was the only comfort she had ever known.

At last, Vicky just held me. I said that I had delivered Lily up to strangers. She said she knew I had only done what was best for her. I told her it was all wrong. I was all wrong.

She held me for a long time and then went over to the piano and began to play. It was dark by then, the sudden blanket darkness of the East. With a full moon and a few bright stars.

Imran and Feroz were standing by the window. At one point Feroz said to me.

"Come. You should see, Juanita. This is what history looks like."

I walked over to the window and looked out. The old city was in flames.

He said gently, "It's war. This is what you have protected your child from. Many will die before this is over."

I stayed with them that night. The next morning I went to Eva Maria's. She arranged for my things to be brought from the Braganza. I never went back there.

Chapter Eighteen

I felt odd at Eva Maria's. I wasn't sure if she was my greatest friend or my bitterest enemy. I knew she had told Abdi both of Lily's birth and our struggle to survive. She would have taken a pragmatic view of that: whether he "stumped up" and supported us or took her away, either would have seemed a good outcome to her. She thought I was mad not to take the *Begum's* money. After Lily left it was offered again, but I wanted no part in that. I tried to explain to Eva Maria that I would not sell my child, but she didn't understand. She just thought it was stupid. To her, everything was for sale. But whatever her motives and feelings were, she took me in, housed me in a large and comfortable room at the back of her bungalow, away from the main part, and let me begin to absorb what I had done.

For the first few days I was overwhelmed by loss. My mind a kaleidoscope of Lily—her smiles, her gurgling laughter, her frowns and cries. The drying milk in my breasts made them feel like blocks of wood, burning and painful, a reminder of when we had been one, a time when only she and I seemed to exist. Since they had put her on my tummy with her cord still attached and she had opened her great dark eyes, looking at me with that curious, unblinking stare, we had lived only for each other. I had carried her in my body and after she had left it, in my arms. In her short life, we had never been apart. If I was lost without her, how could she survive without me? Would she know a depth of misery and fear no less profound because she could not articulate it? Would they be cross with her if she cried?

These thoughts racked my waking hours. Then came the dawning realisation that the man I had loved so intensely and unwisely had decided that the only way he would care for our child was to take her from me and cut me out of her life. At last, I had to face the truth. Abdi had hurt me in every way he could. He had thrown away my love and he had stolen my child. I could feel hatred rising in me. If it would not have hurt Lily, I could happily have cut his throat and watched him die.

I did not cry at first. But when I did, I cried for a long time. Eva Maria let me go through this Calvary alone. She saw it as a rite of passage. She came to see me, to check that I had regular food and drink, she sat with me but did not try to talk to me. She said, "There is nothing I can do to get you through this. You will either sink or swim," and on that Darwinian note she left me. I thought she must have been through this herself, or something very similar. She had never hinted at any living child, but then she never would. She could have had seven and you would never know. Had she been through the same process herself? Or were her abortions so late and the babies within her so developed that their induced deaths haunted her?

She left me to wallow for three days. Then on the evening of the fourth, she came into my room, practically threw me into the shower, washed, set and dried my hair and put clothes out for me on the bed. I dressed, she put my make up on and fixed my hair.

She could make me look human, but my eyes were raw with tears and my face behind its' painted mask, ached. She poured whisky down my throat and took me out.

All the usual suspects were assembled in the lounge of Faletti's. Minus Imran and Vicky. Ethel waved at me from across the room. I turned my head away. I didn't want to know her now.

Eva Maria sat me next to a man called Philip Waldron, ICS I think. He ordered drinks and tried to talk to me. I listened, making cursory replies, trying to wash away the lump in my throat with whisky and failing. I stared into the distance, not really there at all. I focused on the doorway and wished I could get out through it.

As I was staring at the door, Lal walked in. I had not seen him for years. Not since he had stayed at the Waldorf in London at the beginning of the War. We had had a brief but intense affair and then he had gone to Scotland to join his squadron. He was in the RAF, too. I had written to him, but he had never replied.

He saw me, hesitated, then walked on to join his own party of friends. I thought he doesn't even want to know me now and who could blame him? If I had changed as much on the outside as I had within, I must be unrecognisable.

I turned back to Philip and attempted some degree of conversation. Then I noticed Lal looking at me. I smiled sadly at him. He seemed like a ghost from the past, a reminder of who I was. He was very elegant in his beautifully tailored evening dress. Tall and slender, he always did make other men look like cattle. He shook his head, grinned and came over. He held out his hand.

"Come on. Let's go." I clutched his hand like a drowning man and scrambled to my feet. Muttering a cursory apology to Philip, we left.

He walked across to his car and got in. I smiled. A long, low sports model. Classy and fast, just like him. He leaned across and opened the passenger door. I got in.

"What the hell happened to you?" He turned the key in the ignition and drove off without waiting for an answer.

"Oh, you know... Life," I replied attempting a flippancy which fell flat on its face. "You? Still living in palaces?"

"Not always. You?"

"Hardly living at all." There. In almost no time I had crumbled. He glanced at me and his face was so full of warmth and sympathy, that tearfully, accompanied by sobs and hiccups because I had had a lot of whisky and it had gone straight to my head, I told him everything.

He stopped the car and listened. It all came flooding out—the war, Yolanda's death, leaving Mother, the breakup with Rikh, Abdi and how he had rejected me, my adventures with Eva Maria—the whole sorry tale. And then Lily—how I had failed her utterly and given her away. I howled for the child I had abandoned. He handed me his handkerchief.

"Blow your nose. Because you do look a bit awful like that." I did so.

"God, you've been a fool." There was no denying that. Then his whole stance softened and he put his arm round me. "But who isn't? Hell, you've been in the wars..." He lit us a cigarette and we shared it. I felt safe in the shelter of his arms.

Lal did not gush and he did not judge. He listened. We talked for a long time. I poured out all my pain in a flood of alcohol and tears. At the end of it, I turned to face him.

"I had all these big ideas, but I've failed everyone. I've hurt those who were stupid enough to love me and clung to those who didn't love me at all. I'm an idiot and a bastard," I finished with the emphasis of the truly drunk.

"That's quite a confession." He turned to me and gently pushed a lock of hair out of my eyes.

"Well. My life hasn't exactly been a series of triumphs, either. In fact, since we last met, it's been one cock-up after another."

For the first time since Lily left, I smiled. A real smile, not a clown like grimace. Just like before, when we talked there was an ease, an honesty, an instant depth I have never felt with any other. We resumed where we had left off and despite everything that had happened to both of us, there was no awkward beginning and no fear of an end.

Then he told me about his life—his time in the air force, the crash that had broken his spine, all his own fault, he said and the co-pilot had been killed, the year he had spent in the military hospital in Poona, learning to walk again.

Lal made light of his appalling injury, but I wondered if that was what had dented his prior assurance. He was doubtful now. A year is a long time to spend in hospital, he said, plenty of time to think.

"Then I married. That was a complete fiasco," he said. "We were rushed into it. They wanted me to have an heir before I killed myself and she was nineteen."

I must have looked blank because he went on, "That's quite long in the tooth for a Punjabi princess." He stared into the darkness and his face took on harsh, bitter lines that were not there before.

"We were suitable in title only."

"Oh dear."

"Recipe for disaster. Two spoilt brats longing to break free. Instead, we were like a pair of convicts chained together."

"The ball and chain..."

"Precisely. They married us off as soon as I got back

from Poona. Paired off like pedigree dogs. Money, land and mountains of gold changed hands. The festivities went on for a month. Everyone was ecstatic. All we had to do was live together."

"How did that go?"

He shrugged. "It was all right at first. We sort of circled round each other politely for a while. We didn't know each other from Adam. I only met her twice before the wedding."

He looked bleak.

"We did our duty. Then we got to know each other. It was ghastly."

I had to laugh. "It can't have been that ghastly."

"You'd be surprised." Not really.

"But you had a child."

"We did. And the wonder of that carried us along for a bit. Then it all fell apart."

"Why?"

"We had no real reason to be together. Duty, rank, money, doesn't exactly add up to a marriage, does it? Not my idea of one, anyway."

Didn't I understand that? I said nothing. It was my turn to listen.

"In the end we hated each other. I irritated her beyond belief and she appalled me. She was thick as a plank and a bit nasty, if you want the truth. Treated the servants like dirt. Always a bad sign."

He sighed heavily. "By the time the boy was two,

jumping out of the window began to look like a good idea."

"Poor Lal."

"Yes. Then she shot me."

"What?"

"With my own gun. Good job she was a rotten shot or she'd have killed me."

Now I was shocked. "What happened?"

"I ducked and she missed. Well, she winged me. Caught my shoulder."

"God! Why did she do that?"

"She accused me of running round with other women."

"Were you?"

"Yes." He paused. "After that, neither of us were very keen on close proximity. So she took her money and my child and went back to her family."

He faltered here. "He's a lovely little chap. I miss him. But not her."

He always laced any account of his feelings with an almost flippant sarcasm, but it was clear to me that whatever he had done to provoke it, he had been very hurt.

He looked at me wearily. "You and me—two of a kind?"

He went on, "One rogue seeks another. Miss Batt always said that."

I remembered his great love for Miss Batt, his British nanny. He had spoken of her often in London, quoting her clichéd maxims always, as if he hoped her well worn wisdom would rescue him now as no doubt it had in the past.

"She was your guiding star, Miss Batt, wasn't she?"

"Yes. I suppose she was."

"Yolanda was mine."

"I remember her. At the Waldorf. Stunning girl. Face like a Madonna and mind like Albert Einstein."

She was and it was an immense comfort to me that he had not only known her, but also seen what she was. We sat in companionable silence for a long time. Dawn was breaking when he drove me back to Eva Maria's.

I have often marvelled at the random good fortune of our meeting again and wondered what my life would have been had Lal not walked into Faletti's that night. It was not a given that we should meet again at all. It was actually quite unlikely. War had taken him away from me in London and kept him away from me in Lahore. For years we were never in the same place at the same time. And, even when we were, we did not move in the same circles. He knew Imran by sight, they belonged to the same clubs, but they were never friends. Lal was never part of the pro-Independence intelligentsia. In fact, he rather despised it. We met again by chance. I think they call it serendipity.

I saw him almost every day after that. He would collect me in his car and take me away. We mostly avoided the centre of town and the places I had frequented with Abdi and Eva Maria. Often he took me out of Lahore altogether, driving for miles out into the countryside. He showed me his India—the tiny villages, the sunlit fields of rich farmland, the wide rivers of the Punjab. Although I could quarrel with his noblesse oblige attitude, I could not fault his concern. He wanted 'his villagers' as he called it to be 'dragged into the twentieth-century.' He wanted them to have wells, clean water and irrigation systems to protect them against drought and flood.

His India was not Gandhi's dream of a pastoral idyll, "Everyone living together in an ashram" as he rather dismissively put it, but he did want a better life for those he was responsible for and he had a fair idea of how to get it.

Our relationship was forged during those drives. As India revealed herself to me, so we talked at great length or hardly at all. We were wary of involvement and each other and terrified of feeling even a fraction of what we had felt before. Our lives had taught us to distrust our feelings and our senses. He would always hide the depth of his emotions under a veil of sardonic humour, but underneath he was almost as bruised and hurting as I was. He felt the loss of his son keenly.

"I've been cut off completely. A blank cheque—that's all I am to her—and she'll make damn sure that's all I am to him too. A blank cheque with a title. As far as she's concerned, my only use to him is as a corpse."

When he said this his face assumed harsh, bitter lines. He carried a picture of his son in his wallet. He looked at it often. But only when he thought he was alone. Who could understand his loss and shame better than I?

On the days that we did not go into the country he took me a little outside town to the Shalimar Gardens. I had not seen them before. They were a revelation and a delight. An enclosed garden of tall trees, fountains and terraces, dotted with pavilions of delicately carved marble, inlaid with *petra dura*, it had been conceived as a garden of paradise. The Moghuls believed paradise was a garden and in this lovely place, they came very close to it. The gentle symmetry of arches and colonnades, of pools and flowers, imposed calm. It was a place of restoration. We both loved it and we went there often.

Eva Maria was not thrilled by my constant absence, but to her undying credit, she let me be. I don't think she approved of Lal, whether because he brought her no profit or because she distrusted any association with the opposite sex that was not based on money, I don't know. I didn't think of her much at that time.

Lal and I did not make love for some time. We embraced often, but more as friends than lovers. After a while, I wondered why he did not desire me. He had been such an ardent lover in the past. I felt torn—I shrank from the prospect of physical intimacy, but I feared the lack of it, seeing it as a precursor to rejection.

In the end I said, "You don't want me anymore, do you?"

He looked at me in genuine surprise, "God, yes. But it's become tainted for you."

It had. It was now a tangle of pain, loss and profit—all inextricably linked.

"So, we will wait and see." And so we did. For a long time.

After about a month, I told him I wanted to leave Eva Maria's. That being there, despite her kindness, only took me back into the past. To say nothing of the constant terror that I would see Abdi, or someone who knew him far too well. That was my idea of hell now. I told Lal that I wanted a job. To stand on my own two feet. To find a place of my own.

"Good." he said. Nothing more.

The next time I saw him he told me he had found me a place for the time being. It was a hotel, the Imperial. Not quite as grand and stylish as Faletti's or the Braganza, in fact, it was a bit sedate, favoured by the landed gentry of the Punjab, but no less comfortable for that. I said I had a little money, but not much. He said I should pay what I could and he would make up the difference until I was back on my feet. He made it sound only a matter of time. His confidence in me was infectious. Although I looked for Lily everywhere I went, I no longer cried for her every night.

I ignored Christmas that year. Although I didn't imagine that a Christian festival would be celebrated in the *Begum's* household, I couldn't bear to think of Lily spending her first Christmas without me. Christmas trees and lights were all over Lahore, even that year, because India was still

British—just—and Lahorians loved a party. So I hoped that Abdi with his childish love of any festivities, would spoil her a little.

One evening as we drove down the Mall, I told Lal that I would have loved to see Lily's face when she saw her first Christmas tree, all lit up with decorations and the star. To my surprise, he said the last time they were together he had made a Christmas stocking for his son, filled with sweets and toys, as Miss Batt had always done for him and his brother and sister. He said his wife had disapproved vociferously, but he hadn't cared, his reward had been the child's delight as he unwrapped his presents.

I asked him why he never referred to his son by name. He said it was less painful, somehow. A generalised term like son or child avoided the trigger of memory. I said Lily had always been Lily to me. Herself. Utterly unique. He nodded, then said very quietly, "his name is Karam. It means generous of spirit—which is what I wish for him."

We held hands then and turned our backs on Christmas, thinking of our lost children. On Christmas Day we took a picnic and headed out of the city, shunning all parties and dinners, and walked for miles through fields of early growing wheat, feeling the sun on our backs and staring at the distant horizon. Alone together in the vastness of India, we managed to avoid the festive season. We stayed away for just over a week, staying in the government guest houses that then dotted the landscape. They were basic but clean, with a minimum of comfort.

We didn't care. Lal showed me his farms and villages. Tiny hamlets, where the villagers greeted us with garlands and touched Lal's feet in obeisance. I could not approve of that. But I remember the bright colours of the women's saris, the children playing in the dust and the smoke rising from the cooking fires in the early evening. The pale green sea of field after field of early wheat blowing gently in the wind.

In January, Imran came to see me at the Imperial. He looked grave. We sat with Lal in a quiet corner of the lounge. Imran got straight to the point. He told us that things in the city were bad and about to become much worse.

The Governor of the Punjab, appalled by the apparently incontrollable rise of armed militias, had declared both Muslim and Hindu organisations illegal. He had then arrested their leaders and raided their headquarters. It was a belated and flat-footed gesture, Imran said. Everyone who could lead was now in jail. Even Feroz. The situation was untenable, he said.

"Too much too late," commented Lal. Imran agreed and went on to say that all public meetings and gatherings had been banned. When news of these measures spread throughout the city, everyone ignored the ban and the marches and demonstrations increased.

Lal said that Lahore was becoming a madhouse.

"You should consider leaving. Both of you." I knew how

much it hurt Imran to say that. It underlined the failure of everything he had worked and hoped for.

I said that I would never leave Lahore while Lily was still here. At that Imran looked awkward. I wondered if he knew something I did not. But before I could ask him, he moved the conversation away from me, asking Lal how the current situation would affect him. Lal admitted it would be a disaster, as his ancestral home and lands would be in India, and those he could never leave, he declared categorically, but the vast proportion of his wealth, in terms of farmland, properties and money, etc, would rest in Pakistan. Without this, he feared he would become a paper tiger, with palace and title but none of the wherewithal to maintain it.

They discussed their fears for the Punjab. Lal pointed out that the division that was provisionally proposed, was insanity, as it would run from north to south and all the roads, railways lines and irrigation canals that had been the foundation of the area's prosperity, ran from east to west. He stated that fifteen million Hindus, sixteen million Muslims and five million Sikhs were all inextricably interspersed throughout the eighteen thousand towns and villages of the province and that to separate them would be an impossible and abhorrent task. One he doubted could be achieved without huge bloodshed, as none of them would be torn away from their homes and land "without a fight."

Imran nodded, suddenly looking old and tired. His hair

now grey, his face set in lines of resignation and despair, he had aged ten years in the three that I had known him.

He stated that a similar situation existed in Bihar. The conversation ended in an uneasy silence. We agreed to skip lunch. No-one had the stomach for it. Imran left. A lonely and disillusioned figure. At one point he looked at me and paraphrased Yeats. "Those I fight I do not hate and those I guard I do not love."

I knew what that meant. He had made his choice. Despite his hatred for the League's methods and his real distrust of Jinnah, Imran would never leave Lahore. He would throw in his lot with Pakistan. Lines were being drawn in the sand and we would be separated by them. Lal understood. As we watched Imran leave, he said, "we will lose the best like him and be stuck with the worst," he said. I didn't know about that, but I did know that we would be with India and that so much that was part of us would be left behind in Pakistan.

Later we heard that the Governor had released the leaders who were in jail. Imprisoning them had done no good at all. In fact, it had made things worse.

In February we watched from the broad windows of Imran's apartment as a massive Muslim League procession marched into the centre of Lahore. His apartment building now had an armed guard at the door. The crowd was in an ugly mood. Bricks had been thrown and one of them killed. All shops and businesses were shut and the windows boarded up.

At first all we could hear was an ominous quiet, followed by the muffled, shuffling sound of thousands of marching feet and then, as they grew closer, the roar of the crowd. "*Pakistan zindabad*", Long live Pakistan, followed by "*Hindustan Murdabad*", Death to India.

We watched the seemingly endless column file past. When they reached the High Court, they ransacked it, tearing down the Union Jack and raising the flag of the Muslim League. The police arrived far too late and, as the terrified barristers and judges fled the building, they were greeted with a barrage of tear gas. Lal said if it wasn't so awful, it was almost comic.

In response to this, the Sikhs, on orders from their leader Tara Singh, formed small fighting units called *jathas*. The Sikhs are a proud and martial people. They had conquered the Punjab and even held Afghanistan, which no-one since, not even the British, had been able to do. Lal was very proud of this. Tens of thousands of Sikhs, like him, had volunteered and served in the War. Lal said that most of them had returned with their uniforms and weapons. He said if Tara Singh wanted an army, he wouldn't have to go far to find one.

It didn't take long for Lal's fears to become reality. Riots spread throughout the Punjab—in Ludhiana, Rawalpindi, Multan and Amritsar. Villages and towns burned, many were killed and the police seemed powerless to stop it. The army had not hesitated to use full force in defence of the Raj, but now in the face of inter-communal violence, looked away and did too little too late. The British were finished in India and they could not wait to leave.

So a spark became a flame which became a conflagration. It spread across that infinite and beautiful land, from hill to plain, from ocean to desert, consuming everything that lay in its path.

Chapter Nineteen

A few days after Lal went away for a while. He went back to his palace from time to time, never for very long, but just to see that all was well there. I stayed very quietly when he was gone, rarely venturing forth. Even the Imperial was guarded now.

Frankly, I was not so much afraid of the rioters as of seeing Abdi. I felt only pain and disgust at the thought of him now. And as my disgust of him was largely disgust of myself it was an uncomfortable feeling, and one which, with my usual heroism, I avoided. So I planned a few days of reading and quiet walks. I was given a rude awakening on that score. When I left the hotel early one morning, I was stopped by an armed security guard. He asked me where I was going. Only for a stroll, I replied. He looked grave and said, "Strolling no longer safe, Memsahib." I said that surely the vicinity of the hotel was all right. He said, "Gangs are marauding. With knives." I smiled at his syntax.

"It has become necessary to check all comings and goings for safety of bona fide guests," he announced importantly. "Hotel is now guarded front and rear."

He said if I still wanted to walk he would get one of his men to accompany me. And so we set off down the road, me and my unlikely shadow, a burly Sikh in a policeman's uniform. The absurdity of it made me smile. It reminded me of London and the India League when walking to the pub on the corner with Krishna Menon, we would be tailed by a miserable looking member of the Metropolitan police. He always looked miserable because he was always wet. It rained a lot that year.

We took a sedate stroll around the block and then returned to the Imperial. I don't think Dolber, my guard, was very keen on walking. He wasn't very keen on talking either so it wasn't very enlivening. But perhaps he had troubles of his own to concern him.

The smile was certainly wiped off my face when Lal returned. He told me it had taken him hours to get out of Lahore. The inner road was closed off because of rioting and the Grand Trunk Road was choked with refugees, heading west. Thousands of Hindus and Sikhs, he said, with bullock carts piled high with their possessions. He had seen an old man clinging to the back of one of these overladen carts like a bunched up despairing monkey, and a naked baby swaying precariously, perched on top of a sack of rice on the back of an emaciated bullock, while his mother trudged wearily alongside. The air was thick with smoke, he said, they are burning the crops in the fields to drive people out.

His homecoming to Lahore was even worse. As he had walked down the broad, leafy street towards his home, he noticed that crescent moons had been painted on the exterior walls of some of the houses. He said that was when he began to feel afraid. Some of his neighbours' houses were burnt out. Blackened shells were all that remained of once palatial homes. Tennis courts and swimming pools had been vandalised. The whole area was deserted and an uneasy quiet reigned. When he reached his house he saw that *goondas* had smashed in the front door. The trunks that had been stacked in the hall, padlocked and corded, carefully packed with silver, carpets and paintings, were broken into and the contents stolen or destroyed. The little tables inlaid with silver and sandalwood, centuries old, were reduced to matchsticks. Even the trunk that contained his clothes and personal effects—photographs, letters, his personal papers—had been ransacked. Though he did find a rather nice pair of Savile Row trousers in a crumpled heap by the back wall, he said wryly. I hugged him in sympathy. He pulled away.

"It's much worse than that."

"What happened?"

Haltingly, he told me that two of the servants had volunteered to stay behind. Lal had sent the others to the

Fort some weeks before. The *Chokidar*, who had guarded the property from his hut by the gate for as long as Lal could remember, had tried to defend the house and been stabbed. He died in the garden that was his home. Lal had found him there. Of the other man, there was no sign.

"I knew him all my life. He was an old man. He shouldn't have died like that. I should have made him leave." He walked over to the window and looked out, his voice choked with tears.

"I hope to God the other one got away." Then he noticed the guard at the rear of the hotel.

"I hate this town. If you're lucky it's a prison, if you're not, it's hell on earth." As we looked at the now permanent pall of black smoke rising over the old city, I could see what he meant.

Then he looked back at me. "We have to get out of here. Find out where Lily is. If they haven't taken her to a safe place, we will."

He was making me remember why I had loved him so much. Without fuss or condition, those he loved he looked after.

I rang Eva Maria. If anyone knew of Lily and Abdi's whereabouts it would be her. She told me she too was preparing to leave. She said many others already had. She was surprised I was still in Lahore. She was going to Simla with Derek. All in a flat, matter of fact tone. She said that he had become a big pal of hers. She went on to say, "Funny chap, your doctor friend. Not quite what he seems, is he?" No, indeed. Then, with the rough London edge that always broke through and betrayed her in rare moments of emotion, she asked if I wanted to go with her. If so I should get my skates on and get over to her place toot sweet, she said. She had an awful French accent for someone who claimed to be Belgian. She said she didn't know about Lily, but she would find out.

As ever, she was as good as her word. She rang back about an hour later. A very anxious hour in which I paced the hotel room like a caged animal and Lal sat, waiting with me. I was torn, longing for Lily to be safe and far from all danger, but guiltily hoping she was still in Lahore so we could take her.

Then Eva Maria rang and said that Lily was safe and sound with the *Begum* in her house in Murree and that she had been for some weeks. She said, "The child is apparently well and happy."

I prayed to God she was right. There was now nothing to bind me to Lahore. Lal was impatient to leave. The next day, he came and went, seeing people he knew, pulling strings. In the end he managed to get us a place in a British army convoy headed for the military base at Dehra Dun, a hill station in the foothills of the Himalayas. There was an elite army base there—it sounded like a sort of Indian Aldershot. We would be safe there, he said. It was no longer safe for us to drive alone. People had been killed on those roads. He said even with the convoy, he would be armed. He had a revolver in the glove box of his car, he said, just in case. Then he asked me if I could shoot. Of course not, I replied. Thank heaven for small mercies, he said, grinning. For a brief moment, the old Lal was back.

I packed and we left the next morning at dawn. As we left, I looked back at that once beautiful city and wept for all that I had found and lost there.

About fifteen miles out of town, we joined the convoy. Once again, I was travelling under the aegis of the British Armed Forces. It had a familiar oddness to it. *Deja vu*, only this time by land not sea. So we fell in, taking our place in a long line of military trucks and jeeps, armoured cars and lorries bristling with guns. There were a few private cars other than us in the convoy, but not many. A Raja and his family who had equipped and funded a regiment during the War and as such was entitled to the honorary rank of their commanding officer. That apparently meant that he could "apply for the protection of Her Majesty's something or other" Lal said. He then said sheepishly that, his air force service apart and he had ended up a Squadron Leader, he was also an honorary Brigadier, for the same reason. We laughed like drains over that one. Brigadier Blimp, I used to call him when he resorted to bossiness, born to command. He took it very well.

Despite the circumstances, slowly and tentatively we were beginning to laugh again. After Lily went, I had thought I would never laugh again. I didn't want to. Tears seemed more appropriate for the mess I had made of my life and the harm I had inflicted on others. But it was easy to laugh with Lal. We were amused by the same things. He had a profound sense of the absurd but his wit, although trenchant, was never spiteful. There was no malice in him; it was just not in his nature. As I watched him, cool and confident, take our place in the line, I felt safe. The trembling wretch in my heart was still when I was with him.

Chapter Twenty

It was a slow and ponderous journey. We left Lahore at seven in the morning and arrived in Dehra Dun after ten that night. Long after dark, we finally drove into the base, leaving most of the convoy behind, and carried on down a long, tree-lined avenue to the club. It looked imposing and very large, with a grand stone portico and ivy clad walls. A sort of Palladian refuge. Lal had arranged for us to stay there. He was greeted effusively by Mr Bedi, the Club Secretary, a plump, compact, little man suave in black jacket and pin striped trousers, whose neat black hair, glued to his head with Brylcreem, gave him the air of a painted doll. He looked a bit like the General Manager at the Waldorf. But without the roving hands, I hoped.

Lal signed the register and we went upstairs, tired and not very clean. We had supper in our rooms and soon fell asleep.

The next morning I was awoken by the sunlight. Not the

harsh, unforgiving light of the plains, but a soft, diffuse glow. I looked out of our window and saw the distant blue line of the Himalayas. The landscape had a quiet, timeless grandeur. I looked down and saw long shadows on the grass. Legions of men were silently tending the lawn. Sweeping up the fallen leaves, cutting, trimming, creating patches of bright vivid colour—the pink and purple of bougainvillea and petunia—among the lush green grass. The brow of a gentle hill and the shade of tall trees.

Lal woke and we went down to breakfast. The club was a gracious and spacious place. Long corridors lead to oak panelled rooms with honour boards and silver trophies, quiet lounges and a library, an imposing dining room and an even grander ballroom. With a sprung floor, said Mr Bedi with pride. We had our breakfast on the deep, shady verandah overlooking the gardens. Despite the sun, it was chilly in the early morning, with a heavy dew. I had to go back to the room for a cardigan.

The club, like others, had been created to form a bastion of British colonial life—one of privilege and strictly kept rules. A place where the Raj could find repose under an alien sky. But the War had changed everything. Now the club's clientèle, formerly so predictable, was a motley bunch. Among the old guard, the retired majors and their desiccated wives, were sprinkled a goodly shower of a more cosmopolitan crew. Those, like me, who were not the backbone of the Raj, but oddballs seeking a place of safety. We were to be granted sanctuary. But only if we were Europeans: unaccompanied women mainly. Otherwise the old rules or prejudices—applied—Officers in the Armed Forces, senior ICS, Indian princes with officer rank only. If you didn't fit into any of that, your fate was not their business. You could be raped, murdered and left to die in a ditch for all they cared.

After we had finished breakfast, Lal's great friend joined us for coffee. A smiling, red faced man, running to fat, he introduced himself to me as "James Wilkinson, Colonel retired, Sandhurst Returned." I hadn't a clue what that meant, but he evidently felt it was a complete life history. I later discovered it actually was. He had been an army engineer and he had helped Lal introduce new wells and irrigation canals in his villages. A gentle man with a whimsical sense of humour, he was clearly very fond of Lal. Later Lal went out to make some phone calls and Colonel Wilkinson stayed with me drinking coffee.

"He's quite something, isn't he?" He said watching Lal as he disappeared into the shadows of the club interior. I didn't reply.

"A one off. Dynamic. Most princes don't really give a damn about their subjects. He does."

He leaned across and shook my hand. "Call me Wilkie, m'dear. All my friends do."

I became very fond of Wilkie. He was one of nature's gentlemen, a man who saw a great deal and said little. I don't know what Lal had told him about my history, but he treated me with a quiet courtesy, an unintrusive protectiveness, as if he knew that I had been hurt and he didn't need to know why, he just wanted to make things better.

He loved India. He saw all her complexities and contradictions. When I asked him, rather tactlessly, if he, like most of the other diehards in the club, would return 'home' after Independence, he looked sad.

"No. I don't think so."

I was nosey enough to ask why.

"I don't really know England. Not my home in anything but name. Sandhurst Returned, you see," he repeated, as if that explained everything. I had to confess I hadn't a clue what that meant. He smiled.

"Born here. Father and grandfather in the Indian Army, also born here. Whole bunch of us only "returned" to Blighty for school and Sandhurst, then back here to join the regiment."

He cleared his throat. "So I don't think of "going home" because it isn't, if you see what I mean. India is my home. Though I don't quite know how or if I'll fit in. To the new order."

I did see. I saw that generations of men and women had made India their home, despite their denial of it. I also saw that they would never fit in to the Britain I knew. Men like Wilkie and Lal, and my friend, the Nawab, had looked at the prospect of Partition and a new, independent India and seen that history was leaving them behind. Everything they had been born to would vanish, turning them into anachronisms overnight. They had no real future at all.

That morning, Wilkie pointed out some of the club residents to me. There were the Cathcarts, Richard and Lavinia, senior ICS. They had a faded, ill tempered air as if they knew their day was done and they had been short changed. A pinched retirement in some shabby English town was now the best they could hope for, not the glowing sunset in Simla or Nainital, living in quiet affluence, tended by servants, playing bridge and golf, that they had always dreamed of. Here they clung religiously to the rules and regarded the new guests with horror, making their savage disapproval abundantly clear. Lal and I were reduced to helpless giggles later that day, as we sat in the library, hidden by our newspapers, in the deep armchairs, as the Cathcarts walked though, from bar to verandah, gimlets in hand and discussed us thus, chewing us over and spitting us out with distaste.

"I don't know why he's running around with her. Very *declasse*. Or she with him? Couldn't she find an Englishman? She looks right enough," he said.

"She's a Mrs Rikh. Bedi told me." Pamela replied darkly. "What do you make of that?"

"Oh dear. A taste for dark meat."

"Indeed." They strolled past us, bigoted and unseeing.

"How old do you think she is?"

"Impossible to tell under all that paint."

"She could be forty." I was twenty-six. I hoped Lal wouldn't laugh out loud.

"You can never tell with her sort." And on a cloud of spite, they wafted out into the garden, like a pair of malevolent ghouls.

Lal guffawed. "Now you've met the bitch brigade. Not restricted to the female sex, you'll observe. If anything, the men are worse."

He was right there. I soon learned that the most vicious, virulent gossips were often men, unattractive and uninteresting, the ones you would always turn down.

Then there was Gloria, the Anglo-Indian and very beautiful girl friend of Kitou, a dissipated Indian prince. The Cathcarts reserved their special vituperation for her. Lal commented "Poor old Anglos, raised to think they were a cut above, but actually despised by all." I thought they were just jealous of her youth and beauty and made a point of always talking to her. She was a sweet girl, but terribly vacuous. Lal thought she was a "grade A ninny. Looks like a dream, but being with her would be a nightmare. A very boring nightmare."

I didn't like that attitude. "What's the difference between her and me?" I was about to add that we were both mistresses of aristocratic Indians. But he jumped in, "a few million brain cells."

I began to feel sorry for Mr Bedi. He was the one who had to field the outbursts of malice, the groundless complaints, the tearful and very public wailing of Gloria when Kitou once again let her down in one way or another. He did a lot of that. I told her she should leave him. She shrugged and said she loved him; she knew he was a bastard, but she couldn't leave him and in any case, where would she go? And who was I to judge her for that? I said nothing, just made sure I was there to listen when she was distraught and wanted to catalogue Kitou's many atrocities. They had an awfully familiar ring to them.

Mr Bedi carried on through it all, marshalling this motley crew into something resembling good order, like the Captain of the Titanic. A ship of fools sailing into a very uncertain future. He ran the club with skill and efficiency, somehow if not reconciling, then at least maintaining a truce between the old guard, who wanted nothing to ever change and the flotsam and jetsam of war, like me, who disturbed the status quo just by being there. But we were young and still alive, and at no occasion was this more apparent than at the Saturday Dinner Dance, held in the ballroom. We wanted jazz and swing, they clung to Begin the Beguine and the Viennese waltz. We wanted life, love and laughter, they hid behind prejudice and habit. We saw them as ossified old fossils, pickled in alcohol, relics of a bygone age; they saw us as an outrage and a threat, determined to smash the old order and destroy their values. They weren't far wrong. These chasms of difference showed themselves in outbursts of spleen on one side and not very gentle mockery on the other. Poor old Mr Bedi somehow managed to keep the peace. He smoothed the ruffled feathers of the old and sympathised with the impatience of the young. At the time I thought he was a hypocrite. Now I think he was rather admirable.

Despite all this, we settled easily into life in Dehra Dun. It wasn't difficult. For us both, after the roller coaster of our lives in Lahore—it provided a hiatus. This quiet backwater gave us time to heal, time to reflect. Although I was far from Lily, and I missed her and grieved for her loss, I knew she would be well cared for and loved. The *Begum* had made that clear. I just hoped that I could find her again, as she had promised. Dehra Dun and its calm gave Lal and I time and space to rediscover each other, to be together without external pressure, to talk, which we did endlessly, and to find the courage to love again.

Lal wasn't there all the time. His land agent, Master Catar Singh, came to see him regularly. When he told Lal there was trouble in one of his villages, Lal would always go to sort it out. These absences alarmed me. I feared for his safety. He also had to go to Delhi to attend the Chamber of Princes. They were endlessly debating their fate in the new order and not much liking the prospect. Nehru was a socialist and they could not expect to enjoy the same privileges that they had under the British. Despite that, their wealth, influence and vast landowning still made them a force to be reckoned with. To say nothing of their private armies. There was even talk of some of the larger kingdoms refusing to join an independent India.

When Lal was gone, I missed him very much. Not just because he fixed everything for me, but because I could at last begin to admit that I loved him. I missed his body beside mine, our long, eclectic talks—we discussed everything from cooking pots—he favoured stainless steel and copper, he said (he who had never so much as fried an egg in his life!) I had only known aluminium—to politics, family and religion—neither of us was very much in favour of the last two, to silk scarves and who served the best food in Lahore. The food in the club was rubbish, we agreed. Most of all, I missed his jokes. Our love and laughter.

When he was away, I was not bored. Lal had arranged for me to help Mr Bedi in the office during the afternoons. After the Waldorf, it was child's play, but it kept me busy, gave Mr Bedi a well-earned 'breathing space' and gave me a small income that I could offset against my bill, which made me feel independent. And then there was Peggy.

She breezed in one afternoon as if she owned the place and asked me the price of the cheapest room. She was wearing a nurse's uniform complete with cape and cap. A 'bottle blonde,' her hair was so bleached that it was almost white and she had a vicious perm that did nothing for its condition. She had lovely skin though, soft and flawless, what we called 'peaches and cream' in those days.

Glancing down the register, I asked if we were expecting her.

"I doubt it," she replied. That puzzled me because

people like her, in uniform, were usually booked in by the unit they belonged to or were accompanied by a club member. At that point Mr Bedi emerged from his office, where he had been snatching a quick forty winks, to see what was going on.

"Q.A." she announced importantly.

"Queen Alexandra's Imperial Military Nursing Service," she proclaimed with the careful enunciation usually reserved for tongue twisters.

She grinned confidently at us. "I'm the same as a Captain. Equivalent rank."

Mr Bedi was deeply impressed. He stood up straight, as if to attention and began to sign her in. I was less convinced. The QAs were an elite, military nursing group that had a certain cachet. Tracing their origins back to Florence Nightingale, long before Queen Alexandra had given them her patronage, they were usually recruited from the upper classes. Many of them were debutantes. This girl was not one of them. Nothing about her, from the Irish accent she had not yet learned to disguise to her deep red lips and painted nails, looked either posh or medical. I had known QAs in London during the War. Two of them stayed at the Waldorf from time to time when they needed a break from the hoi polloi of the nurses' home. They had a very distinctive uniform. She was not wearing it.

She saw me hesitate and give me a fleeting, anxious glance. Mr Bedi turned to get her key. Then she winked at me and put her fingers to her lips.

I smiled at her and she beamed back at me. She had a rather wonderful smile, her ebullient good humour was infectious. Picking up her battered, cardboard suitcase she went off with Mr Bedi to her room.

That evening, as I was sitting with Wilkie in the bar, she walked in. Wilkie nearly fell off his stool. It was quite an entrance. She was transformed. She looked wonderful. The thick stockings and lace up shoes had gone along with the starched uniform and stiff collar—now she wore a low cut dress of soft, cloudy blue that clung to her and showed off her figure. It wasn't perfect. She was not really that good-looking, but she could make you think she was. She had something that made you want to look at her. An odd air of childlike innocence and worldly astuteness. There was no doubt in my mind that she'd been around the block a few times, but she carried herself with a kind of fragile bravado that was very endearing.

The bar fell silent, staring at the newcomer. She smiled brightly at everyone. No-one spoke to her. The women glared at her and the men gawped at her. They were a dismal bunch. Now she just looked anxious and very alone. I slid off my stool and went over to her.

"Hello, Nurse...?"

"Peggy."

I wasn't going to question her. "My name's Nita. Will you join us?"

She smiled gratefully. "Thanks for the rescue."

"Think nothing of it. And take no notice. They're all toothless anyway."

Wilkie was scrambling to his feet. "I'll get us a table."

While he was organising that we stood together, bearing the full brunt of the old guards' glare.

"Not very friendly are they?'

"No."

"What have they got against us?" She lumped us together right from the start, but she wasn't wrong.

"We're under a hundred? We've still got a pulse?" She laughed aloud at that, a hearty guffaw that attracted even more disapproving glances. She fitted in even less than I did. She would liven things up all right. I liked her immensely. We became firm friends and we stayed so for many years.

Peggy was a godsend when Lal was away. She was lively and provocative company and she would not let me mope. She dragged me out for walks in the nearby forests and trips into town to scour the shops. She ate with me and insisted I turn up in the bar in the evenings. "I'm not facing that shower on my tod," she would say, although she made friends with everyone in the end. No-one could withstand her relentless good nature for long. Gloria and Kitou took to her at once. Even the old guard softened their stance when Mrs Phillimore fell over in the gardens and cut her eye quite badly. Peggy took charge and cleaned and patched her up with professional dispatch. She was a nurse all right, and probably a good one, but she was never a QA. Never in a million years.

Chapter Twenty One

One morning about two months after we arrived in Dehra Dun, Lal was away on one of his trips to Delhi and I was sitting in the library reading 'Great Expectations'. I always found that book a consolation. I could identify with Pip's appalling behaviour and his redemption gave me hope. Peggy was in town at the hairdresser being "dyed up" as she called it. So, it was one of the rare occasions when I was alone. Anyway, that morning I received what I can only call a visitation.

A tall, impossibly grand Sikh, clad in gold brocade coat, spotless white trousers and shoes that shone like glass, was ushered in with great pomp and ceremony by Mr Bedi, who stood by my chair and muttered out of the side of his mouth.

"His Highness wishes a private interview." I looked up and saw the Sikh towering above me. I didn't know him from Adam.

"Oh... good morning. Who are you?" I asked politely.

Mr Bedi nearly fell over. "Princely family," he hissed. I hadn't a clue what he was talking about. However, I indicated that the Sikh gentleman should sit and Mr Bedi withdrew, walking backwards with his head bowed. The stupid man was practically genuflecting.

The Sikh eased himself into the armchair and regarded me solemnly with a stern, unsmiling gaze. There was an awkward silence. I wondered what on earth he was doing here. He cleared his throat.

"I come here on behalf of princely family."

Oh God, Lal's family. I said nothing.

"We feel his association with you is an unfortunate one."

"Isn't that up to him?" I'd had enough of this with Abdi's set up to last me a lifetime.

"Not entirely. His position is such that the honour of princely family is at stake. He is in deep with you and we are disturbed by future prospects."

His florid language made me want to laugh. His icy glare did not. I may have glared back. He changed his tack. He attempted an avuncular smile.

"You are, no doubt, a charming companion." If anything, this was worse.

"But you have no family, no fortune and no influence." Ain't that the truth, I thought.

I nodded. He crossed his long legs daintily and flicked

an imaginary speck of fluff from his trousers. A strangely nervous gesture, I thought.

"What you do have is a chequered past and unsavoury reputation."

"Brother," Heavens, he was Lal's brother. "His Highness, the Rajasahib needs a helpmeet. A consort. His marriage was not happy."

"Yes, I know."

"But he is young and can marry again. A suitable consort."

No-one could describe me as that.

"One who will help him bear the heavy burden of his rank."

"Shouldn't you be having this conversation with him?"

He shook his head sadly. "Brother is besotted. Wise counsel fell on deaf ears." He must have been taught by Miss Batt too.

He spread his hands wide in supplication. "So I am come here," he announced, looking around the oak-panelled room, lined with gold tooled volumes, as if it were a Calcutta slum. Perhaps it was to him. "To appeal to... to cast ourselves upon your..." here he faltered, "better nature." Definitely Miss Batt. I could hear her maxims ringing through the schoolroom. Here he raised his voice. "Give him up. We beg you. For God's sake, give him up." Sweat was forming a sheen on his forehead.

He stared at me expectantly. Clearly waiting for a response. I had no intention of giving him one. None he would welcome anyway. Perhaps my dealings with Abdi and his family had made me hard. But after all that welter of pain, I had resolved never again to be bullied or harried into giving up anyone I loved.

"I will have this conversation with him. And only him."

He sat back in the chair and rested his head against one of the wings. Exhausted, deflated, he closed his eyes in an attitude of complete despair. Then he opened them wide.

"Silly Billy. I forgot."

"What?"

He smiled. "Nub of the matter. Excuse me." He unbuttoned his jacket and took an envelope out of the inner pocket. He handed it to me with a flourish and stood up.

"We do not wish you any harm," he said magnanimously. "We wish you long and happy life—far from your usual vicissitudes—and far from brother." He nodded.

The interview was over. He left, leaving me with his envelope.

In it was a letter from a highly reputable law firm—offices in New Delhi, Bombay and Lahore—offering me a very large sum of money on the condition that I never see, communicate with, or more quaintly, 'have congress' with His Highness, Rajasahib, Brigadier, Squadron Leader, etc. etc. All his titles were listed and they took up about half a page. On signature the money would be paid into a bank account of my designation.

Once again, people of substance were willing to pay good money to get me out of their lives. Not a flattering thought. The more I thought about it, the more it frightened me. I wanted to be with Lal, to be part of his life, but how could I oppose all this? And would it tear him apart if I did?

I stewed about it for days, but I didn't tell anyone. Certainly not Peggy. I knew what her response would be. I presented the letter to Lal on his return. Immediately, in fact. I couldn't wait to hand it over. It felt like the damn thing was burning a hole in my hand. But I could have waited a bit. The poor man had hardly arrived. His unpacked case was still on the bed. He looked tired and his shoes were dusty. I looked at them. I didn't dare look at him.

"I had a visit..." I began.

"Oh yes? Who from?" He sat down on the edge of the bed and started to unlace his shoes.

"Your brother."

"Poor old you. Pompous sod, isn't he?" He eased one shoe off. "Never mind, his bark's worse than his bite. Certainly a lot longer."

"Not really. He brought me this." I thrust the letter at him. He glanced at it and frowned.

"I'd like a drink first." This was not reassuring. I brought him a whisky and he sat in the armchair and read the letter. Having done so, he laid it down on the table between us.

"It's not a bad offer."

I felt sick. Did he want to get rid of me?

"Do you want me to go?"

"Do you want to?"

I said nothing, sure I was about to be hurt again. In silence, I waited for the axe to fall.

He looked at me for a long time then said softly, "What a daft old goose you are." He grinned wearily.

"No, I was wondering if we should cut and run." This didn't sound like Lal. "Leave it all behind."

I wasn't really listening. Suddenly I was so happy I could barely breathe. He had said the magic word. We. He wasn't thinking of a future without me.

"Perhaps we should just sail away?"

"In a beautiful pea green boat?"

He smiled at that. I knew Miss Batt would have taught him Edward Lear.

"Why not? Just you and me. Leave the whole rotten bunch behind. Sounds like bliss."

He was very tired. He went to bed and within a few minutes was fast asleep. Much later we made love. With one word he had made me happier than I had ever been in my life.

When he awoke the next morning he was angry, very angry. I had never seen him like that before.

"How dare he meddle in my affairs?" He kicked one of his shoes across the room.

"How dare they judge me?"

"I think it was me they were judging."

"Same thing." he snarled. I could have started singing. I was filled with joy. I would never be alone again. Not while this wonderful man was alive. I just wanted to be with him and I couldn't have cared less if we lived in a palace or a shack. Just him. That's all I wanted.

"How dare they offer you money to go away? If they don't want you they can clear out. It's all my money anyway. They're a millstone around my neck. They cost me a fortune and then stab me in the back. They can go to hell."

He summoned his brother. When he arrived, Lal insisted we see him in the library. He also insisted I was present and that they speak English. Then he gave him a complete wigging.

By the end of it, I felt quite sorry for Lal's brother. Lal didn't. He was still angry. A scary prospect. He was irredeemably regal. His scorn was glacial.

"I will not even discuss your predilection for scurrilous gossip and meddling in my affairs. Both are beneath contempt. But I will not tolerate your presumption. You will never make decisions for me. Is that clear?"

His brother looked about to cry. Lal went on, his anger filling the room.

"Need I remind you who I am?"

His brother stammered tearfully. "No, no, dear brother... Rajasahib..."

He bowed. Lal glared at him. His brother kissed his hand and went to kiss his feet. Lal pulled him up.

"Get out. And don't come back until you've learned your place."

I had to smile. Lal was such a combination of medieval king and Victorian nursery.

I felt jubilant, but thought it ungracious. His brother left, a picture of abject misery.

Lal was still fuming.

"I felt rather sorry for him."

"Don't. He should thank his lucky stars. A hundred years ago I'd have had him beheaded."

I couldn't resist. "What a charming family."

He grinned at me. "Not a family at all. Nest of bloody vipers."

He put his arm round my shoulders. "Now. Let's go and find some human beings. We'll have a drink with Wilkie and Peggy. That fool has left a bad taste in my mouth."

We never spoke of it again. He had proved his love and loyalty and in return I gave him mine.

Life with Lal was different. He was bright, funny and interesting. He had been born into a life of immense privilege, and he could be impossibly lordly at times, but he never used his rank or his wealth to manipulate or hurt people. He didn't have to. He was commanding enough a personality without it. With him there was never the undertow of fear, the streak of malice there was with Abdi. Had that given our toxic relationship its frisson, its excitement? I hoped not. I talked to Lal about it. He said only a coward rules through fear. He made me very happy.

Shortly after the visit from Lal's brother, Rikh called me. I had not heard from him for a long time. Not since long before Lily. He rang at a rather awkward time. About seven in the evening when the lobby was thronged with members and their guests, meeting and greeting, chatting and laughing, dawdling on their way to bar or billiard room.

I took the call at first in reception, but after a few seconds I asked Mr Bedi to put the call through to one of the booths. This done, I squeezed into the tiny space and shut the sliding door.

Rikh said he had had a hard time tracking me down. I supposed he had—via the Braganza, then the Imperial and now the club. I said never mind, you've found me now, trying to be cheerful and friendly. I always found it strange, hearing from Rikh. The sound of his voice, once so familiar, now so infrequently heard, had the unnerving habit of transporting me back instantly into the past. London, a chilly green spring and the dust filled rooms of the India League.

He cleared his throat. He only did that when he was anxious. Whatever he was about to say would not come easily to him.

"It's been more than two years..." he began. Two years in which so much had happened. It seemed like a lifetime. In many ways, it was.

"I think it is time now to put our affairs in order."

"Do you mean divorce?"

He coughed and when he spoke his voice was scratchy. "Yes. I think so."

He said he had met someone. A widow named Mina, he said. An Indian wife who could be everything to him that I had not, I thought. Did it give me a pang? A moment of sadness, regret? Yes, it did. But I despised myself for it. There was no excuse for that.

I agreed at once. How could I not? It was not the man, but the artery to the past I was mourning. I told him I would not defend it. I told him I had never meant to hurt him- I wanted him to be happy.

He said he thought he would be—with Mina. He said he would "put the wheels in motion."

We spoke for a short while in a business like fashion, then said goodbye.

Divorce in those days was very different. It was a protracted and complex process which required court attendance and the necessity to prove one's case, even if it were not defended. I hated whole idea of it. It seemed to presuppose we were opposing parties, almost enemies. All our dirty linen, mainly mine, would have to be washed in public. It felt like we were being put on trial. Part of a sequence of events that would prove that we had failed, not that we had grown apart. Never taking into account that we were human beings, messy and fallible, but only that we had broken rules society held sacred and we would be pilloried for it.

The prospect of it depressed me for days. I wanted us

both to be free. I wanted Rikh to be happy. God knows he deserved it. I told Lal straight away. He understood completely. He said he would soon be going through something very similar himself, but he imagined it would be even worse—involving as it did the custody of a child and the division of substantial assets.

"Now you know why I wanted to run away," he said. We held hands a lot that evening. Then as we were going into the dining room, he said, "at least, when it's all done and dusted, we can move on."

"To what?" I asked but he didn't answer, just studied the menu. "Makes you long for Faletti's, doesn't it?" he said. It did. The club menu was an all out embrace of traditional English fare. Not of a high standard. Mutton, stews of the finest leather and vegetables boiled to extinction. A sort of three course school dinner. All pale grey. Except the custard which was a glaring canary yellow. You couldn't believe that you were in India, with all its complex and intense flavours, though I suppose that was what they were aiming for. We both sighed and ordered a drink.

Later on the dance floor as he massacred my feet—Lal was a terrible dancer—he whirled me round and said, "Shall we do it then?"

"What?" I said, wincing with pain.

"Tie the knot." He pulled my arm up and down as if it were a pump handle, but at least he wasn't standing on my feet.

"Are you asking me to marry you?"

"Yes. Triumph of hope over experience, I'd say." And I knew we were safe, because we were back with Miss Batt.

"You want to risk it?"

He nodded emphatically, "You?"

I could have screamed for joy.

"Oh. I will if you will." I never could pull off nonchalance. He gave me a hug.

"On one condition," I said through clenched teeth.

"What's that?" he looked worried.

"I never have to dance with you again."

"Done," he said and together we left the floor.

An incident occurred soon after that that reminded me forcibly that India was not all "silk scarves and bonbons." Another of Miss Batt's sayings. I told Lal it was dreadful. Her platitudes were catching. I was beginning to think like that. I told him I didn't think he had been educated, but rather brainwashed.

"Isn't that true of all educators?" he replied. I thought gratefully of the Godolphin and Latymer and their insistence that I use my brain. However, there was not much evidence of that teaching in my life, so perhaps I was resistant.

"What about the Jesuits?" he finished triumphantly. I gave up. You couldn't win an argument with Lal—certainly not when Miss Batt was in play.

One of her other maxims was "What can't be cured must be endured." We heard a lot of that one around the time of Partition. I hated it. I couldn't work out what I hated more—its fatalism or its banality. So I changed it to "What can't be cured must be ignored."

I found that worked better for me. I found it particularly apposite when dealing with Lal and Wilkie's endless games of billiards. Many evenings they played for hours after dinner and watching them bored me to tears. So I took to going for a walk instead. I used to walk through the grounds to the river. It was very pleasant, that riverside walk, the air was cool and fresh and as it was rarely cloudy, there was just enough moonlight to see by. I took a torch, but I hardly ever used it. I also found that a brisk walk after the usual lump of concrete that was the club pudding was a good idea if you didn't want to be up all night with indigestion. A *pi dog* usually accompanied me on these walks, falling in behind me when I reached the riverbank and following me as I walked along. He kept his distance, my shadowy companion, and I didn't make any overtures towards him as I was mindful of disease, especially rabies. But he would trot along behind me and I came to welcome his presence. I found it reassuring.

Lal didn't like it. He said he wasn't sure I should go alone. I thought that silly. There were no *goondas* or armed militias in Dehra Dun. And, in any case, I'm not alone, I said. A rather sweet dog always follows me. Wilkie and Lal exchanged glances.

The next night he offered to accompany me. So we strolled along hand in hand and at one point, he turned and looked behind him. Then we went on. It was all very pleasant.

When we got back to the club he said, "No more nocturnal walks for you."

I couldn't believe my ears. He never laid down the law to me. Was the prospect of marriage turning him into Rikh?

I must have looked rebellious because he grinned. "Your Fido's a leopard," he said.

I didn't need any more persuasion to stay in after that.

Chapter Twenty Two

While we remained safe in our colonial backwater, outside things were moving fast. The new Labour Prime Minister, Clement Attlee, was committed to ridding England of her imperial trappings and in particular, the jewel in her crown, India. In this he was the antithesis of Winston Churchill. In a statement to the House of Commons, on the 20th February 1947, he declared that Britain would end her rule in India by no later than June 1948—in other words, a mere sixteen months ahead.

I hoped this very finite timescale would bring a much needed note of pragmatism to the proceedings. That such a specific deadline would force the warring parties to come to the table and find a solution everyone could live with. Both Lal and Wilkie thought that was idiotic. Lal even said so. He pointed out that no progress at all had been reached in discussions between the Congress Party and the League. I countered that perhaps the sacking of the old Viceroy, Lord Wavell and the appointment of Louis Mountbatten might bring some new dynamism into talks that had degenerated into turgid and formulaic recriminations. Wilkie said darkly that Mountbatten was dynamic all right, that his wartime acts of daring do had resulted in the sinking of every ship he had ever taken command of. I knew this was an exaggeration, but there was likely to be a kernel of truth in there somewhere. Wilkie was not given to extravagant statements. He would never have said anything like that without cause.

Lal said his fear was that Nehru and Jinnah would continue going "round and round the garden," getting nowhere, while the British drew increasingly unrealistic boundary lines and after months of pointless wrangling and pontificating, during which India would tear herself apart, British rule would simply "time out," leaving the country to anarchy and chaos.

Mountbatten took up his post at the end of March, proudly declaring on arrival at Palam airport that he was the last British Viceroy and he had come to assist in the birth of a new nation. Seeing that scion of the British royal family arrive in Delhi to dismantle the keystone of the Empire, reminded me again of the days in the India League when many of our fellow citizens had regarded us as dangerous revolutionaries, even traitors. I knew the current situation looked grim, but I could never regard an independent India as a catastrophe and I felt proud that I had been a tiny cog in that mighty wheel. I thought of the heroes of our movement, Gandhi, Nehru, and the suffering and imprisonment they and their followers had endured, and hoped with all my heart that India would take her rightful place in the world, at liberty to explore her own destiny, unshackled and free at last.

What Wilkie and Lal regarded as my naive optimism seemed to have been proved right. There was a brief hiatus in the violence in the beginning of April when Mountbatten and Jinnah engaged in intensive talks to try and find agreement. They went round in circles. Mountbatten's optimism seems to have been as out of touch as my own. He hoped Jinnah would listen to his arguments and that when the actual scope of this 'moth-eaten Pakistan' became clear, he and his League members would revert to their place within a united India with special privileges and safeguards for all Muslims.

In the meantime, the Sikhs were preparing for war. The prospect of a divided Punjab, or even worse a Punjab within Pakistan, was anathema to them. They would never accept either. Lal said they would rather kill everyone in the Punjab first. Wilkie showed me an advertisement in a Lahore newspaper calling on all Sikhs to contribute to a five million Rupee war chest to buy arms. Tara Singh wanted to seize power when the British departed and take the Punjab as part of an independent Sikhistan, rather than have it fall to Jinnah. The royal family of Patiala, particularly the Maharajah, backed this idea with an enthusiasm that stretched to a private army and almost unlimited funds. So Lal was very busy these days, travelling to and fro Delhi to attend the Chamber of the Princes.

It was during this time that I received notification from the High Court of Lahore, Family Division, to attend the initial hearing of my divorce. Wilkie had been down to Lahore the previous week to attend to business at his bank. The Cathcarts went with him. Lavinia had gone shopping. Essential supplies, she said. She made it sound like the dawn raid on Dieppe. Wilkie said, although it felt odd because there was now an armed guard in the European carriage of the train, it was actually quite safe. Their entire trip of several days had passed without incident.

Lal wasn't happy about my going alone, but he could not accompany me. His presence was required in Delhi and he said that me being seen around Lahore with my very conspicuous boyfriend, i.e. him, could lead to accusations of 'collusion.' Apparently, this could have a dire effect on the divorce. Judges were very strict in those days. I thought it was absurd. I had openly lived in Lahore with two men, neither of whom was my husband. It was hardly a secret. My association with Abdi had been the talk of the town and my relationship with Lal was common knowledge. They were both fairly eminent individuals and in neither case did we hide away. But it didn't matter because he couldn't come with me anyway. Wilkie told me to "err on the side of caution and give the old city a wide berth" and I told him I certainly didn't want to hang around in Lahore. I couldn't think of anything worse, so I would take the overnight train there and another one back the same night. Lal thought I should stay over, but I didn't want to. Lahore was nothing but a catalogue of past pain to me now. I would attend the court as required and leave at the first opportunity. I wasn't exactly looking forward to seeing Rikh again either.

Lal had arranged for me to have a meeting with his solicitor in Lahore, a Mr Kingaby, formerly of Lincoln's Inn, who would accompany me to the court and introduce me to the barrister. Wilkie kindly took me to the station at Dehra Dun in his car, an old Riley. It had cracked leather seats and reeked of pipe tobacco. The car was like its owner, reliable and trustworthy, if not smart.

The evening I left I was assailed by a roller-coaster of memory. My first meeting with Rikh, our wedding during the war in London, our arrival in India, and our journey by rail to Ambala. The prison our marriage became and then Abdi. A sorry tale that became sorrier. I wondered what my mother would think.

So it was that with all this maelstrom of emotion churning around inside me, I boarded the train to Lahore. It was a long journey, some seven and a half hours, and it went via Ambala, where part of the train terminated. I wondered if Rikh would get on the train there and thought how ironic it was that the two of us, who had travelled from Madras to Ambala by train as man and wife, starting this great adventure of our lives in India together, should now be ending it like this, separately but by the same means.

Wilkie carried my overnight bag to the first-class European compartment and saw me safely ensconced on the train. Then he left. I was alone. There was no-one else in the carriage, though there was a large crowd further down the platform, pushing and shoving their way on to the train. Women and children were clambering into the purdah carriage, a crescent moon chalked on the carriage door for the illiterate, all of them laden with bundles and boxes, the immense amount of luggage no Indian will travel without.

It was a warm, airless night. I opened the window and soon after the train puffed its way out of the station and began to gather speed. It was about half past ten. The club had given me a packed supper for the journey, sandwiches wrapped in a damask napkin and a flask of coffee. I took a peek. Mutton sandwiches. Pale grey bread and chunks of dark grey meat. It looked fibrous and tough. Not very appealing.

I took out my book and tried to read. After a while, the guard came in to make up the bed.

He did so and then he locked me in from the outside. All the couchette compartments had an interior latch, so the passengers could sleep undisturbed, but this was a proper exterior lock with a key. One I did not possess. I didn't like that at all. I asked him sharply what he thought he was doing.

"New regulation. For your safety, Memsahib. Guard is on patrol in corridor. If you need toilet, better go now. If you need in the night, he will let you out and see you back in." He then proceeded to lock me in.

I really didn't like that at all.

I remember that night and the following day as a series of images, a slide show rather than a chain of events. I have no coherent memory of it at all.

I remember it was hot and stuffy. A cloudy, moonless night. The decorated glass shade of the overhead lamp, a garland of flowers etched around the fluted edge, and the soft pool of yellow light it provided. The rough, hairy velveteen that covered the seats and the cool crisp linen of the sheet laid on top of it. I must have slept, but only fitfully.

It was impossible to rest for any decent period of time because of the constant stopping and starting, the shunting backwards and forwards as the train uncoupled outside Ambala. Then we went on towards Lahore. I fell asleep. At one point I awoke. The train had stopped again. I couldn't see why. We were in the middle of nowhere. I looked out of the window, but I couldn't see anything. The darkness was thick and impenetrable. I heard nothing except the squeaky protest of the brakes. I got back into my makeshift bed and tossed and turned some more. I felt tired and grumpy. A sleepless night before going to court. That was all I needed. Cursing, I fell asleep.

I woke as the train pulled into Lahore. I dressed hurriedly and waited for the guard to liberate me. He took his time. I could hear voices, shouting, a whistle, and then a soft whoosh as if water was coming out of a hose. I waited some more. Finally, he came and unlocked the door. He looked ashen. I wondered why.

I took my bag and stepped down onto the platform. Then I heard a shrill, harsh animal cry. I turned and looked back. The bodies of women and children were being lifted out of the purdah carriages and laid on the platform. Black and white blood stained bundles, some pathetically small. A never ending line, three deep. At the far end a station guard was hosing blood from the platform.

A little boy, who could have been no more than four years old, squatted beside the lifeless body of his mother. He spoke to her softly, patiently waiting for her to wake.

Her face was uncovered, her sightless eyes turned towards the sky. A mute accusation. Her features were already pinched and set like stone. Around him, total chaos.

I made my way out of the station, shaky and ashamed. We had come to India, blind with arrogance, preaching Christianity and the rule of law. We had robbed them blind for three centuries and now were leaving them a charnel house. Like my peers, I turned my back on the undefended dead, sickened by the knowledge that while that massacre of the innocents was taking place I was safe and sound, locked in and guarded, saved by my white skin.

I took a taxi to Faletti's and rang Lal.

Late that night, he came to get me. He drove all the way from Delhi with a guard from the Rajputana Rifles. God knows how he got hold of him.

Mr Kingaby came to Faletti's at the appointed hour. I could not stop shaking. I told him I was sorry. That I had seen dead people before. Brought out of the rubble after a raid in London. Lain on the ground covered by St John's ambulance blankets, I said. Then I began to cry. The boy haunted me. How could I have left him? Who would comfort and care for him? A scrap of life alone in a sea of death.

I waited at the court. The solicitor spoke to the barrister who arranged for the court hearing to be postponed to a later date. Rikh came to see me in the waiting room. I don't know if he was supposed to do that. I told him what I had seen. He patted my hand. A woman was with him. Mina? I don't know. I didn't ask. The solicitor took me back to Faletti's.

When Lal came, he took me in his arms. The next day, with our guard, we drove back to Dehra Dun. Everyone was very kind. Even Lavinia.

Lal and I were always together after that. When he had to go to Delhi, I went with him. We clung to each other now, knowing how fleeting life is and how rare this love.

We were in Delhi when Independence was declared on

the 15th August. There were fireworks and celebrations. The previous day, Pakistan had celebrated a separate independence.

By the end of it, between one and two million people had died and fifteen million people had become refugees. They formed the greatest migration of human souls in the history of the earth. The true numbers will probably never be known. A great nation was free. It was a bungled and bloody birth.

Lal and I stayed together through thick and sometimes very thin. Through his family's fierce and protracted opposition—they plotted to tear us apart for decades—through our own foolishness. The cataclysmic rows and thoughtless affairs, the bruised pride and hurt feelings. And still, despite everything, the love. That seemed to endure everything we could throw at it.

We lived well after Partition in Delhi, in a lovely house near the Lodhi Gardens. A life of leisure and opulence. Cars, jewels, diplomatic parties and summers in Simla and Kashmir. Too good to be true. And so it was. With Partition and Nehru's abolition of the powers of the princes and then their privy purses, Lal's wealth shrivelled away and we moved to London. The city of my birth. Full circle.

He died far too early and far from home in the general ward of a London hospital.

He died alone. His last act of love was to send us away. Our son and I. To spare us the pain of watching him die.

He was born a prince, but he died like a king. He was my beloved.

I never heard from the *Begum* again. For years Lal and I tried to find Lily. But she had vanished, trapped behind a closed border I could not penetrate, between two countries that were at war.

I always wished I could talk to her. To tell her that I loved her then and I love her now. I read that adopted children often feel that maternal rejection is their fault. That they feel not only abandoned, but unworthy. So, as I have failed to find her and tell her face to face, I want to state this now. She was a perfect child. There was no fault in her. Only me.

My life has been utterly conditioned by war. Without war, neither my mother nor my father would have been in London. Without war, Rikh would not have been 'returned' to India and I would certainly not have been 'returned' with him. Without war, Lily would not have been born. Without civil war, Lal would not have been dispossessed.

War changes everything. It flings people apart like flotsam and jetsam—throwing them together and tearing them apart. It breaks the fragile ties of time and place and forges new ones of brief but white-hot intensity.

It churns everything up, careless and random, and hurls people round the globe bringing untold heartbreak in its wake. But still I count myself lucky. How could I not? I survived when so many others did not.

We are midnight's legacy. History's heirs. The past defines us and we define the future. There is no escape from that.

Acknowledgements

My first and greatest thanks must go to my husband, Mike for his open-hearted generosity in letting me plunder his history and ransack his memories. He is the beacon and guy rope of my life. I also owe huge thanks to our daughter, Ilona Mannan, whose literary gift so far exceeds my own, for her patience, insight and meticulous help with both texts.

I am also grateful to my publisher, Patricia Borlenghi, whose incisive yet sensitive notes have been invaluable.

I also wish to thank:

Nadia Ostacchini, a beautiful and dynamic powerhouse, who with great charm and purpose, found me my publisher.

Penny Culliford, a gifted writer and wonderful human being, for her friendship, encouragement and profound and unshowy kindness.

Acknowledgements

Thanks too to Paul Anthony Barber for his encouragement and support and to Teresa Jennings for her perceptive and unstinting kindness and help.

And then there's Jenny. Jenny Patrick has been the midwife of most of my creative endeavours for more years than either of us would care to admit to. First as an actress and then a writer, she has bullied and cajoled, encouraged and inspired me, always with love and laughter, making me feel that the better acted scene, the more expressive phrase was within my grasp, if I would only reach for it. She has egged me on relentlessly and I have been infinitely richer for it.

Mr Bhola, in the bookshop of the Imperial Hotel, New Delhi, patiently and diligently shared his encyclopaedic knowledge of Partition and found many of the important and comparatively obscure sources mentioned overleaf, all of which proved invaluable.

Bibliography

Lahore by Pran Nevile. Penguin

Liberty or Death by Patrick French. Harper Collins

Indian Summer by Alex von Tunzelmann. Simon & Schuster

Plain Tales From The Raj edited by Charles Allen. Andre Deutsch

Freedom at Midnight by Larry Collins and Dominique Lapierre. Harper Collins

Midnight's Furies by Nisid Hajari. Penguin India

The Other Side of Silence by Urvashi Butalia. Penguin India

Train to Pakistan by Khushwant Singh. Roli Books

The Punjab by Ishhaq Ahmed. Roli Books

Other title

War Changes Everything by Melanie Hughes

Illegitimate Nita was born during the First World War.
When her mother marries, she despises her stepfather. At
grammar school she meets Yolanda who introduces her to
the vibrant Italian community. The two young women
become involved in the left-wing intellectual life of
London in the 1930s. She meets Rikh, an activist in the
India League.When war is declared, Rikh is seconded to
Bomber Command and they marry in haste. While Rikh
is away, she meets Lal, an Indian prince, and they have a
whirlwind love affair. As the war engulfs the world, Rikh
is posted back to India and Nita goes with him even
though their marriage is unhappy...

Publication date: 30 September 2017

Paperback edition ISBN: 978-0-9955386-5-8